TEN

A Her Russian Protector Novel

Roxie Rivera

Night Works Books
College Station, Texas

Author's Note

The prologue of this book contains descriptions of violence against women that may be triggering to some readers.

If you or someone you love is experiencing domestic violence, please seek help.

In the United States, call 1-800-799-7233.

or

Text START to 88788

PROLOGUE

*I*F I DON'T *escape tonight, he's going to kill me.*

Gritting my teeth, I choked back the groan of discomfort that threatened to escape my lips. I controlled my breathing, inhaling slowly and deeply and exhaling just the same. It was impossible to ignore the tightening band gripping my hips and thighs now.

The aching had started earlier in the evening, after Kiki had put his hands on me, squeezing my neck until I hovered on the edge of unconsciousness. After he made me do vile things to earn his mercy. After he repeatedly slammed his fist into my back and ribs until I was sure he would kill us both.

All because I smiled at the old man next door. Smiled which, according to Kiki, was a sure sign I wanted to fuck Juan. You know, the same way I apparently wanted to fuck every single man who crossed my path.

Funny how Kiki accused me of doing the thing he was actually doing every night. He thought I didn't know, but I did. I knew everything now. All of it. Every single nasty, dirty detail of what he had done and who he truly was.

I have to get out.

It was now or never.

I could not bring my baby into this world still chained to

this monster. I could not bring her back here to live with a man who would surely abuse her. More than anything, I feared he would kill her in one of his violent rages.

God, how did I get here? How had I gone from a straight-A student with my eyes on a full-ride basketball scholarship to Baylor to this? To a pregnant high school dropout, barely eighteen years old and married to a man who was nearly thirty and regularly beat the shit out of me?

Abandonment issues. Daddy issues. An abusive, junkie mother. A desperate need to be loved, to feel special.

No more.

I have to get out.

Right now.

I bit my lower lip as another wave of pain began, this one curling low and deep before spreading out toward my hips and thighs. I had expected labor pains to feel like period cramps on steroids, but this was something else entirely. The nausea-inducing ache in my thighs and hips shocked me. It was relentless, and I didn't know how much longer I could keep quiet.

As I sat up, I closed my eyes, shutting out the dizzy spin of the dimly lit bedroom. I wasn't sure if the headache and dizziness was a side effect of the near strangulation earlier or some kind of complication. The last six days had been hard on me. Headaches, swelling, a strange sense that something wasn't right.

Kiki wouldn't let me go back to the doctor, not after the nurse had asked him to step out of the room at my thirty-two week appointment. She had seen the marks on my upper arms while taking my blood pressure. I had lied, of course, and told her I had lost my balance and banged into a door. Looking back, it wasn't a very good lie, and she hadn't believed me. She had told me that I could get help, but I had asked her to let Kiki back into the room.

I would never forget the pitying, disappointed look on her face. She didn't understand. She couldn't understand. That one simple act of asking him to step outside the room had guaranteed my ass was getting beat as soon as we got home. The longer he was forced to wait outside the room, the worse it would be.

No matter how much I had assured him that I told her nothing, he wouldn't believe me. He had decided then that it was better for me not to be influenced by nosy white ladies with savior complexes. He was convinced the nurses and doctors would lie to take our baby away from us, a Black teenager and a Latino. He had a lot of strange conspiracy ideas like that. Everyone was always against him, and nothing was ever his fault.

Like when he knocked me around after that prenatal visit.

He didn't want to slap me or kick me in the legs and back. He hated having to discipline me, but I pushed him too far. I broke the rules. I let that woman embarrass him by sending him outside of the room like a child. I had undermined him, and I had to learn my lesson.

As the memory of that beating faded, I reached up to touch my right ear. It still rang, a soft and high-pitched whine that never left me. A constant reminder of his open-handed slap and the battery that followed.

Get up.

Stop thinking about the past.

Get up and get out.

I glanced at the open bedroom door. Kiki's loud snores echoed through the small house. It was a creaky, rundown mess he had inherited from his grandmother. It was nothing like he had promised when he convinced me to marry him and run away from Houston together. There was no picket fence, no roses out front, no brick sidewalk, or tall shade trees.

No, he had brought me to a hellhole. This San Antonio *barrio* was among the most dangerous areas. The house behind us ran a pit bull puppy mill that smelled horrendous in the scorching Texas heat, and the dogs barked all hours of the day and night. When they weren't barking, they were rattling the chain link fences of their kennels and snarling viciously. The inhumane treatment made them mean and dangerous.

Kiki kept talking about getting one of Roberto's dogs as a pet for our baby. Knowing how much Kiki enjoyed the dog fights on the outskirts of town, I didn't trust him to bring home a docile animal. He would want one quick to anger, a bloodthirsty mongrel that would stalk my baby and hurt her.

Last week, a neighbor two houses down had been shot over a set of rims. Literally gunned down in the street over a few hundred dollars. The old lady on the corner had been beaten and robbed after her grandson messed up a drug deal. Cartel knee breakers had put the hurt on her to draw out her grandson and get their money or product back.

And, of course, there were the hookers.

Houston had the Bissonnet Track, and San Antonio had Guadalupe and Zarzamora. I had grown up around pimps and prostitutes. My uncle was one of the biggest names in the skin game back home, but the trade here felt different, dirtier, grimier.

Even before the first girl turned up dead behind the tire shop, there had been an ugly feeling in the air at night, a stifling and oppressive sensation that left me uneasy and on edge. Then the second girl had been found under a tarp in a junkyard. By the third, I had started to wonder if the killer lived on our street or somewhere nearby.

Crime shows always said serial killers hunted where they lived. It made sense the person hiring those girls, assaulting them, torturing them, and killing them would be familiar with the area. The disposal sites weren't easy-to-reach areas, and there were never any security cameras or footage.

That was the thing that made me curious. The security cameras, I mean. It was a detail that was easy to overlook or shrug off. Maybe I never would have put two-and-two together if I hadn't found that box—.

I gasped softly as I felt a pop inside of me. A moment later, warm fluid trickled down my thighs. I stared down at my lap in horror and panic. *No, no, no.* This was happening too fast. I wasn't ready to run yet. I needed a few more minutes. I had to make sure he was passed out real good before I crept to the front door.

Clearly, my baby had other ideas. I clutched my belly, awed at how stiff it was as another contraction started to tighten up my muscles. As I stroked the curve of it, I realized I hadn't felt her move in a while. She was pretty big now, judging by how high up I could feel her feet and how low down she sat in my pelvis. I had read online that babies ran out of room to roll and flip around as they got bigger.

When had I felt her kick last? After Kiki put his hands on me? I must have. Definitely. I was certain she had kicked a few times as I cleaned up from his assault, wiping the blood from between my butt cheeks and wincing at the throbbing pain of being forced to have sex that way.

As the contraction ended, I leaned forward for a better look at the fluid trickling out of me. It was supposed to be clear. That's what the books and baby websites said.

But mine wasn't.

It was bright red and tinged with a strange greenish-black sludge.

Oh no.

No.

No.

No.

All thoughts of my safety fled. I needed to get to a hospital right now. I needed an ambulance.

There was no time to wait. I stood up, bracing myself on the wall by the bed as another wave of dizziness hit. My head was killing me, and my feet were so swollen and puffy that it hurt to walk on them. Still, I kept moving toward the bathroom and the burner phone I had bought with a stash of coins and dollar bills I had been collecting while doing the grocery shopping. I kept the phone in a box of tampons, one of the few places Kiki would never look.

Carefully, I closed and locked the door to the bathroom. *Please*, I prayed, *please let him stay asleep a little while longer.*

"Bexar County 9-1-1. What is your emergency?"

I quickly rattled off the address, desperate to make sure they had that vital piece of information before anything else was said. "I'm in labor, and I'm having complications. My water just broke, and there's blood and that green-black stuff."

"Meconium," she said, and I could hear typing in the background. "We're sending an ambulance right now."

"And the police," I insisted, gripping the burner phone so tightly my fingers went numb. "Please, you need to send the police in here first. My husband tried to kill me earlier. He strangled me, and he beat me. He hurt me, and he won't let me see a doctor."

All the horrific abuse I had been holding inside came tumbling out as I gripped the phone, my only lifeline. "Please, help me. Please. He's going to kill me and our baby."

"Ma'am, police, and EMS are on their way. Are you in a safe place?"

"I'm locked in the bathroom." I glanced at the flimsy, hollow door, wondering how long it could possibly withstand an assault from Kiki. "But you have to hurry. Please."

"Ma'am, we have help coming as fast as possible. Tell me about your labor. When did your contractions start?"

"Maybe four hours ago?" I was a bit confused about the time actually. "Maybe not," I admitted. "My head is all fuzzy. I'm not sure."

"It's okay. What's your name?"

"Nisha."

"Nisha, you stay strong, and you stay hidden. We are coming to help you. Officers will be on the scene in—."

"Nisha! Who you talking to?" Kiki growled through the bathroom door.

I nearly screamed. With the phone in one hand, I pressed against the door with the other in a desperate attempt to keep it closed. "No one, baby. I'm feeling a little sick."

"Bullshit!" he snarled and thumped the door with his fist.

"I know you're talking to someone in there. Do you have a phone? What did I tell you about those goddamn phones?"

"I don't have a phone." My voice shook, and I could hear the dispatcher trying to coach me. "I know I'm not allowed to have one, not after I called Uncle Nicky."

Kiki rattled the door handle, and when it didn't open, he kicked the door. "What did I say about locked doors?"

"No locked doors in your house," I repeated, my heart hammering against my ribs. "I'm sorry. I just...I wanted some privacy. I...my stomach hurts real bad."

"Open. The. Door. Now."

I didn't. For the first time in years, I refused to follow his order. "No."

"What did you say? Nisha! Open this goddamned door now!" He kicked and banged on the door, and I could see the ratty old hinges ready to give at any moment. "Open the door!"

"No!" I let the phone drop to the floor and put both hands against the door. "I'm not opening this door! I'm not letting you hurt me anymore!"

In the distance, police sirens grew louder. I was so close to escaping. So close.

"Did you call the police?" He slammed both hands against the door and unleashed a tirade of fuck and bitch and every other terrible, degrading thing he could think of at me. "After you made me teach you a lesson? After you made me hurt you? Because you won't follow the rules? Because you want to act like a whore smiling and shaking your ass at every man on this street?" He punched the door, and the cheap wood splintered. "I swear to God, Nisha, when they get here, you better tell them the truth."

"I will," I promised, my voice shaking and my hands trembling. "I'm going to tell them everything, Kiki. I'm going to tell them to look in the shed. I'm going to tell them to look at the security systems you serviced. I'm going to tell them you killed those girls."

"What did you say?" Kiki hissed through the door. It was that demon voice of his, the one that told me the worst pain of my life was coming my way. I wasn't deeply religious, but there were moments when I truly believed the Devil lived inside Kiki.

I couldn't back down now. I don't know where that flare of bravery—or stupidity—came from, but I wanted him to know that I *knew*.

"I said I know you've been picking up prostitutes. I know you did it back in Houston, and you're doing it here, too. Except now, you don't have anyone keeping you in line, and you're killing these girls. You cut off their—."

A second too late, I heard the metallic *thunk* and *clank* of a shotgun being racked. It was a sound I had heard dozens of times. Kiki liked to scare me with his sawed-off Mossberg when I stepped out of line, like the night he found out I had called Uncle Nicky and asked for a bus ticket back home to Houston.

I stumbled backward in an attempt to get out of the way, but I was too slow. There was no escaping the blast that tore through the cheap door—and right into me.

CHAPTER ONE

"HEY, NISHA, CAN I show you a photo of my monstera?" Billie Garcia, our salon's receptionist, dropped into the open seat at the round table in the employee lounge. "Oh! Is that gumbo?"

"It is." I held up my spoon like a sword and playfully stabbed it in Billie's direction. "And, no, I'm not sharing!"

"Selfish much?" Billie frowned and reached for her battered *My Little Pony* lunchbox. "I guess I'll just eat whatever slop my sister made."

I rolled my eyes at Billie's drama llama act. "Your sister is an executive chef for the most popular vegan restaurant in town!"

"Yeah, like I said," Billie reiterated with an aggrieved huff. She opened the lid on the neatly packed container of food and carelessly discarded the sweet little hot pink sticky note with a message from her sister. "See! Can you imagine serving this to someone you supposedly love?"

I wasn't a big fan of overly complicated vegan food filled with strange meat substitutes, but this dish was simple and looked incredible. "Was it that? Chickpeas?"

"Chickpea tagine with North African spices served over mint and dill infused couscous with coriander garnish," Billie described in a haughty voice.

I shrugged. "I'd eat it."

"I'm happy to trade."

I pulled my last serving of Uncle Nicky's gumbo closer. "Pass."

Billie pouted and stabbed her fork into a meal that had obviously been cooked with love. She put the first bite in her mouth and grimaced. After swallowing, she said, "Well, it's not the worst thing she's ever cooked for me."

"You know, for someone who lives rent-free in her sister's house, taking up space that her sister and brother-in-law would probably love to dedicate to their own hobbies or even a baby, you sure do complain a lot."

"Oh, my God. Remind me to never schedule Jamie with you ever again," Billie remarked with an eye roll. "You'll give her ideas about charging me rent or giving me a move-out date."

"Uh-oh," Savannah butted in as she joined us at the table. She plopped down across from me with a delivery bag that smelled spicy and delicious. "Did big sister give you the time-to-fly-the-nest speech?"

"Not yet." Billie scrolled through her phone. "Here. This is Monty, and he's suffering. Look, Nisha."

I took the phone from Billie and studied the sad plant on the screen. "You're giving him too much water. Let the soil dry out between waterings. Poke your finger down into the dirt a few inches. If it's moist, don't water. If it's dry, take the pot to the sink or tub and set in a few inches of water. Let it sit and soak up from the roots."

"And that's it?" Billie seemed disappointed. "No special

food or fancy fertilizer or expensive lights?"

"Nope." I returned to my gumbo. "Stop drowning it."

"Oh. Well. All right." Billie's attention turned to Savannah's lunch. "Is that butter chicken?"

"Yes." Savannah eyed the receptionist's dish. "Did your sister make that?"

"Yes. You want some?" Billie asked hopefully.

"Want to trade half?"

"I will literally let you have all of it for one single naan."

Savannah snorted with amusement. "Calm down and grab a bowl from the cabinet."

I shook my head as Billie scampered off to the supply of melamine dishes Holly kept in the salon's lounge. "That girl is a mess."

"Yep," Savannah agreed. "But the clients love her and she's a hard worker."

"I think a lot of it is an act." I lowered my voice. "She likes being the baby of her family, being spoiled and coddled."

"Well, we all have to grow up someday."

I shared a knowing glance with Savannah. Like me, Savannah had been forced to grow up too soon. Abandoned as a baby. Foster care. Failed adoptions. Never having a family or belonging. Savannah had learned to be independent at an early age.

My life's trajectory had followed a similar path. When I was four, my father was killed in a robbery gone bad. By the time I was eight, my mother had run off to Dallas and then Tulsa with some washed-up cowboy she had met at the rodeo. Last I heard, Mama was waiting tables in a truck stop diner up near Little Rock. The cowboy was long gone, and Mama was on her fifth or sixth marriage by now, still nursing a wicked heroin addiction.

I'd had Mimi June, my grandmother, of course, and Uncle Nicky to keep an eye on me. All things considered, my childhood had been pretty good. Church. Dance classes. Girl Scouts. New clothes and shoes whenever I needed them. A dog and two love birds. A big garden out back and my own swing set.

I had lived in one of Houston's less-than-stellar neighborhoods, but our house was the nicest in the whole ward. Nobody ever hassled or bothered me. I never worried about walking to and from the school bus or riding my bike around the neighborhood with my friends. Everybody was always so nice to me.

It wasn't until later, around fifth grade, that I finally figured out why my life seemed so much different than my peers. I was the niece of one of Houston's most dangerous men. My beloved, silly Uncle Nicky was called Nickel Jackson on the streets, and he controlled a huge swath of Houston's criminal underworld. No one was brave or stupid enough to go against him or hurt his family.

Not until Kiki.

The worst mistake I had ever made.

The man who had left me scarred body and soul and mind.

The man who I hoped would rot and die in prison.

"So," Savannah said in a sing-song voice, interrupting my troubled thoughts. "Guess who is coming to the salon today?"

"The weatherman who makes you sweat like a July heat wave?" I teased.

Billie laughed as she scooped most of the chickpea dish into Savannah's takeout container.

Savannah pursed her lips. "He does not make me sweat!"

"Ma'am," I said with a pointed look. "Don't lie to me. I know panting when I see it."

Savannah glared at Billie who was giggling now. "He does not make me pant. I am not a panter! Or a sweater! I am not interested in Travis!"

"Sure," I remarked with faked sincerity.

"He has a girlfriend!"

"So do most of the guys who hit on me," Billie said. "Even a wedding band doesn't stop some of these two-timing motherf—"

"Billie!" Savannah hissed.

"Fluffers," Billie finished with a dramatic flourish.

"Uh-huh. Sure." Savannah turned her frustrated gaze back to me. "As I was saying," she emphasized each word, "one of *your* favorite guests is coming to the salon after lunch."

"None of my favorites are on my books today."

"I didn't say he was on your book," Savannah clarified, looking like the cat that got the cream. "He's on Holly's."

Him? On the outside, I remained cool and calm, but inside, nervous butterflies swarmed my belly. Surely, she didn't mean…?

Billie frowned as she dragged her naan through the rich buttery sauce in her bowl. "There's no one on Holly's book today. She had me block it off last month so she could dip out early for her flight to LA with her mom."

"Oh, did she?" Savannah pretended to be surprised. "Well, that must have been my mistake! But, that's okay. I'm sure

Nisha will be more than happy to squeeze him into her chair."

"Savvy!" I glared at her, hoping my narrowed eyes would take away from the obvious flush of excited nervousness. "You didn't!"

"Oh, I definitely did. Ten will be your last appointment of the day."

Ten.

Anton Vasiliev.

The big, huge, sexy-as-hell bodyguard who shadowed Vivian Kalasnikov.

The outrageously handsome man who had been openly flirting me with for almost two years.

The first man to ever make me feel needy flutters and that dark, curling, squeeze of desire between my legs.

The only man I had ever fantasized about, turning off the lights in my bedroom and using my favorite toy while thinking of his rough, tattooed hands touching my body.

"Right." Suddenly flustered and no longer hungry, I gathered up my lunch mess and left the table. Savannah called out after me, obviously regretting her little trick, but I ignored her as I cleaned and dried my vintage Tupperware and packed everything back into my lunch bag.

"Nisha! Wait!" Savvy chased after me, blocking the doorway of the employee lounge. "I'm sorry! I'm so sorry! I just meant it as a little joke. I didn't think—." She shook her head. "Look, I'll find someone else to cut his hair, and you can leave early if you'd like. It's just—well, I thought you two were flirting. I didn't realize he made you uncomfortable."

"He doesn't make me uncomfortable." As much as I wanted her to grovel, I didn't want her to think she had misread a situation and put me in danger. "The opposite actually."

"Okay?" Clearly confused, she asked, "Are you not interested? Are you seeing someone?"

"I don't date, Savvy. You know that. Everyone knows that."

"I mean, there's not dating and then there's living a celibate life like a nun," Savannah said. "I mean, I grew up with nuns, and you are definitely not nunnish."

"Is that even a word, Savvy? Nunnish?"

"Don't try to distract me with a language discussion! You know my nerdy crossword puzzle-loving ass is unable to ignore any talk of vocabulary."

She was right. I had hoped she would go off on a tangent about the etymology of nuns and let me escape without any more uncomfortable questions about my love life and my infatuation with Ten.

"Listen," Savannah stepped closer and put a gentle hand on my shoulder. "I am sorry, and I will fix this. I shouldn't have played games with your feelings. That was wholly inappropriate of me."

"Goodness," I said, taken aback by her apology. "How many hours are you spending reading all those HR newsletters that drop into your inbox?"

"Nisha!"

"Okay! All right." I held up a hand to stay her next words. "I am not mad at you. You didn't offend me. We're fine."

Savannah nodded, but I could see that she remained uncertain. "I'll see if Tiara can stay late and take his appointment."

God help me, but I felt the most intense and awful flare of

jealousy at the very idea of Tiara Woodruff putting her hands on Ten. She was the sweetest woman. Her life revolved around God and family and her role as a cheerleader for the Texans. She only worked part-time at Allure during football season and had a waitlist five miles long for appointments. She wouldn't purposely try to flirt with Ten, but there was just something about her that made men into slobbering idiots in her presence.

"No!" The word came out harsh, and Savannah seemed visibly surprised. More gently, I said, "No, it's fine. I'll do it."

Savannah's surprised expression turned sly. "Okay."

"What?" I asked, irritated that she had seen right through me. "I'm sure she has choreography training this evening. She can't be late."

"Sure." Savannah nodded smugly. "That's definitely why you're worried. Her schedule, right? Definitely not her fingers running through Ten's hair at the shampoo station."

"You're impossible." I stomped away in a huff, ignoring Savannah's laugh and the burning streak of jealousy that scorched my heart at the very thought of Tiara putting those neatly manicured nails anywhere near Ten's scalp.

Get a grip!

Of all the men in Houston, why did it have to be Ten who affected me like this? Why did it have to be a man who was the absolute worst choice? A man who went against every single rule I had made for myself after Kiki?

No criminals. No gang members. No made men. No felons or prisoners.

Ten checked every one of those, probably twice or more on some of them.

He likely didn't meet any of my other criteria either.

Stable white-collar job? Homeowner? Retirement savings? A good relationship with family? Education beyond high school?

He was all wrong for me. Completely. Totally. Wrong.

But I wanted him.

I wanted him in a way that I had never experienced.

I wanted him to kiss me until I was breathless, to manhandle me into bed and do dirty, filthy things that made me scream with joy.

I wanted to know what it felt like to have his mouth on me, to have those strong, scarred hands gripping my thighs as he pushed them wide open and lashed me with his tongue.

I wanted to know what it was like to be fucked by a man who looked at me like I was the sexiest woman he had ever seen. I wanted to be worshipped and treated like a queen.

I wanted Ten, even if just for one wicked and wanton night.

An idea struck me as I walked toward the lobby of the salon to greet my next client. What if I propositioned Ten to give me exactly that? What if I indulged myself this once? Satisfied my craving for Ten and then moved on to someone more suitable?

Would he agree? He seemed down for that type of arrangement. No strings. A fling. He got what he wanted. I got what I wanted. No attachments. No trouble.

It could be that simple.

Couldn't it?

"Nisha." Mandee, one of our interns, intercepted me before I made it to the lobby. Her green eyes were wide with concern, and she glanced nervously behind her.

"What's wrong?" Her body language had me on alert. Was it a problem client? Had someone crossed a boundary with her?

Mandee stepped behind the fancy backdrop we provided for guests to take photos for social media and gestured for me to join her. Lowering her voice, she said, "There's a woman at the reception desk who says she's your husband's lawyer."

My stomach dropped, and my heart pounded. Mouth dry, I said, "Kiki is my ex-husband."

"I know, but that's what she said. She has that creep with her. You know, that Chad Whatshisface that's always on TikTok and FB with his lives on crime scenes? He's recording everything on his phone and a Go-Pro." Mandee wrung her hands. "Tiara is up there right now trying to get rid of them. Do you want me to get Billie to throw them out? Or Savannah?"

As much as I would prefer to let someone else handle this, I shook my head. "I've got it."

When we drew near the lobby, I heard Tiara's raised voice. "You shouldn't be here! This is not—."

"Is there a problem?" I asked, lifting my shoulders back and assuming my best professional voice.

"Mrs. Acevedo, do your clients know that your husband is a serial killer?" Chad Asshole shoved his phone in my face, and I reared back to avoid getting hit.

"My name is Ms. Nisha Jackson," I clarified calmly. "That monster is my ex-husband."

"But do your clients know what kind of woman is cutting their hair?" Chad insisted, shaking his phone at me.

"They know she's a fighter who survived what you can't even imagine," Tiara hissed before smacking the phone out of the way.

Guilty about the way I had imagined her rubbing her perfect hands through Ten's hair, I smiled gratefully. "Thank you."

"Chad, step back." The attorney looked fresh out of school. She had that nervously arrogant energy about her, like she wanted to project cool, collected professionalism but didn't have the experience to back it up. The polyester shine of her trendy but cheap SHEIN pantsuit didn't help.

She was obviously doing the best she could on a small budget, and if she wasn't here to harass me, I would have pointed her in the direction of resale shops that served professional women just starting out in their careers.

"Ms. Jackson," she said too loudly. "I'm here to—."

"Let's speak in my office." I cut her off before she could say his name. I pointed at the man with a phone in my face. "And you need to take your phone and recording equipment outside. This is a private establishment that provides spa services. We do not allow our guests to be recorded."

"My name is Chad—."

"Did I ask your name?" I interrupted brusquely.

His face turned red. "You don't have to be—."

"Sir, this is private property, and you are not a guest. Take your phone and go." I glanced at Tiara. "Call the police to have him removed."

"With pleasure," she said brightly smiling at the creep.

"You," I narrowed my eyes at the attorney, "can follow me."

As I spun on my heel, I tapped slipped my earbud in place and clicked the call button on the salon headset, "Billie, get Savannah to the front, please. We have a problem."

"On it."

When I led the attorney through the employee access door to the back of the salon, I nearly collided with Savannah. She spared a withering glare at the lawyer trailing me. From the looks of it, she had gotten an update from Tiara at the front.

"If she gives you any trouble, I'll trespass her myself," Savannah warned. "I'm not in the mood for games."

When we reached my office, I let her step inside first.

"I'm not here to play games. I'm here on behalf of my client."

"Your psycho serial killer client?" I pulled the door shut behind me.

"Alleged," the lawyer insisted, and I wheeled around on her in shock.

"Convicted," I corrected. "Tried. Convicted. Sentenced. Appeals denied."

"Not all of them." She lifted her chin higher. "We are filing new appeals based on new evidence that has come to light."

"Uh-huh." I rolled my eyes. "You realize you're not the first lawyer he's tried all this nonsense with, right?"

"I'm the first lawyer who has stepped back and looked at the entire case—including you."

Her remark had the hint of a threat to it, but I just shrugged. "And?"

"And Kiki's DNA was not the only DNA recovered from the evidence you conveniently discovered in the shed behind his house."

"Our house." I emphasized. "I was married to him. And, yes, obviously, I touched the box when I found it. I touched what was inside because I didn't know what I was looking at and couldn't make sense of it." I crossed my arms. "This was all covered in the trial. The same trial that countless appeals have found was conducted correctly."

"Yes, but I'm able to put forth a new motive. You were a jealous, abused, toxically co-dependent child bride who would have done anything to get revenge on your husband. You had a history of violence."

"A history of violence? One time." I held up a finger. "Once. When I was a teenager. I made a mistake." I blinked as her insinuation registered. "Are you accusing me of—?"

"I'm not accusing you of anything, Nisha. I'm giving you a chance to tell the truth about what really happened to those prostitutes. I'm offering you an opportunity to get in front of the scandal that's about to erupt."

I stared at her. The haughty, smug expression on her face burned me right up. Was this bitch for real? Standing here in my office accusing me of—what? Being the real killer? An accomplice?

"Get out." I wrenched open my office door. "Get out of my office. Get out of our salon. Now."

She didn't move. "Nisha, if I walk out that door, I'm not coming back with a better offer."

"Good." I pointed at the open doorway. "Get the fuck out of my face."

She bristled at my rudeness and stormed out of my office. I stepped into the hallway and found Tiara and Mandee, looking on anxiously. Tiara rushed to my side and gave me a hug. "Are you okay?"

"I'm fine." It felt good to be hugged by a friend. It centered me back in the moment, and I managed not to get dragged back into the emotional hell of my memories.

Savannah appeared at the end of the hallway. She took one look at me and asked, "Do you want to go home early?"

"No." The last place I needed to be was alone with my thoughts. "I'm fine."

"She's not fine," Tiara protested. "Look at her. She's shaking!"

"I'll be fine." I gently extricated myself from Tiara. "I have a client waiting."

"Savannah." Tiara shot her a look.

Savannah shook her head. "Nisha wants to go back to work. I think that's the right decision."

Tiara and Mandee trailed me to the lobby where my client was waiting patiently. As much as I appreciated their concern, I had a job to do. Kiki had already taken so much from me. I wasn't going to let him interfere with my livelihood.

But even as I sat my client down in my chair and began to chat with her about amping up her highlights, I couldn't shake the feeling that something terrible was just around the corner.

CHAPTER TWO

A S TEN STEPPED out of his Tahoe, he scanned the parking lot for any signs of trouble. Even without Vivian and Lev in his care, he remained ever vigilant. Getting a haircut wasn't usually dangerous, but this wasn't any old hair salon. Holly Phillips was part-owner of Allure and also the girlfriend of Kostya, the Kalasnikov family's semi-retired cleaner.

And, of course, there was Nisha Jackson.

The woman who had taken his breath away at that first meeting. Beautiful, sexy, curvy Nisha fucking owned his heart and soul—and she didn't even know it.

In the early days of knowing her, when he shadowed Vivian to her salon appointments, he tried to hide his interest. He wasn't stupid. There was no way a woman like that would ever want a man like him. A criminal. A felon. A tattooed killer in the Russian mafia. He was lower than shit on the bottom of her designer high heels.

She was unattainable. Strong. Sophisticated. Successful. Nisha's ideal man was probably a lawyer or a doctor or a wealthy businessman. She deserved a man who could give her whatever she wanted—a house, luxury vacations, kids.

Yet, try as he might, he couldn't shake his infatuation with her. Over time, that lustful interest deepened into gut-gnawing unrequited love. It was pathetic, but it was the truth. He was a ridiculous, love-sick asshole.

And, because he clearly hadn't suffered enough, he had allowed Vivian to meddle and arrange this haircut. She had successfully manipulated and played matchmaker for most of her friends, and now she seemed to have set her sights on him. She couldn't fathom that some people weren't meant to be happy or that she couldn't solve everyone's problems.

Frankly, Ten was of the mind that Nikolai needed to tell her no more often. The boss spoiled her, and it only encouraged her pushy behavior. Like taking it upon herself to call the salon and book an appointment for him with Nisha. What did Vivian think would happen? That Nisha would gaze down at him while she shampooed his hair and fall madly in love with him?

With an irritated grunt, he slammed his door and locked it. He crossed the parking lot with purposeful strides and entered the salon. He always expected to be smacked in the face with the chemical scents of hair dye and whatever other complicated concoctions the women here mixed together in the name of beauty. Somehow, Holly kept the place smelling clean and bright, like crisp morning air and fresh oranges. The air purifying setup in here must have been outrageously expensive which probably explained the eye-watering prices for their services.

"Hello!" Billie greeted from her spot behind the reception desk. "You can take a seat if you'd like, and I'll let Nisha know you're here."

"I'll stand." If he sat, he would start fidgeting. Up on his feet, he felt calmer and in control.

"Would you like some water? A mimosa? Coffee or tea?" Billie offered after using her headset to contact Nisha.

He shook his head. "I'm good."

"Ten?"

At the sound of Nisha's husky voice, his mouth went suddenly dry. Maybe he should have taken that water, after all.

The moment he laid eyes on her, he was overwhelmed by needful yearning. Even in her simple, all-black outfit, she blew him away. Not that anything about Nisha Jackson was ever simple. She toed that line of professional and sexy, showing just a hint of skin to drive a man wild.

The fluttery top she wore today had short sleeves and a dip right in the front that gave him a very much-appreciated glimpse of her cleavage. Her tight pants highlighted her thick thighs and that fat, spankable ass that made his brain go numb and his dick stand at attention. He wouldn't let himself imagine what she was wearing under those pants. He could only control himself so much, and if he started thinking about running his hands over her plump bottom and giving it a good smack before diving in with his tongue—.

"Ten?" Nisha brows drew together. "You all right?"

"Yeah. Sorry." His face flushed, and he was certain she knew exactly what he was thinking. She narrowed her eyes a bit. *Fuck. Busted.* In a rush, he blurted out, "You look beautiful today. Not just today," he hurriedly clarified. "Every day. Always. *Blyad.*" Shit. Fuck. Shit. "What I meant to say—."

"Bro," Billie cut in dramatically and slashed her fingers across her neck. "Stop digging."

"Right." His ears were burning, and he felt ridiculous and flustered like he was fourteen again, his voice cracking when he tried to ask out Daria Kwiatkowski in front of all her friends.

Nisha smiled gently. "Come on. Let's get you in my chair before you open that mouth again and say something really silly."

Billie giggled, and he shot her a glare. Most people would immediately clam up and apologize, but not this girl. She was like an annoying kid sister who always had to poke and prod.

"Wait! Nisha! Tell him about the lawyer and that mother-fluffing podcaster!" Billie's interjection drew a glare from Nisha.

"What lawyer?" He didn't like the sound of it, and the way Nisha was trying to throw eye daggers at Billie convinced him something troubling had happened.

"It's nothing," Nisha insisted.

"Her ex-husband's lawyer showed up here with a nosy butthead," Billie said in a rush. "The podcast guy was, like, all up in Nisha's face and started saying really inflammatory stuff about what kind of woman she is like he wanted to rile up our clients. Savannah threatened to kick his ass all the way to Louisiana, and he scuttled like the cockroach he is."

"Thank you, Billie," Nisha muttered.

"What?" Billie gestured at him. "Look at the guy! You think that wiener weasel Chad is going to bother you if Ten gives him a visit to straighten him out?"

"I don't need Ten to fight my battles for me."

"No, but I will," Ten said, catching Nisha's eye. "I know you can handle your own business. There's nothing wrong with outsourcing the dirtier work."

"Thank you, but no." Nisha glared at Billie who looked

obscenely proud of herself. "Listen, let's get you back to my station."

He let the subject drop, but he intended to follow up on this podcaster and the lawyer. But there was something he wanted to know from Billie first. "Motherfluffing? Wiener weasel?"

"I'm not allowed to use the bad words up here," Billie said in a stage whisper. "Mommy Savvy charges me five dollars anytime I let the naughty words fly."

"Uh-huh," he said dryly. "Well, you sound ridiculous."

"Ridiculously adorable," Billie countered with her trademark grin.

"I don't know how you handle this all day." He gestured toward Billie. "Just nonstop sunshine."

"No one else can figure out the client booking system," Nisha remarked. "She keeps it just disorganized enough that she'll always have job security."

He fucking believed it.

When they reached Nisha's station, he warily eyed the chair. "I'm not sure I'll fit."

"I fit," she said reassuringly.

He frowned. "You're also a foot shorter than me."

"But a foot wider," she remarked lightly.

"Hardly," he grumbled, not at all happy that she would put herself down like that. Feeling more confident now that they were alone in her corner of the salon, he lowered his voice so only she would hear. "I meant what I said, Nisha. You're beautiful. Today. Yesterday. Tomorrow. You're the hottest fucking woman in this city."

She gulped with surprise. "Ten."

He stepped closer than he had ever dared. When she didn't immediately step back, he took that as a good sign. She wasn't putting up walls today. She was letting him in, and he was going to go as far as she would let him.

Her perfume tickled his nose, and he wanted to lean in and drag his nose along her neck and pulse points, to scent her like the dirty dog he was. "You smell good."

She swallowed hard again, and her gaze dropped to his chest. "It's Lost Cherry." She finally dared to lift her gaze to his. "Tom Ford."

He made sure to burn that piece of information into his brain for later use. He locked eyes with her, taking in the dark pools that seemed suddenly hazy. Feeling bold, he admitted, "I didn't come here just for the haircut."

"I figured as much." Her gaze flicked to his mouth and then back to his eyes. "You've never been subtle about your interest, even if I don't understand why a man like you would want anything to do with me."

"Stop," he commanded, not wanting to hear any of that nonsense. "Let's get real, Nisha. You're my superior in every way. I'm lucky you're even letting me stand this close."

She lifted her chin. "I'm considering letting you get even closer."

His lips twitched with a smile. "How close?"

"I haven't decided just yet." She poked his chest with her forefinger and gave him a little shove. "Be a good boy, and we'll see."

If ever there was a woman who could drive him to his knees with one little finger, it was Nisha. "Yes, ma'am."

Her eyes sparkled with amusement. "Sit."

He did, but as he'd expected, it was a tight squeeze.

"Okay, I apologize. You were absolutely right. Let's try the barber chair station."

He hefted his bulk out of the salon chair and trailed her to a station near the front of the salon. It gave him another chance to study the swing of her full hips and the lush curve of her bottom.

There were only two spots dedicated to men, not surprising considering their clientele was overwhelmingly female. He got comfortable in the chair and caught Nisha furrowing her brow. "What's wrong?"

"I've never used this thing before so I have no idea how the footrest works. Maybe Billie does? I can't even tell you how many times I've caught her after hours pumping these chairs up all the way and spinning in them like a preschooler on a sugar high."

"Yeah, that doesn't surprise me at all."

"To be fair, she's amazing with kids who come in and are a little nervous. She's great with Chess's daughter. They play barber shop and sing songs while they wait and Billie always has a stash of Reese's cups at the front desk for her."

Nisha crouched down to examine the chair more closely, and she wobbled on her high heels. She reached out to steady herself, grasping his bare arm. Her grip seared him, and he wished more than anything that she would leave her brand on him. "Sorry!"

"It's fine." He fought the urge to place his hand atop hers, to stroke her soft skin. "You okay?"

If she was flustered, she didn't show it. She rose gracefully and then pressed a lever with her toe. The footrest dropped, and she knocked him out with her smile. "There. Fixed."

"Thanks." He missed the heat of her hand on him as she stepped behind him. Her height and the added lift of the high heels meant she didn't need to adjust the chair. In the mirror, her breasts perfectly framed his head, and he couldn't help but wonder—.

"So—what were you thinking?"

His brain fritzed for a moment, and he almost blurted out the filthy thought he was having. "Uh—a trim?"

"A trim?" She eyed him skeptically. "Do you know what I charge? You could have gone to Great Clips if you only needed a trim."

"Vivian insisted."

She tilted her head. "Do you do everything she insists?"

"You've met her. She's bossy."

"I never took you for the sort of man to be bossed around by a woman."

"Depends on the woman," he remarked, pinning her with a heated gaze.

"Uh-huh," she intoned dryly.

His flirtatious reply died on his lips. Nisha combed her fingers through his hair, lightly scratching her bright aqua nails along his scalp, and he shuddered at the incredible sensation. It traveled right down his spine, settling low in his groin. *Fuck me.*

"You okay?" She held his gaze in the mirror, her movements paused as she waited for his reply.

"Yes," he ground out, worried he was going to embarrass himself with a groan. She started to drag her nails through his hair again, and he felt himself start to lean back, desperate for her to keep her hands on him.

"You and Wilford would get along like two peas in a pod." She scratched her nails against his scalp, this time with enough pressure to make goosebumps break out on his skin. "Just don't bite me the way he does when I stop."

"I hope you're talking about a pet." He gripped the arms of the chair, the leather squeaking under his tightly clutched fingers.

"My cat," she clarified. "He looks just like Wilford Brimley."

"The diabetes commercial guy?"

"Yeah, and Quaker Oats," she said, gently removing her fingers from his hair. "You have very healthy hair and a squeaky-clean scalp."

"Is that strange?" He figured she wouldn't mention it if it wasn't.

"Considering most men use a shampoo and body wash combo like they're still teenagers? Yes."

"I buy my products separately," he assured her.

"You do seem to be a man who takes care of himself." She opened a drawer at the hair-cutting station and retrieved a cape. "Do you want a shampoo?"

"Yes." He craved the feeling of her hands on him again. He wanted to close his eyes and revel in the sensation of hot water and thick lather and her nimble fingers gliding along his scalp.

"Okay." She draped the cape around his shoulders and fastened it in place. "This way."

The shampoo chair was surprisingly comfortable, even for a man of his size. He shifted a bit to get his neck in just the right place. She gently cupped the back of his head, guiding his movements. This close, her scent wrapped around him, invading his nose and lungs and settling deep inside. He wanted to stare up at her gorgeous face, but he felt suddenly awkward and nervous.

Was she scrutinizing him? Was she counting the scars on his face? The small dent on the upper left side of his forehead where he'd caught a rock thrown by his cousin? The old acne marks hidden under his beard? The melted plastic spoon turned prison shiv that had sliced open his cheek? Was she drawing lines between the splatter of freckles on his forehead and cheeks like a connect-the-dot page in a child's coloring book?

"Let me know if this gets too hot," she warned before turning the spray nozzle onto his scalp.

"I will." He relaxed into her skilled hands, closing his eyes and enjoying her touch. She worked slowly, wetting his hair and gently scratching his scalp. She moved away briefly and returned with shampoo that she lathered into his hair. It felt so good.

Too good.

He hadn't been touched like this in a long, long time. Sure, there had been some one-night stands and hookups between his release from prison and now, but they were always the same. He seemed to only draw the attention of women who wanted a good time. They saw a man who was built like a bear, nearly seven feet tall and muscular, and wanted to be man-handled and fucked hard. They wanted wild and hot and dangerous.

But he craved something else.

He craved tenderness. He craved intimacy. He watched

Nikolai with Vivian and Sergei with Bianca and envied their marriages. He wanted that. He wanted a wife and a family. He wanted the nice house and the kids in soccer and gymnastics and vacations to Disney World every summer.

But he would never have those things. He was tainted, and no woman would ever want to tie herself to him. Even if Nisha gave him a chance to take her out, the odds were against him.

He knew all about her ex-husband, Kiki. They had run in the same underworld circles, and Kiki's reputation as a hair-trigger psycho was well known. More than once, Kiki had tried to provoke him, but Ten had refused to give in and take the bait. There were rules, and Nikolai didn't fuck around when it came to keeping the peace.

When it came out that Kiki was a serial killer, Ten hadn't been surprised. No one who lived in the darkness of their world was. Kiki and that *pederast* Adrian Umansky and their partner Fat Tony had been under suspicion by the boss and Kostya. There was something wrong about those three, and Nikolai and the cartel should have never allowed the trio to work together on drug and gun runs. Everywhere they went, violence followed.

Tony. Ten's jaw tightened with hatred. That piece of shit was the reason he had gone to prison. Ten had done his time without complaint. He kept his head down, played by the rules, and got out on parole as quickly as possible. Now, he was on the outside, enjoying his freedom, and Tony was rotting six feet underground in the Forest Park Cemetery in Webster.

The jingle of Nisha's gold bracelets filtered through his thoughts and brought him back to the present. She had rinsed the shampoo and applied a conditioner, massaging it into his hair until his shoulders slackened and his scalp tingled.

"Don't fall asleep," she teased.

"I've been chasing after a crawling baby all day. I've got maybe 5% left in my battery."

She laughed softly. "Lev is a sweetheart. Those eyes and that hair! He's adorable."

"He knows it," Ten grumbled. "He's got everyone wrapped around his finger like a little prince."

"Well," she said, turning on the water again, "he kinda is a little prince."

"Kinda." Nikolai and Vivian were the king and queen of Houston's underworld.

"It's good practice chasing after Lev," she said and rinsed his hair. "I mean if that's something you want in the future."

"It is." He cracked open an eye to judge her response and caught her smile. "What about you?"

Her smile faded, and she turned off the water. She reached for a towel from a nearby shelf, and with her back turned, she said, "Yes. I'd like to have kids someday."

"I'm sorry," he apologized, silently berating himself for upsetting her. "I shouldn't have asked such a personal question."

"It's fine." She smiled down at him, but it wasn't as genuine. "It's a touchy subject for me."

"I'm sorry." He felt even worse now. He didn't know everything that happened to her while married to Kiki, but he should have remembered she had lost her baby. He should have been more careful with her.

"It's fine." She patted his shoulder. "We're fine."

He wasn't so sure of that. She dried his hair and beckoned him back to the barber chair. He stayed silent as she grabbed her tools from her station. Their friendly banter had cooled, and he wasn't sure how to get back on track. Maybe he had blown it for today and should let it go.

She worked quickly and efficiently, her scissors snipping and the comb sliding through his shaggy hair to separate the short sections. There was none of the gossip and laughter that he normally heard among the clients and their stylists. Every now and then, their gazes would clash in the mirror, and she would smile and then glance away quickly.

You fucked it, Anton. You fucked it up good.

When she finished the cut, she began to style his hair. He never used products in it, but he had to admit it looked nice. "Do you sell this stuff?"

"Yes. Would you like to buy some?"

"Yeah." He watched her apply some kind of mousse that smelled woodsy and clean to his hair. "That's all there is to it?"

"That's it. You have great hair so you don't need much." She grabbed a fat, fluffy brush and cleaned the clipped hairs clinging to his skin. "Do you want me to hit you with a blow dryer to get all of this off?"

"No, I'm headed home to shower."

"Hot date?"

Seizing his chance, he said, "Only if you're available."

Suddenly demure, she glanced away and seemed very interested in dusting his neckline with the fluffy brush. "My book club meets tonight."

"Oh."

"But I'm free tomorrow night."

He met her heated gaze, and there was no mistaking the

flash of excitement in her dark eyes. His heart thumped wildly in his chest. "Dinner?"

"I'd like that."

"Can I have your number?" He shifted in his seat and retrieved his phone from the pocket of his jeans. "So we can work out the details?"

"Sure." She took the phone from him and sent herself a message so he would have her phone number. "I'm out of the salon by five tomorrow, but I have Pilates until six."

"How about eight?" He hesitated before adding, "I can cook for you if you'd like."

"You cook?" She playfully narrowed her eyes. "Well, now my interest is piqued. I'd love to come over for dinner."

They firmed up their plans as she walked him to the front desk and grabbed the products he wanted to try from the nearby shelves. She smiled at him one last time before leaving him with Billie who nosily asked him what he was going to cook for Nisha.

"She had gumbo for lunch today. Don't make anything similar to that. Oh—you forgot to boop the card reader." She gestured to the device mounted on the counter. "Definitely skip any of that funky Russian food with cabbage or beets. There is nothing sexy about cabbage or beets."

"Noted," he muttered, wishing the card reader would hurry up so he could get out of there. "And Russian food isn't just beets and cabbage, Billie. That's racist as hell."

She wrinkled her nose. "I don't think that's the right word for it. Stereotyping? Profiling?"

"It's a rude assumption is what it is."

"You're right. I will chastise myself properly during my evening prayers. Flogging. Hairshirt. The whole bit. Straight back to my Catholic roots."

"Are you like this at home?" Ten knew her big sister and couldn't fathom how she handled Billie.

"Jamie encourages me to work as much as possible."

"I bet she does."

"Hey, make sure you get a good dessert for dinner." She put his products into a small paper bag stamped with the salon's logo. "Like a really good one. Something fancy but delicious from a bakery. If you can't get to a real bakery, H-E-B is fine, but stick to the stuff in the bakery case."

"Anything else?"

"Well…"

"I was kidding." He snatched the bag and receipt from her hand. "See you later, Billie."

"Bye! If you need help planning your menu, I'm happy to help! Unless you're going to make vegan food in which case, you're on your own!"

Shaking his head, he left the salon and wondered how Billie had ever managed to get hired at Allure. Then again, a spunky chatterbox was the perfect fit for the reception desk. God help whatever man was crazy enough to fall in love with her.

He had just reached his Tahoe when his phone began to ring. He unlocked his door and answered. "Yeah?"

"Ten. It's Kostya. Get to the storage center as soon as you can. We have a problem."

The call ended before he could reply. Dread washed away the excitement of finally securing a date with Nisha. Whatever awaited him at the warehouse was surely going to fuck up his plans.

CHAPTER THREE

LATER THAT EVENING, when I stepped out of the bar and grill where my book club met, I was taken aback to see Detective Eric Santos leaning against my Rubicon. We had practically grown up together, living on the same street and going to the same schools. Our relationship was one of a brother and sister so I scowled and called out, "You better not scratch my paint with all that flashy nonsense on your belt."

Eric laughed and shoved off the Jeep. "Sorry, Cinderella. I'll step away from your pumpkin."

"The color is Punk'n Metallic, Detective," I corrected with playful haughtiness. "And I love it."

"It suits you." Eric stepped forward, and I hugged him tightly, giving his back a quick pat.

"It's been forever since you've visited." I stepped back and studied his face. The tension in his expression made me nervous. "What is it?"

"Something has happened."

"My uncle?" My stomach dropped like a runaway elevator. "Has there been a shooting?"

"No, no, no." Eric hurriedly clarified. "Nicky is fine. I mean, he's up to no good with his business, but he's fine."

"Eric!"

"It's Kiki," he blurted out. "He escaped from his prison transport."

"What?" Staggered, I took a sharp step backward and gripped my handbag. My fingers flexed, ready to snatch open the door of my Jeep and grab the P200 SK hidden away in my glove box. Normally, it was in my bag, but the restaurant didn't allow weapons inside. "He's a convicted murderer on death row, Eric! How the hell did he escape?"

"He's sick, and his lawyer filed a bunch of motions until TDCJ agreed to have him moved from the Polunsky Unit to the prison hospital in Galveston for a workup."

"And, again, he's on death row! Who the fuck cares if he's sick and suffers and dies in his prison cell? Not me! Not the families of the women he killed!"

"Nisha," Erica interjected gently. "I know it doesn't make sense, but it's the law. We can't mistreat prisoners because they're monsters."

"Well, someone needs to change that law," I stubbornly argued. "Look where it's gotten us." Another troubling thought hit me. "Did he kill someone to get free?"

Eric nodded somberly. "Two guards and a retired couple he carjacked."

That ever-present tinnitus in my right ear seemed to grow louder. I was probably imagining it, but there it was all the same. "So far," I corrected, holding Eric's solemn gaze. "How close is he?"

"We don't know," Eric admitted. "He escaped right near Shepherd so he's probably in Sam Houston National Forest."

I snorted in disbelief. "He's probably in Houston, trying to catch my scent so he can finish what he started in that bathroom back in San Antonio."

"Maybe." Eric seemed unable to agree to something so obviously bad for me.

"I assume he didn't manage this alone. He's not that smart, you know. He thinks he is. He really believes all the bullshit his mother told him when he was a kid, that he's such a smart boy and so special. But, actually, he's an idiot."

"He definitely had help," Eric confirmed.

"The lawyer? She came to see me today. Brought some idiot with a phone and GoPro to record the whole thing. We threw him out, but I let her talk to me in my office."

"What did she want?"

"She was making threats about me being the real murderer. Something about a motive and new witnesses." I rolled my eyes just thinking of her stupid spiel. "It was just horse shit."

"Maybe."

"Eric!"

"I didn't mean you being innocent is a maybe! I meant her threats. Robin Harris has connections to some of those groups that work to free unjustly convicted inmates. She's also very popular on the podcast true crime circuit."

"The what now?"

"Podcasts. True crime. Amateur investigators. Robin made trouble in San Antonio before coming here. Kiki isn't the only defendant she's championing."

"Well, considering how easily she's been bamboozled by Kiki, I suspect her other clients are just as guilty."

"She got one of them cleared of his charges and two others reduced sentences."

"Oh, well that's just great!"

"That's not going to happen with Kiki. He confessed. His DNA was all over the victims and the knife they found in the house. Even if he managed to get out of those charges on some bizarre technicality, he attempted to kill you while police were right outside the front door. It's on the 9-1-1 call." Eric hesitated. "He also killed your baby."

A wave of nausea left me lightheaded. My dinner swirled in my stomach, and I swayed as the horrible memories of that night came rushing back.

"Nisha!" Eric engulfed me in his arms, cradling me close and bringing me back to reality. "You're okay. You're okay."

"I'm not okay." I closed my eyes and held tight to my friend. "I'll never be okay. I should have known Kiki would never let me escape. He's going to finish what he started and kill me."

"Don't say that!" Eric urged. "You are not going to die."

"We're all going to die, Eric. It's just a matter of when." I didn't often let myself sink into such moody nihilism, but it felt appropriate in that moment.

"Yeah, well, I'd rather us be old and wrinkled and surrounded by kids and grandkids and great-grandkids when we go." He gently pressed me away until we could look each other in the eye. "You and I have a lot of living to do, Nisha."

"You're right." I held tight to his hand. "I'm not letting that piece of shit Kiki take anything else from me. If anyone is going to meet our maker, it's going to be him."

Eric didn't scold me for basically confessing to a plan to murder my ex-husband if I got the chance. Instead, he nodded in agreement. "I'll help you in any way I can."

I understood what he meant. He wasn't talking about

helping me as a police officer and a detective. He was talking about helping me as only a true friend could. He would take off his badge and pick up a shovel if I asked him.

"Lean on your uncle," Eric counseled. "He can probably protect you better than we can. If there is some friction with the cartel and the Hermanos, hopefully, he has some pull to get you clear of it."

"And if he doesn't?" I didn't ask my uncle questions about his business or look too deeply into what was happening in our neighborhood. The less I knew the better, but now I worried I might not have the security I assumed.

Eric hesitated. "I can reach out to my cousin."

"Vivian? I thought you two weren't close anymore."

"It's complicated." Eric scratched his jaw. "We've made amends since Lev was born, but there's still bad blood with her husband."

It seemed he couldn't even bring himself to speak Nikolai's name. I wasn't aware of everything that had gone down between the two men, but it had to do with the only woman Eric had ever loved. All these years, we had thought she was dead, but apparently, she was living her best life in Asia after Nikolai helped her escape her father's clutches. It was like something out of a telenovela.

Thoughts of Vivian and Nikolai spurred images of Ten. If I called him, would he come? Would he keep me safe? Or would he take one look at my messed-up history and run like his ass was on fire?

No. Ten wasn't like that. I had seen him with Vivian and the other women in her group of friends. He would never allow anyone to threaten a woman and especially not one he wanted for his own.

I flushed, overcome by the notion of being Ten's woman. Was that what he wanted? Was it what I wanted?

What would he be like as a partner? As a lover?

He would never hurt me or hit me.

Ten was a criminal, but Nikolai would never leave Ten alone with his wife and child if there was even a sliver of doubt regarding his honor.

"Nisha." Eric reached out suddenly and drew me between his body and my Jeep. Guarding me with his back, he stiffened and let his hand fall to the sidearm at his hip.

I didn't understand what was happening until I heard a revving engine and squealing tires. I flinched and drew back against my Jeep, fully expecting to be shot at or worse.

A vehicle braked. Eric's arm twitched. A door slammed. And then—

"Nisha!" Ten shouted my name.

Startled, I peeked around Eric's shoulder. The Russian be-hemoth stormed across the parking lot, closing the distance between his Tahoe and my Jeep with determined strides. His expression was hard, and he glared at Eric. "Ten?"

"Are you okay? Did something happen?" He glanced around the parking lot. "Why the hell aren't there more cops here? Why doesn't she have an escort?"

"Hey, back up!" Eric shouted and stepped to the side, blocking me from view. "Put your hands up where I can see them."

"Are you fucking serious, Eric?" Ten squared his shoul-ders. "We're doing this? Now?"

"Show me your hands."

Ten mockingly raised his hands and made the nastiest face at Eric. "Happy?"

"Not when you're around," Eric grumbled, moving his hand away from his sidearm. "Why are you here, Ten? Shouldn't you be checked into your halfway house? I wouldn't want you to miss curfew."

The ugly way Eric spoke shocked me. I understood his protectiveness toward me, but he was taking it too far.

Ten didn't miss a beat. "Says the man who still lives with his mother."

I winced at that low blow. Eric's mother had been unwell for years, and he had moved back in to help. Granted, there were some tight apron strings between them.

"I don't have a curfew," Ten said, his gaze meeting mine over Eric's shoulder. "And I have my own home."

"That your mafia boss pays for in exchange for you babysitting his wife," Eric spat back.

"Don't hate on me because I make more money than you doing half the work," Ten remarked. "It's not my fault you flunked out of college and had to get a job as a policeman. Maybe you should have taken the test to be a garbage man instead."

Eric took a step forward, and I latched onto his arm. "No! Stop! Both of you!" I shot Ten a perturbed look. "You apologize right now."

"What?" Ten reared back in shock. "I will not!"

"Yes, you will." I moved between the two men, holding tight to Eric to keep him from leaving. "And then Eric will apologize to you."

"The fuck I will!"

"Well, if you two can't get along, I have nothing to say to either of you." I shrugged. "Your choice. Apologize or lose my number."

Ten huffed—actually huffed—like an irritated dragon. "Fine. I'm sorry, Eric."

He didn't mean it, but I couldn't exactly order him to change his feelings. Still, it was a start.

"Eric?" I prompted with a raised eyebrow.

"Yeah. Fine. I'm sorry, Ten."

"See?" I beamed at both of them. "Was that so hard?"

Eric's phone rang, and he shifted out of my hold to retrieve it. "Detective Santos. Uh-huh. Yeah." He glanced at his watch. "I'll be there in twenty."

"Everything okay?" I noticed the grim set of his mouth as he slipped his phone into his pocket.

"No." Eric looked at Ten. "Felix Osorio is dead."

"Dancing Bear?" Ten seemed taken aback. "I saw him a few days ago. We have the same PO."

"Not anymore. Someone slit his throat and shoved him in the ice machine in a motel laundry room." Eric gestured between Ten and me. "I don't know what this is, and I don't like it. But—if you're here because you care about her, take her home and stay with her tonight."

Ten nodded. "That was the plan."

"Wait. What does this Bear guy have to do with me?" I had never heard his name in my life, and I couldn't understand why his murder had rattled Eric enough to make him ask Ten for a favor.

"He was a connection between your ex and the cartel," Ten explained, his gaze never leaving Eric's face.

I frowned. "No, that was Adrian Umansky."

Ten shook his head. "Adrian was a driver on loan from us. The three of them—Adrian, Kiki and Tony Guerrero—would meet Dancing Bear to pick up the cargo and get their destination assignments."

Rattled by how much Ten knew about my ex-husband, I gawked at him. He must have realized how much he had revealed in that statement because he wouldn't meet my eyes.

All this time, I had assumed he knew a little about me. It was hard to keep secrets in Houston when your uncle was a high-ranking underworld kingpin, and your ex-husband was a notorious serial killer. Still, it had never occurred to me that Ten might have actually known Kiki.

As if reading my mind, Ten finally said, "We'll talk when we get back to your place."

"Go now." Eric glanced back at the restaurant. "It's not safe here. Too open."

"Agreed."

"Be careful, Nisha." Eric reached for me, drawing me into a lingering embrace. I closed my eyes and squeezed him back, praying silently that he wouldn't get caught in the crossfire of my messy life.

"You be careful, Eric."

"I always am." He pivoted toward his vehicle and left.

"I'll follow you." Ten gestured to my Jeep. "Are we stopping anywhere?"

"No. I planned to go straight home."

He nodded. "Get in. Lock your doors. Drive normally. When you get to your house, pull into your driveway but not into the garage. I'll check your garage and house to make sure it's safe."

"And what if it's not?" I grabbed his hand, suddenly fearful he would get hurt. "What if something happens to you?"

Ten's big, warm hand settled along my cheek, and I couldn't help myself. I leaned into his touch, wanting to remember the heat of his skin on mine for the rest of my life. "Then it happens to me and not to you."

"Ten," I said, desperate for him not to get hurt, not when things were just starting to get interesting between us.

He leaned down and kissed my forehead. It was the sweetest, gentlest kiss, and it made my lower lip wobble. How long had it been since someone had shown me such tenderness? He stroked my face and said, "Get in your Jeep."

Wordlessly, I nodded and got behind the wheel. He waited until I started the engine and fastened my safety belt to close the door. Once I hit the locks, he backed away and returned to his Tahoe. I made sure he was behind the wheel and ready to go before pulling out of the restaurant parking lot.

He followed close behind, never allowing more than one car to get between us. The way he drove convinced me he knew exactly where I lived. Had he driven by before? Maybe parked on my street and thought about ringing the doorbell? Asking if I wanted to hang out? Was he keeping tabs on me? Making sure I was staying safe? Or was it jealousy that motivated him? Was he afraid I was seeing someone else?

All thoughts of Ten fled when I reached the four-way stop where I normally turned left to go down my street. The space outside my house was packed with strange vehicles. People trampled my front yard and sat on my porch swings and rocking chairs. Some of them had lighting setups with them, and all of them had phones in their hands.

Journalists. Podcasters. Nosy assholes.

Panicked, I turned in the opposite direction, praying none of them had seen me at the far end of the street. Ten followed close behind, and I wasn't sure what to do. At the next stop sign, I scrambled for my phone and called him. He answered as I dropped my phone in the cup holder. "Nisha."

"Ten, what do I do? Where do I go?"

"You can come to my place." His voice filled the interior of my Jeep, the soothing baritone pulsing out of my speakers. "You'll be safe there. My condo is gated. You won't be bothered there. At least for tonight."

"I don't have any clothes—and Wilford!" I couldn't leave my fur baby all alone with all those weirdos. "I have to go get him."

"I'll go get him," Ten said calmly. "Let's go to my place and get you safely behind a locked door. I'll go back to your house and get the cat and your clothing and anything else you need."

"He's mean," I warned. "Like I have to give him sedatives before I take him to the vet because he's very quick to swipe with those murder mittens."

"His *what* mittens?"

"His claws," I clarified.

"I've been cut by worse," he assured me before rattling off his address and then asking me to let him pass me so he could take the lead.

Ten lived in the River Oaks area, not in the super bougie and ultra-expensive part where Vivian and Nikolai had a house obviously. Nearby in a nice but more affordable section.

His condo was on the bottom floor of a gated complex that had lush, mature landscaping camouflaging its amenities like a tennis court and pool.

I parked in the covered guest space next to his and grabbed my purse and phone before joining him on the sidewalk. "I won't get towed, right?"

He shook his head. "I have two spaces with my condo. I'll bring out the tag later. You can keep it."

Keep it. No return date. Just—here you go.

"Come on." Ten scanned our surroundings as if he expected trouble and placed his hand between my shoulder blades. With a gentle push, he guided me forward. Even though I knew my psycho ex was out there somewhere, vengeful and murderous, I felt safe with Ten.

Safe. With an ex-con. With a Russian mafioso.

But as he carefully positioned me between his body and anyone else who might want to hurt me, I acknowledged he was so much more than those things. I wasn't naïve anymore. I didn't believe I could fix a man. I wasn't looking at Ten as a project. I was looking at him as he was, ugly parts and all.

And I couldn't find a reason to push him away. There was something about him, something underneath that gruff, hard exterior, that left me wondering if maybe he had a secret. All I had seen of him—and admittedly, it wasn't much—convinced me he wasn't a violent brute.

Sure, Nisha, except for the part where he went to prison!

When we stepped inside his condo, I was taken aback by how incredible it looked. Masculine was the first word that came to mind. Leather, wood, exposed brick. Moody shades of gray and hunter green on the walls. Bookshelves crammed with paperbacks and hardcovers. Artwork and black and white photos in antique frames.

A basket of neon green yarn with a terrible crochet chain dangling off of it caught my eye. I glanced at him, and his ears and cheeks turned bright red. He rushed over to the leather couch and snatched up the crochet basket. He tried to hide it behind his back, but there was no escaping my curiosity.

"You crochet?" I hoped he didn't feel embarrassed, but the furious flush creeping up his neck told me otherwise.

"I'm learning. Against my will," he muttered. "It's part of my court-mandated anger management."

"Really?" I had never heard of crochet as a form of anger management, but it made sense. It was a calm, relaxing activity, and one I enjoyed quite a bit. "If you need some pointers, I can help. I've been crocheting since I was a little girl. My grandma taught me."

"Uh, sure. Maybe." He cleared his throat nervously. "I'll be right back."

While he disappeared with the crochet basket, I locked the front door and then wandered around his living room, taking in the art and then finding myself in front of a bookshelf. He had a lot of thrifted hardcover classics and a mix of newer paperback releases. There was a good mix of nonfiction and fiction with a heavy tilt toward science fiction and fantasy and detective novels.

I glanced in his direction as his heavy footfalls echoed on the hardwood floor. "You have a nice library."

"You have a lot of time to read in prison." Ten joined me at the floor-to-ceiling shelf and reached for a title high up at the top. It was well-worn and leather-bound. He ran his fingers over the spine before handing it to me. "I spent a lot of time reading this one."

I tried to read the title but couldn't make sense of it. "It's in Russian."

"Yes." He seemed amused. "Dostoevsky."

"Of course," I murmured, finding it a little funny, too. "*Crime and Punishment*?"

"Yes."

"How do you say it in Russian?" I looked up at him, marveling at how warm he was standing this close. His body heat soothed my nerves and called me closer.

"*Prestupléniye i nakazániye.*"

"Uh," I said with a self-deprecating laugh. "I'm not going to insult you by butchering your language while trying to repeat that."

"There's nothing you could say that would insult or offend me." Ten carefully took the book from my hand, purposely rubbing his finger along mine, and placed it back where it belonged.

"I bet I could"

"Well, for all you know, that's my kink." He grinned down at me, and I felt giddy like a teenage girl in her first blush of romance. "Being insulted by a beautiful, successful woman."

"You're teasing." I turned away, my face burning with excitement and nervousness. I hadn't flirted like this in a long time. Ever since Kiki, I had chosen men who were easy to read and well-behaved. Betas, I guess, you might call them. Nonthreatening. Simple. Quiet. Small. Slim. No one who could hurt me or get the upper hand in a fight. The dates never went anywhere, and I hadn't touched or slept with another man.

But Ten was the complete opposite. There was nothing small or slim or quiet about him. He was big and loud and handsome, and I knew that if I went on a date with him, it would absolutely lead somewhere. Probably a bedroom.

"I can do more than tease if you'd like."

I pivoted at his offer, finding him staring at me in a way that made me feel naked and seen. I gulped and let my needy gaze roam his chiseled body. I was reminded of my silly idea that morning and blurted out, "I planned to proposition you."

Ten reacted with surprise. "What?"

"This morning," I said, turning away again and unable to meet his intense stare. "I had this ridiculous idea that I could just ask you to have sex, no strings attached, and you would be fine with it. That I would be fine with it," I added, suddenly realizing how dumb that was. "But I don't think that's a good idea anymore."

"Okay, *that* would have offended me."

I spun back to face him. He looked hurt, and I felt bad. "I'm sorry."

"I understand why you would want that." He hesitated. "I know your ex hurt you."

"He did." There was no point in lying about it or being cagey. It was all out there in black and white for anyone to read in newspaper archives. "That doesn't mean I should hurt other people."

"You didn't hurt me, Nisha. I would have been offended by the idea of only being good enough to fuck, but I would have understood."

He stepped toward me, and my first instinct was to recoil and hide. Those old habits were hard to break, even after years of therapy for the trauma and betrayal I had endured. Instead, I stood my ground and waited.

Ten moved slowly, cautiously, as if he were approaching a wounded animal. In many ways, I was. His gaze was so soft and kind, and it made me want to weep with relief. "I won't hurt you, Nisha. Not physically or emotionally or mentally. If all you can accept right now is sex?" He shrugged. "Okay. I would be honored to share that with you."

"Honored?"

He chortled. "I'm an ex-con, Nisha. I'm honored you're even willing to step foot into my home. Letting me touch you?" He shook his head. "I don't deserve that, but fuck me if I'm going to refuse the chance."

My heart raced as I gazed up into his handsome face. There was no dishonesty. He was being open and truthful—and it was making my whole body thrum. The sexual tension between us coupled with the adrenaline of fear from Kiki's escape had my emotions amped right up.

I stepped toward him, closing the space between us, and placed my hands on his chest. I was a big girl, heavy and curvy, but he made me feel small. Dainty, even. I spread my hands along his cotton shirt, sliding them up his hard pecs and up toward his shoulders. He leaned down as I touched him and swallowed so hard I could hear it. The vein in his neck jumped wildly, and I had the strongest urge to lick it, to swipe my tongue right over it and feel his heartbeat.

And then my phone rang.

Startled, I broke eye contact and glanced at my purse on the coffee table where I had left it. My first instinct to ignore the call was squashed by Ten gesturing toward my bag. "You should take that. It's probably important."

"Right." I nodded and reluctantly stepped away from him. As I reached for my phone, I looked back at him. Ten wiped a hand down his face, and I couldn't tell what he was feeling. Regret? Frustration?

Whatever it was, it would have to wait. When I answered the phone, I heard the voice that stalked my nightmares.

"Nisha. I'm coming for you, baby."

CHAPTER FOUR

WHEN NISHA DROPPED the phone, Ten rushed to her side. She shook so hard he feared she was on the cusp of a seizure, and her eyes were wide with terror. "Nisha?"

She threw her arms around his neck, clutching onto him so tightly he nearly choked. She was strong, much stronger than any other woman he had encountered. Her sharp nails dug into the meat of his shoulders, and he winced. He didn't ask her to let go or push her away. He suffered through the pain, desperate to calm her.

"Nisha." He wrapped his arms around her body, drawing her in tight. "It's okay. You're okay." He cupped the back of her head and pressed his cheek to her temple. She trembled, and he was certain she was having a panic attack as her breaths grew shallow and short. "Nisha, talk to me."

"Kiki," she finally managed and buried her face in his neck. He felt the smear of hot tears on his skin. His heart broke, and he held her even tighter. "He's coming."

Ten would kill him. There was no question about it. "He's never going to touch you again."

"He will."

Ten hated that Kiki had destroyed so much of Nisha's life. He hated that she could be so easily reduced to this terrified, shaking, sobbing mess by that psychotic, abusive piece of shit. The death sentence Kiki had been handed down by the jury wasn't enough. With appeals and now this escape, he had continued to torment her and the families of his victims.

"I'm so sorry, Ten." She sobbed against his neck. "I'm so sorry."

"For what?" he asked, completely befuddled.

"For dragging you into this."

"You didn't drag me into anything. I came running willingly." He eyed the sofa and steered her that way. She never let go, and he didn't mind the awkward pace. Holding her like this, feeling the curves of her body against his, giving her the comfort and protection she needed, was worth the slight ache in his back and the worry he might clumsily step on her.

"Wait. I'll squash you." Even in her distress, she worried about her weight and hurting him.

"Maybe I want to be squashed by you." He dropped down onto the couch and dragged her with him. She sat stiffly at first, trying to keep as much of her weight off of him as possible. He gripped her hips and pulled her down firmly against him. It wasn't meant to be sexual, but there was no mistaking the flash in her watery eyes as their bodies connected. "I like you just the way you are, Nisha. All of you."

She studied his face, and she must have seen something that convinced her of his genuineness. She relaxed and shifted a little more, straddling him with her knees on either side of his thighs. She rested her face in the crook of his neck, and he embraced her, holding her close and rocking gently. She sniffled a bit, her breaths coming in shuddery waves as she cried softly. Eventually, she stopped, and he thought she must have fallen asleep until he barely heard her whisper, "Thank you, Anton."

His heart skipped a beat. It has been a long time since anyone had called him by his real name. Not since his father had died. Hearing Nisha say his name felt intensely intimate, and he liked it. He wanted to hear her say it again.

"You used my name."

She leaned back until their gazes met. Her brow furrowed, and she asked, "Is that okay?"

"It's more than okay." He wiped the slick of tears from her face with his thumbs. "I didn't know you knew it."

She lowered her gaze as if suddenly shy. "I asked Bianca about it the last time she was in my chair."

"Sneaky," he teased and wiped the last bit of wetness from her skin. "You could have asked me."

"I could have," she agreed, "but I like to gossip with my clients."

He laughed. "Yes, I'm quite aware of all the whispering and gossip that goes on in that place. Kostya teases Holly that he should have it bugged so he can keep abreast of the latest news in town."

"What's his deal?" Nisha ran her finger over the neckline of his T-shirt. "Like what does he do exactly?"

"He works in private security."

She rolled her eyes. "Sure he does."

"I can't tell you what you want to know." Ten didn't want to have secrets between them, but Kostya's secrets weren't his to share. "Whatever you're imagining is probably correct."

Ten eyed the hastily discarded phone on the floor. Carefully, he shifted Nisha off his lap and retrieved her phone. The screen had locked so he handed it back to her. "Can you let me see the number he used?"

"Yes." She used her face to unlock the phone and gave it back to him. "I don't even know how he found my number."

"You'd be surprised how easy it is to find information like that." He studied the phone number. It was a local area code. Probably a burner given to him by the person helping him with his escape. "We need Kostya."

"Will he want to get involved?"

"He already is." Ten fished his phone from his pocket and called Kostya on his private line. The cleaner answered on the second ring. "Where are you?"

"My place," he answered in Russian and glanced at Nisha. "With her."

"Her house is all over the fucking news. I do not want to see your face online or on television."

"Neither do I. Listen, he called her."

"He? Kiki? When?"

"A few minutes ago. I have the number."

"I'm coming over." Kostya abruptly ended the call.

Ten pocketed his phone and turned back to Nisha who stared intently. "Kostya is coming over to look at your phone. I'm going to have him sit with you while I run to your place and pick up the things you need. Give me a list that has enough clothing and other things for a few days." He hesitated before adding, "We might need to leave Houston for a bit."

"Can you leave? Just like that?" She bit her lower lip with concern. "I don't want you to get in trouble with your parole officer."

"We won't go that far." He also had some concerns about

his PO being a hard ass. He had worked his program exactly as it had been outlined.

> Six years in prison plus the 197 days of time served in the county jail while awaiting trial and twenty out of twenty-four months of supervised release completed.
>
> Time in the halfway house.
>
> Supervised living with Ivan and Erin.
>
> Gainful employment.
>
> Obtaining a home.
>
> Getting his driver's license back.
>
> Attending anger management courses.
>
> Staying out of trouble and away from other felons and ex-cons.

"I will not let you get into trouble for me," Nisha stated resolutely. "I am a big girl, and I can handle myself. I appreciate everything you've done and offered to do for me, but I'm drawing the line at you getting picked up for a parole violation."

"You really think I'm going to let you deal with this all alone?"

"Let me?" She shot to her feet, and he realized too late he had made a mistake. "No man *let's me* do anything. I am a grown woman, and I make my own choices. Do not think that just because I'm half in love with you that you can ever tell me what to do."

Her heavy breathing and that finger stabbing the air did crazy things to him. He seized on her last sentence and asked,

"Only half?"

She gulped and suddenly seemed very interested in his bookshelf. "Love was the wrong word."

"Was it?" He didn't think so. "We've been doing this dance for almost two years, Nisha. I flirt with you. You pretend not to like it. Now, we're standing here in my living room, and you admit what I already know to be true. I know it's true because I crossed the halfway line a long time ago."

Her gaze snapped from the bookshelf to his face. She tilted her head and scrutinized him. "You feel that strongly about me? When we've never even been on a date?"

"I tracked you down at a book club to make sure you were safe. I brought you into my house to protect you. I called in the most dangerous man in Houston to sit with you. I'm about to brave a cat with murder mittens for you." He took one step toward her with each statement. Looking down at her, he said, "I don't need to take you out for an overpriced steak to know that you make my heart stutter and my brain go stupid and my cock ache."

"Was that supposed to be romantic?" she asked, her lips twitching with a smile. "Because, if it was, maybe leave the part about your dick out the next time."

"Noted." He leaned down and captured her pouty lips in a tender but promising kiss. She gripped his waist, and he tangled his fingers in her tight curls, tilting her head back and her chin up so he could kiss her the way she deserved. Her tongue was shy against his, but he didn't mind taking it a little slow. There was plenty of time for the heat and passion he craved.

"Ten, what are you doing to me?" she asked in between

feverish kisses. "You're making me break all my rules."

"Good." He slid his hand down her spine to cup her incredible ass. He gave it a squeeze and then stabbed his tongue against hers again. She whimpered, and her fingernails dug into his waist. He groaned against her soft lips and rubbed her ass, wondering how long he had until Kostya showed up and ruined everything with his grumpy bullshit.

Nisha's phone rang again, and he fought the urge to throw it out a window so he could get right back to getting her onto his couch and out of that blouse. Instead, he eased off their kiss and let her answer. He noticed the hazy satisfaction in her dark eyes, and the slick, swollen curve to her lips. He wiped his thumb over his mouth, cleaning off the lipstick that had transferred.

"Hello? Yes, this is Nisha Jackson. Yes, I'm aware of the escape. No, I'm not home. I'm staying with a friend. No, I'd rather not share that information right now. Yes, I understand. Okay. Well, I haven't spoken to her yet, but I will—." She stopped as if she had been interrupted. "Yes, I think that's best. No, I will definitely not be going to work tomorrow, but I think my colleagues would appreciate the extra security. No, I haven't heard from him."

Ten met Nisha's panicked gaze and nodded encouragingly. He assumed she was speaking with the police and agreed with her decision not to tell them about the call just yet.

After she ended the call, Nisha held tightly to her phone. "That was a three-way call with the sheriff and the chief of police. They wanted to offer me extra security and make sure that I was aware of my rights as a victim. They also want me to arrange an interview with my attorney attending."

"I'm sure it's nothing serious." He didn't want her to worry more than necessary. "They probably want to touch base with you."

"Probably." She grimaced. "Why did I lie about the phone call? I should have told them."

"You can tell them tomorrow. If we're lucky, Kostya will find Kiki tonight and—"

"And? And what?"

"And I'll handle the problem."

They stared at each other for a moment, neither of them clarifying what he meant. She must have understood because, eventually, she nodded and said, "Make it hurt."

"I will." That was a promise Ten intended to keep. Knowing Kostya, he would want to get in on the hurt as well. Maybe he'd bring his black bag. God only knew that Kiki deserved to feel real torment.

"Ten?"

"Yeah?" He abandoned all thoughts of making Kiki hurt to focus on Nisha.

"What were you in prison for?"

Hearing her ask about his criminal history knocked the air right out of him. That question would lead to other questions, and he would have to lie to her. He never told anyone, not even his lawyer, what had really happened that night. It was his duty as a street soldier to protect the *bratva*, and he had without complaint.

Still, it twisted up his insides to not be able to tell Nisha the truth, but the secret wasn't his to tell.

Holding her gaze, Ten admitted, "Manslaughter."

CHAPTER FIVE

*M*ANSLAUGHTER.

The word rattled around in my head even after Ten left with my neatly printed and organized list. It kept bouncing around my brain as Kostya hooked my phone up to a laptop and ran some sort of sketchy as fuck program that I was absolutely certain was illegal to possess or use.

Manslaughter.

Ten killed someone.

Obviously, I had known that he had committed a serious crime to end up in prison and not the county clink. I knew he was a felon. I had always assumed it was something like aggravated assault or robbery or some sort of weapons charge.

But now I knew.

And, strangely, it didn't change anything.

Besides, who was I to stand here and make ugly judgments about Ten when I had basically asked him to torture Kiki before killing him? What kind of hypocrite would that make me?

"You're not as chatty as I expected." Kostya startled me with his remark. "We've never spent any time alone, but I see you with Holly when I stop by and you're always talking."

I frowned at him. "I am not."

He glanced away from his laptop screen. "You are."

"Well, maybe I am," I said and plopped down onto an empty chair at Ten's kitchen table. "I'm not feeling particularly talkative tonight."

"Understandable." He fiddled with something on the laptop, tapping a few keys and clicking the mousepad. "You shouldn't worry too much. You're probably the safest woman in the city tonight."

"How do you figure that?"

"Law enforcement aside, there are dozens of bounty hunters out to find Kiki. You have me sitting with you, and Ten is like that tiger tattooed on his arm, ready to rip Kiki's head off. There's probably a few family members of victims who are out there looking for him, too."

"Not that many." I didn't like thinking about the trial but there was no avoiding it now. "Only one victim had a family member present. The second girl he killed. Her grandmother came every single day."

"Javier Ochoa," Kostya said, surprising me that he knew the victim's name.

"She went by JoJo," I corrected, hating that the poor girl never had the chance to change her name. "But, yes, that was her birth name."

"I'm not judging." He unplugged my phone from the USB connection and slid it across the table. "Everyone has the right to live the life they want."

"Except JoJo didn't get to live her life," I muttered sadly. "She was only seventeen when he killed her."

"Did you know?"

My head snapped up at Kostya's blunt question. It wasn't

the first time someone had asked me if I was aware that my husband had been killing transgender prostitutes. It wouldn't be the last either. Even so, my stomach churned with shame and guilt. "No, but I should have."

"Why?"

I shrugged. "I don't know. It seems like something I should have known. He was mean and violent and hurt me all the time."

"Sexually?" Kostya asked, and I got the feeling I was being interrogated. There was something about his intense stare that left me feeling compelled to answer him.

"Yes."

"Did he put his hands on your neck?"

I swallowed and reached up to touch my throat. Some nights, when the nightmares and the PTSD were particularly bad, I could still feel his fingers squeezing my throat. "Yes."

"He was homophobic." It wasn't a question.

"Yes." I narrowed my eyes at him. "How well did you know him?"

"Unfortunately, very," Kostya muttered. "You obviously know more about the criminal underworld than most people."

I nodded reluctantly. "I'm well aware that Kiki used to run drugs and guns with Adrian Umansky."

"Don't forget Tony."

How could anyone forget Tony Guerrero? Big, fat Tony with his barking laugh and quick-witted roasts. He could make anyone smile. Well. Not anyone.

I still felt guilty for not going to his funeral or visiting his mother. I had been so wrapped up in my own grief and trauma back then, barely leaving the small apartment in a Dallas medical resort where Uncle Nicky had sent me to heal and recover.

"Have you read all of the case files on Kiki?"

"Most of them," I said and shifted uncomfortably. "Why?"

"There are always things that don't make it into the files." He closed his laptop and sat back in the chair. His posture was relaxed, but his gaze made me feel tense. "You were a child, Nisha, when Kiki groomed you. You were a child when he abused you. You were a child when you got pregnant. You were a child when he married you. You were a child living with a predator, and he fooled you the same way he fooled everyone else. The difference is that when you discovered the truth you didn't hide it. You told the world—and almost died for it."

I couldn't look at him. My mouth was suddenly dry, and I needed a glass of water or something stronger. I stood quickly, the chair scraping across the terracotta-colored floor tiles. Kostya didn't say a word as I opened cabinets in search of a glass and filled it with water straight from the tap. I ignored the chemical aftertaste of the lukewarm water and tried to breathe through the panic threatening to overwhelm me.

"Have you told Ten about your baby?"

I dropped the glass into the sink. Thankfully, it didn't shatter. I spun toward Kostya and leaned back against the countertop. The bite of the quartz lip in my lower back hurt and centered me in the moment. "No, not yet."

"You should. When you're ready," Kostya added gently. "You should tell him all the other things as well. Let him know your boundaries up front. It will make things easier for both of you."

"I know." I had been thinking the same thing. "My therapist and I have done a bunch of role-play sessions where I practice telling a romantic partner about what happened to me and what triggers me and what scares me."

"Ten will be good to you if you let him." Kostya drew a shape on the table. "He's the most loyal man I know."

There was something in the way he said it that piqued my interest. "Is that why he was in prison? Because he killed someone for the family?"

Kostya's head snapped up, and he frowned at me. "You don't know?"

"I didn't feel comfortable digging."

"He beat a man to death, but there were extenuating circumstances."

I gawked at Kostya. The same gentle hands that had comforted me had pummeled a man to death? The same sweet and tender man who had cradled me on his couch had brutally killed someone?

"What circumstances? Extenuating how?" I needed to know all the nitty, gritty details.

"There was a fight. It got out of control." Kostya wouldn't meet my gaze, and I knew there was more he wasn't telling me. "Ten pleaded guilty to a manslaughter charge. The DA gave him a break because of what they found at the scene. Ten had never been arrested or in trouble. Model citizen," Kostya joked with a harsh laugh.

"What did they find at the scene?"

"It's not important."

"It is."

Kostya speared me with a glare. "Are you always this argumentative?"

"Worse."

His mouth quirked with a smile that faded as soon as he spoke. "Child pornography."

I reared back with disgust. "What? Is that why Ten beat him?"

"Part of it," Kostya said evasively. "There was a kid involved. His mother worked at Samovar so it was a family situation. You understand?"

"Yes," I said quietly. "Who was it? The man he killed. Not the kid involved."

Kostya seemed taken aback. "Tony. Didn't you know that?"

At a loss for words, I sat there, mouth agape. "Ten killed Tony Guerrero? But I thought...? It was a drug deal gone bad. That's what they said."

"Who said?"

"Uncle Nicky."

"I'm sure he did," Kostya agreed. "You were not in a good place mentally. Imagine if he'd told you that a friend you had trusted and known was part of a pedophile ring operating right here in town?"

"I would have ended up on a 72-hour hold." I wasn't kidding or being hyperbolic. There was no way I could have handled a life-shattering discovery like that so soon after losing my baby, learning my husband was a serial killer and playing the role of star prosecution witness in his trial.

"It was hushed up by the police and the cartel and everyone else on the street. That was a secret so heinous no one wanted to spread it. Once Tony was dead and Kiki went to prison?" He slashed his hand through the air. "It was done and buried."

"Yeah, but what about Adrian?" I had always wondered about Kiki's longtime partner. "He went missing around that same time, right?"

"He did."

"Chess reached out to me, asked me if I knew where he was or where he might be hiding." She had been in a similarly bad place as me at the time. Pregnant. Seventeen. Alone. Abandoned. Her story had a better ending than mine, though. "I didn't know anything, and I felt so bad for her."

"Things turned out fine for Chess."

"And Adrian? Did he go home? I always just assumed he must have tucked tail and ran back to Russia."

"Yeah, that's a fair assumption."

I suspected that was as close to confirmation as I would ever get. "I can't imagine how stressful that is for Chess. Having to wonder if Adrian is going to pop back up in her life and ruin everything."

"The odds of that happening are almost zero."

I hoped so for Chess and Callie's sakes. Another thought struck me. "Wait—was Adrian like Tony?"

"Adrian didn't get off on hurting kids the way Tony did, but he enjoyed the money he made filming it."

"What?" I swayed with shock and horror. "They filmed the crimes?"

"We always suspected they were part of a bigger operation, probably international."

"If Tony was…? Was Tony involved in Kiki's crimes? I mean. The police would have…? Right?" I couldn't finish a single thought. My brain couldn't make sense of these new details. "Were they working together? Hunting together? Killing together?"

"Nobody but the men who were involved know what really happened."

I thought back to the days following Kiki's arrest, as I recovered in the hospital. The memories were fuzzy, but many of the questions I had been asked by detectives had been repeated at later dates. After Adrian had gone missing, after Tony had died, I had been visited one last time by detectives. "There was a murder they asked me about," I said, my gaze fixed on the chair in front of me. "A boy from Carrizo Springs."

"Derek Miller," Kostya said, jolting me out of my daze. "He was fourteen. A hitchhiker. Runaway. His body was found dumped by the Rio Grande not far from—."

"Laredo," I murmured, mentally building a map. "That was one of their stops on the circuit." I glanced at Kostya. "Of course, you already know that."

"Houston. San Antonio. Del Rio. Laredo. Corpus Christi. Houston." He listed off the cities Adrian, Tony and Kiki visited while transporting guns and drugs for the cartel and Russian mafia. "And there are bodies all along the route. Most of them young boys or transgirls. Runaways. Prostitutes. Kids that no one cared about and wouldn't be missed."

"So, you think that the three women in San Antonio weren't Kiki's only victims."

"I know they aren't, and I know there are more across the border."

My knees went weak, and I staggered to the chair and flopped down onto it. I felt dirty and grimy and wanted to puke. "And you think Kiki, Adrian, and Tony were in it together? Why didn't the police tie them to the crimes?"

"They tried. I have contacts on the inside who told me about their attempts. There was a burn pit behind the house where Adrian and Tony took their victims. They were able to match most of the bones to missing boys from the area. As to the others? The women Kiki probably killed?" Kostya shrugged. "Like I said—no one gives a shit about those kinds of kids. They're disposable nobodies. The ones that were recovered were badly decomposed or there was no DNA. They weren't going to waste time on bad cases. Think about how many rape kits go untested just here in Harris County, Nisha. The police are looking for reasons not to get involved."

"It doesn't make it right. Those families deserve to know what happened to their loved ones."

"They do."

"Where did it start?" I had always wondered when and where Kiki's madness began.

He nodded. "I'm fairly certain they started in Acuña. They would cross the border at Del Rio and visit the whorehouses there after making their cash drops. I fielded a complaint once from a cartel-protected madam down there. Those three were getting rough with her girls, usually at the same time."

I grimaced at the mental image of Kiki and his partners triple-teaming a prostitute. What was wrong with them? Why had they been so vile? Why did they have to spread pain wherever they went?

Why hadn't I seen what they were? Why hadn't I realized the three of them were such disgusting animals?

"There was a dead hooker—late twenties, not easy to

clock, hadn't had bottom surgery—and she was last seen with them. She was found a few weeks later, wrapped in garbage bags and buried in a shallow grave." Kostya grimaced. "I don't think they meant to kill her. I think they probably got into the room with her and realized things were not what they expected. They got mad, violent. They got a taste for killing, for power and pain, and they couldn't stop."

"And all that time I was dating him and living with him and sleeping with him." I shuddered with revulsion. "I told my therapist how he used to come back from his trips relaxed. He was so much nicer to me. I thought it was because we were toxic together, and he was relieved not to be around me for a few days. I never thought…"

"That he was getting a fix? That he was scratching an itch that wouldn't go away?"

"Something like that." I thought of Kiki, somewhere in Sam Houston National Forest, hiding in the trees or an abandoned campsite. "I always wondered if there were more victims. After I found…" I couldn't bring myself to say the words. "The cuts were so clean. Like something you would see a butcher or hunter do, you know? And he wasn't any of those things. He was, frankly, useless at most things, but those cuts?" I shook my head. "I had the feeling he had practiced."

"I suspect you're right."

"I wonder if he still hates himself as much as he used to," I remarked while tracing the wood grain of the tabletop. "I think that's why he did all those horrible things to me and to those women. I think he couldn't bear to admit he wasn't straight as an arrow. His culture, his upbringing, the streets, his gang— they wouldn't accept or allow him to be whatever he was. I think it festered inside him, turned him rotten and nasty, and he hurt people to make himself feel better."

"Men like that don't change," Kostya warned. "He's been sitting on death row for years now, waiting for the needle to go in his arm. If anything, he's meaner and more hateful. Everyone knows what he did. Everyone knows his shameful secrets. That humiliation twists a man. Whatever Kiki is now—it's dangerous."

"Do you think he'll come to Houston to kill me?" I had to know. I could tell Kostya had his fingertips on the heartbeat of the underworld, and it was clear he understood the darkness inside men.

"Yes." Kostya shifted in his seat and retrieved his vibrating cell phone from the front pocket of his jeans. "Among other things."

Among other things? He left me wondering what the hell that meant as he went to answer his phone call in another room. I didn't bother trying to listen. He was speaking in rapid-fire Russian. Most of me didn't even want to know what he was saying. It was probably something that would get me in trouble.

My phone rang, and I warily eyed it. Haunted by the memory of Kiki's voice in my ear, I didn't want to answer it. Kostya returned to the kitchen and found me staring at the still-ringing phone. He seemed to understand my hesitation and picked it up. He read the screen and thrust it at me. "It's Holly."

"Oh." I took the phone, but it went to voicemail before I could answer. I started to call her back, but she beat me to it. I answered on the first ring by tapping the speaker phone option. "Holly?"

"Oh, my gosh! Nisha! Are you okay? Mom and I just got back from our hike and the bonfire, and I had, like, fifty messages and phone calls. Are you at home? I'm going to call Kostya as soon as we get off the phone. He'll keep an eye on you."

When she finally stopped long enough to drag in a breath, I said, "Holly, he's here with me now."

"Oh. Is he?" She seemed surprised and then exhaled with relief. "Thank God! Listen, I know you two aren't very close, and I know he can be a bit scary. Underneath the intimidating outer shell, he's a really good man."

"So, he's like an onion?" I asked, catching Kostya's eye. "Shrek-like, you might say?"

Holly laughed. "Yes, but I don't think he'll appreciate the comparison."

"He doesn't," Kostya grumbled.

Holly gasped. "We're on speaker? Come on, Nisha! You should have warned me!"

"Sorry."

"Kostya, are you taking care of her? Promise me you'll keep her safe," Holly pleaded.

"I'll keep her safe," he promised, his expression softening as she spoke. There was no doubting how much he loved her. I didn't know everything that had happened after Holly, Savannah, and Lana had been kidnapped, but I knew that he had been badly injured trying to save her. He still moved more stiffly and slowly than he had before the kidnapping. Not that it made him any less terrifying.

"What are the police saying?"

"Nothing much," I said unhappily. "I don't think they know much more than we do."

"Surely, they'll find him quickly? Right?" she asked hopefully. "He can't have gone far after hijacking and killing that couple."

"He abandoned that car in a cemetery near Oakhurst," Kostya announced. "That was the call I just took," he explained. "He's either on foot, or he was picked up by someone else."

"Oh, no," Holly murmured. "What are we going to do?"

"*We* aren't going to do anything," Kostya remarked with a frown. "You're staying in California with your mother where I know you'll be safe and won't get into trouble."

"I mean, Mom and I will probably get into a little trouble," Holly argued. "It's kind of our thing."

Kostya sighed, and I almost felt bad for him. She was the sunshine to his grumpy, and it must have been exhausting. "Let's try not to have another international incident."

"No promises," Holly said. "Listen, Nisha, I had a few texts from Savvy. She thinks it might be best if you don't go to work tomorrow. Unless you feel like you would be safer surrounded by friends and clients in which case, please, come to work."

"No, I'm staying home. I don't want to put anyone else at risk." I remembered the mob of citizen journalists outside my house. "I don't want podcasters and YouTubers and all the other idiots in town who think they're legit journalists stampeding the salon either."

"Ugh." Holly made a disgusted sound. "Kostya?"

"Yeah, I'll handle it." There was an unmistakable spark of glee reflected in his eyes.

I shot him a perturbed look. I suspected Holly's expectations of handling it were far less mean and nasty than his.

"So, Mom wanted me to let you know that you are more than welcome to use her place as a hideout. Savvy has an extra key if you need it. The whole place is locked down like Fort Knox. Or, you can head to our beach house. It has an electronic lock so I can generate a code for you."

"Thank you. I'll keep that in mind." I really didn't want to run, but if it was the only way to survive, I would take my purse and race out the door with nothing but the clothes on my back. "I'm actually at Ten's place right now."

"Uh? WHAT?" Holly practically squealed. "When did this happen?"

"This? There's no *this*." I lied right through my teeth. "We're just—."

"Friends," Kostya interjected with thinly veiled amusement. I scowled at him, but it didn't have the effect I'd hoped.

"Uh-huh. *Friends*." Holly laughed. "Yes, I, too, was once *friends* with Kostya."

"Okay," I said, irritated. "Are we done?"

"Fine. Yes. But you better call or text me in the morning to let me know you're okay! I want updates from both of you," Holly demanded.

"Yes, dear," Kostya intoned dryly.

"All right, boss." I matched his tone.

After Kostya promised to call Holly, I hung up and glanced at Kostya. "So—the car?"

"Abandoned. No leads. No evidence."

"And you know this how?"

"I have my ways." He looked at his watch. "Ten should

have been back by now." His gaze darted to the front door and then he pulled out his phone. "If he doesn't answer my message, I'm sending Boy to check on him."

A vise of worry squeezed my heart. "You don't think…?"

"It would take a bigger man than Kiki to get the drop on Ten." Kostya typed out his text. "But, since we don't know how Kiki escaped or if he has help, I'm not taking any chances."

My stomach was a swirling pit of anxious nerves as we waited for the reply. When it came less than a minute later, I clutched the edge of the table, expecting bad news.

Kostya chortled. "Well, it's worse than I thought."

"What?" I gripped the table tightly, my fingers turning pale at the tips. "What's wrong?"

"He's with your uncle."

"Oh, shit."

CHAPTER SIX

WHEN TEN PAUSED at the same four-way stop where Nisha had panicked earlier in the night, he noticed a cop car parked outside her house. There was a smaller crowd of idiots with phones corralled on the public sidewalk outside her fence. Not wanting to be seen, he chose to continue straight for a few blocks to the neighborhood park.

He found a spot under a street lamp. The light flickered, and swarms of bugs fluttered around it. He figured this was the safest place for his Tahoe and killed the engine.

Not far away, a group of kids loitered around one of the covered picnic tables. The scent of strong, high-end weed hit him as he stepped out of his Tahoe. There were worse things a bunch of teenagers could be doing this time of night. He sure as hell had at their age.

"Hey!" Ten called out, his deep voice carrying over their banter and music. "You want to make some money?"

One boy stepped forward, silently acknowledging himself as the leader of the group. Baggy shorts, an oversized Givenchy tee layered over a white tank, Nike Dunks, and a bright red Supreme cap tilted to one side. Half his hair was braided. The rest was shaved close to the scalp. Judging by the amount of money the kid was wearing, he was either a dealer or the son of one. "Yeah. What do you want?"

"Can you watch my Tahoe while I handle some business in the area?"

The kid looked him over. "You part of Nikolai K's crew?"

Ten nodded. "Yes."

The kid glanced back at his friends. The tallest of them shrugged, and the leader turned back to Ten. "You're not here to kill anyone, right? Like you're not handling *business*?"

Ten shook his head. "I'm picking up some stuff from my girlfriend's house. There's a cop car out front, and I'd rather not deal with them tonight."

"I understand, man. My whole damn street gone crazy tonight with that psycho serial killer on the loose." The kid nodded. "A'ight. We'll watch your Tahoe, man."

"What's your name?" Ten asked as he reached for his wallet.

"Carter."

Ten committed the name to memory and handed over two crisp hundred-dollar bills. "The rest when I get back, yeah?"

"Sure." The kid gripped the money, but Ten held tight.

"If you pull any shit, Nickel Jackson will be the first call I make. Understand?"

"Yeah. I know."

Ten let go of the money, and the kid wandered back to his friends. He was fifty-fifty on whether the kids would still be there when he returned. If he had told them he was there to get something from Nisha Jackson's place, the kids would have been more likely to be helpful. He wasn't ready to spread that news around town just yet.

It shouldn't have mattered. He and Nisha were adults.

They should have been able to do whatever they wanted, but the real world wasn't that simple. He practically lived with Nikolai and his family, and Nisha was the favorite niece of Nicky Jackson.

There was a reason most of the families in town didn't allow their people to co-mingle. If his relationship with Nisha took a bad turn and things got ugly, Nikolai and Nicky would be dragged into it. Sides would be taken. Demands would be made. It would be a shit show.

Not that he was going to let that stop him. He cared about Nisha—a lot. All that talk back in his living room about half and maybe more than half had confirmed what he had long believed. There was a reason he had walked into that salon with Vivian. There was a reason Nisha had crossed his path. He wasn't a religious man, but he did believe in fate and the universe having bigger plans for him.

So, no, he wasn't going to walk away from the chance to have a relationship with Nisha. It was going to be messy and complicated, but he hadn't ever liked doing things the easy way. Nisha was special, unique, and she was worth the effort.

When he reached the alley that snaked through Nisha's block, Ten scanned the area to see if there were any more of those nosy assholes lurking in the shadows. He crept down the skinny street, sidestepping potholes and wrinkling his nose at the eye-watering stench coming from one particular dumpster. One of Nisha's neighbors must have run an in-home daycare. There was no other explanation for the overpowering wave of dirty diapers that slapped him right in the face.

He'd never been a man with a weak stomach, but there had been more than one occasion where Lev had a surprise that left him green at the gills. He had been shocked the first time he had discovered just how gross babies could be. Not that it had put him off having children of his own someday.

He approached the back gate of Nisha's property. He was tall enough to reach over the top of the privacy fence and pull the latch. As he did, he decided he would be adding a lock to this gate as soon as this mess with Kiki was finished.

The brick paver pathway meandered from the back gate to a patio. Solar lights lit the way. She had a few bird baths and a small fountain that burbled away in the corner of the yard. The landscaping was dense with layers of flowers, shrubs, and small trees. She obviously had spent a lot of time making this backyard a peaceful oasis.

When he reached the backdoor, he used the key fob she had given him to deactivate the alarm. He unlocked the door and moved carefully to make sure her cat didn't try to escape. There was no sight of Wilford or his murder mittens as he entered and shut the door behind him. Nisha had warned him he might have to chase down the cat, and he wasn't looking forward to it.

Nisha loved technology, and it was evident throughout her renovated home. She had turned on the lights using an app on her phone and given him a tour of her space through security cameras inside the house. He kept meaning to add smart home features to his place but hadn't gotten around to it yet. Mostly because he didn't want to feel as if he were being watched around the clock. He'd had enough of that doing his stretch.

Keeping an eye out for the cat, Ten crossed the living room and ducked down the hallway. He had explained to Nisha that he would check the house for any problems before gathering up the items on her list. To the left, there were two doors, one closed and one open. He chose the closed door first. There was a silly sign on the door barring all cats. It made sense once he stepped inside and discovered it was a crafting space. Cat hair would be a nightmare to remove from all of her supplies.

There was a big cozy chair by the window and potted plants dangled overhead in those fishnet-looking hanger things that were popular everywhere. He'd banged his head on the ones in Vivian's home studio too many times. The lush vines draped over the sides of Nisha's pots were much greener and healthier than the ones in Vivian's room though. The boss's eye twitched any time he stepped into his wife's studio. Frankly, Ten was shocked Nikolai hadn't rescued the suffering plants yet.

One wall of the craft room was floor-to-ceiling shelves stuffed with a rainbow of fabric and yarn and spools of thread. He walked across the plush and colorful rug, not at all surprised by the bright pops of pink and watermelon green in it. Nisha had a flair for color, and this place where she indulged her creativity was no exception. He had no problem imagining her sitting there in that oversized chair, crocheting while she watched the picture-framed television across the room.

He trailed his fingertips along the soft, fluffy yarn of the half-finished blanket draped over the arm of the chair. Curious, he examined the stitching and marveled at her neat and tight shell stitches. He could barely get through a chain without making a tangled mess.

Based on the size and the buttery yellow and sky-blue pattern, he was certain it was for a baby. Looking at the shelves, it was obvious she made quite a few child-themed items—blankets, hats, stuffed animals. He picked up a big, squishy lion and then the most ridiculous narwhal with a glittery yarn horn. She definitely had a talent.

After he checked the closet of her craft room, he left and crossed the hall to the other door. She had a small office space there. A wooden plant stand by the big window was overflowing with pots. He counted fourteen, all of them different sizes with various succulents. The walls were decorated with glossy photos and watercolor sketches of hairstyles. The bookcase was packed with hair styling texts and trade magazines.

His gaze lingered on the strange contraption in the corner, some sort of cat playground. There was a cat-sized couch and a bed shaped like a fruit tart with blueberry and strawberry plush figures. It seemed that Wilford was allowed in here, and judging from the white fuzz on her black desk chair, the cat had lounged there today.

With the office cleared, he moved down the hall, checking the art deco bathroom with its bushy fern and a guest room outfitted with a quilt that must have taken her dozens of hours to make. He touched the intricate stitches decorating the fabric, marveling at the swirls and shapes. Nisha obviously had a skill for things like this.

It made him think of Vivian. When she had been pregnant with Lev, she had gone to a three-day quilting course hosted by a friend. It had been the only time he had ever seen Vivian fail at anything, but Nikolai still insisted on keeping that lumpy, uneven checkerboard quilt in their media room. Every chance he got, Nikolai used the ugly, misshapen thing for Lev.

At first, Ten thought the boss was poking fun at his wife.

That obviously wasn't the case. Nikolai was proud of her for trying something new and dedicating three days of work to a gift for their home. Vivian might not have seen the beauty in it, but Nikolai did.

After he checked the closet, Ten looked a little closer at the banana-shaped cat bed in the corner. There were toys next to it but no cat. Despite all evidence that a cat lived in the house, Ten had yet to see or smell it. Was it watching from a shelf somewhere? Under a piece of furniture? Waiting for an opportune moment to strike?

Ten crossed the house to Nisha's bedroom. As he approached the open doorway, he heard the unmistakable warning growl of a pissed-off cat. Cautiously, he stepped closer, making sure he gave the cat plenty of time to run if it felt cornered. The growling continued, low and angry, and Ten steeled himself for a painful encounter as he entered Nisha's room.

There in the middle of her king-size bed was the fluffiest, fattest, flat-faced beast he had ever seen. It perched in attack mode, all puffed out and furious. When it began to spit and hiss, Ten pointed a no-nonsense finger in its direction. "Cut that shit out right now, Wilford. You and I don't have to be friends, but we have to learn to exist in the same space."

Wilford hopped aggressively across the magenta and gold comforter, hissing and growling like a psycho. Ten ignored the cat and walked to the closet where Nisha had told him he would find a suitcase. He picked out the one she wanted and the small toiletry case and began to methodically work his way down her list of clothing, shoes, toiletries, and comfort items.

Her bedroom was a riot of magenta, green, gold, and

black. The colors were rich and vibrant like jewels. Somehow, they made the room feel bigger than it was and welcoming. He wanted to drop into the loveseat by her bay window and read one of the books from the table next to it.

It smelled fucking good, too. He had expected to run into that cat smell that seemed to linger in other homes, but there was none of that here. Woodsy, floral, warm. It was comforting.

As he picked through Nisha's neatly organized drawers, he kept his promise not to open two of them that she had told him were strictly off-limits. He badly wanted to know what secrets she had in them. Sex toys, he hoped, and naughty ones they could enjoy together at some point in the future. But he wasn't going to break his word to her.

Besides, her fluffy bodyguard was following him around the room, still hissing and growling. Ten ignored Wilford and his uncanny little fur mustache as he packed up Nisha's things. In the bathroom, he had to check the list four times to make sure he had found every product she wanted.

As he tried to make sense of the different skin care serums in front of him, Wilford hopped up onto the counter. The cat hissed, but Ten wasn't the least bit intimidated. "Listen, Wilford, I've been in smaller bathrooms with much tougher guys than you. Either come at me and get your blood payment or fuck off."

Wilford spit at him and hopped like a rabbit amped up on meth. He jumped sideways and banged into a soap dispenser which startled him. The cat screeched as if it had been touched by a demon and skittered out of the bathroom, knocking over anything in his path. Ten shook his head at the crazy cat and wondered much trouble that furball was going to cause back at his place.

With everything packed, Ten went down the list again, making sure he had gotten all the little odds and ends from different parts of the house. The only thing left to handle was to coax that fuzzy gremlin into the cat carrier. He sighed and glanced at the unharmed skin on his forearms. Soon enough, he'd likely be bleeding and bruised.

This had to be love. There was no other explanation for his willingness to take on a psycho cat this late at night.

Ten left Nisha's suitcases in the living room and grabbed the cat carrier from the hallway closet. He also picked up the cat's favorite bed, a macaron-shaped pink monstrosity, as well as the specific toys he liked, a daisy drinking fountain, and the various bags of treats and pouches of food he needed. Wilford watched from afar, no longer hissing or growling, but glaring silently.

With a tube of his favorite treat in hand, Ten placed the carrier on the counter and faced off with his nemesis. "Okay. Look. I know you don't want to get in this crate. I wouldn't want to get in there either. Believe me. I've been caged. It sucks."

Wilford eyed him warily as if to say, "Go on."

"I'm going to make you a deal. You get in this cage without tearing up my arms, and I'll take you to your mama. You can run wild at my place, and I won't even complain about the hair or the litter box that your mother intends to put in my guest bathroom." Ten ripped open the Inaba Churu tube and wrinkled his nose. "But, if you decide to be a punk and come at me with those murder mittens, I'm calling my friend for one of his special sedatives."

Wilford yowled and began to lick at the air. The stinky treat lured him across the kitchen. He hopped up onto the counter and meowed louder. He hesitated a few seconds before moving two steps closer. Ten didn't move. He held still, holding out the lickable treat, and waiting.

Eventually, Wilford's stomach got the better of him. He licked the fishy treat and then pulled back to glare at Ten. He leaned forward and licked again. Ten squeezed a little more out of the tube, and Wilford gobbled it right up.

Cautiously, Ten reached out and stroked the cat's head. His fur was unbelievably soft and thick. Wilford tolerated the gentle petting, but he swatted at Ten's wrist when he wanted more of his treat. There were no claws so Ten let it slide.

He was squeezing out more of the treat when he heard a key in the front door. In an instant, he was moving toward the living room, ready to fight if necessary. When the door swung open, Ten heard Nicky Jackson's familiar voice shouting at the amateur journalists outside. "Yeah, go back to your mama's couch and cry! You fat fuck!"

Nicky slammed the door behind him and jolted with surprise upon seeing Ten. "The fuck are you doing here?"

Ten gestured to the suitcases. "I'm getting Nisha's clothes and her cat."

Nicky glanced around with narrowed eyes. "Where is that beast?"

"Kitchen." Ten held up the half-finished tube of seafood-flavored paste. "I'm trying to make friends so I can bribe him into the carrier."

"Well, good luck," Nicky said, not making any move toward the kitchen. "That thing is a devil. I keep telling Nisha he needs to be baptized or exorcised."

"I think he's territorial and protective of her."

"Makes two of us." Nicky frowned in his direction. "Or three."

Never one to play games, Ten bluntly asked, "Is this going to be a problem?"

"You and my niece? Only if you make it one," Nicky remarked with a warning look. "I'll tell you right now. The biggest mistake I ever made was not getting involved with her and Kiki. I should have killed that motherfucker the first time he put hands on her, and I should have driven straight to San Antonio to bring her back as soon as she told me she was pregnant. I won't be making that mistake again."

"Why didn't you?"

"What?"

"Kill Kiki the first time he hit her?" Ten leveled an accusing stare at the older man. "You knew what he was like."

"I was wrapped up in my own bullshit back then," Nicky said. "I was fighting for every single square inch of territory I could get. Things got pushed aside, important things. Never again."

"I'm not here to ask your permission to date her. I know I'm not the sort of man you probably want for her. Fuck, I'm not the sort of man she wanted either. She could date doctors or lawyers, rich guys, or athletes. I know where I rank," he assured Nicky.

"And I know what you are, Ten," Nicky replied coldly. "And what you aren't."

Their gazes clashed. "I'm just a man trying to find a good

woman so I can have the life I want."

"I'm just an uncle trying to keep my niece from getting murdered by the serial killer she put behind bars."

"Kostya is with her right now." Ten was sure that would put Nicky at ease, and it did. "She's staying with me tonight. I have a few safe houses we can use. Boltholes of my own and a few that have been offered to me. We can stash her and keep her safe until Kiki is apprehended."

"I don't want him picked up by the police. I want him dead."

"So do I." Flashes of Nisha's panicked face after she answered Kiki's call came to mind. "He called her earlier."

"Kiki?" Nicky was taken aback. "How did he get her number?"

"No idea, but Kostya's looking into it."

"There is absolutely no way Kiki did this on his own. The legal wrangling to get him out of that unit? The escape? Having Nisha's number? Someone is helping him."

"It's probably more than one person," Ten figured. "You've been inside. You know how corrupt some of those guards are. They'll do anything for money."

"Or to keep their families safe," Nicky remarked. "If Kiki still has friends on the outside, he could have touched a guard's family."

"Someone killed Dancing Bear tonight. If that murder is tied to Kiki, he still has contacts out here," Ten reasoned. "If he has contacts doing his dirty work, this gets complicated very fast."

"I already talked to Diego. He says that there's no support for Kiki from the Hermanos or the cartel."

"Do you believe him?" Ten hadn't had many chances to get a good feel for the young kid now running all of the cartel's business through Houston.

"As much as I do any pepper belly."

Ten winced at the slur but didn't call him out on it. There was no point with these older guys who were set in their ways.

"What about Adrian?"

Ten suppressed the jolt of panic that name inspired. "What about him?"

"He went missing after you killed Tony," Nicky reminded him unnecessarily. "Maybe he's back."

"No, he's not." Ten knew that with absolute certainty.

"How do you know?"

"I just do." Ten really didn't want to talk about this with Nicky. He barely liked talking about it with Artyom and Kostya, the other men who had been there the night it all went to hell.

"Uh-huh," Nicky murmured unconvinced. "Well, you should get rid of her Jeep until Kiki is caught."

Glad for the change of topic, Ten nodded. "I was thinking about that on the drive over here."

"Orange!" Nicky clicked his teeth. "I don't know what possessed that girl to pick that color!"

"It's a happy color."

Nicky scowled at him. "It's obnoxious." His gaze moved suddenly to the floor near Ten's feet. "Like that evil beast right there."

Ten glanced down and found Wilford rubbing against his jeans, leaving white hair on the denim. He frowned but decided this was better than being scratched.

"You best get on out of here before those assholes out front decide to try peeking in the windows." Nicky eyed Wilford with distrust. "Let my niece know I'm staying the night here at her place."

"Alone?" Ten didn't like that idea.

"Yes. Alone." Nicky acted affronted. "Son, I may be old enough to be your daddy, but I can defend myself and my family."

"I didn't mean—." His phone vibrated, and he retrieved it from his pocket.

"Problem?" Nicky asked as Ten answered the message.

"Kostya. Checking in."

"Remind him he owes me for the poker seat I gave up for that judge he bought." Nicky glowered. "And I don't mean cash."

Ten did just that. "He responded with a thumbs up."

"Yeah. He's been sitting around with his thumb up his ass alright," Nicky muttered.

Ten smiled and typed that right back. Seconds later, Nicky's phone rang. He glared at Ten. "Did you—?"

"Come on, Wilford. Time to go."

Nicky shot him the finger as he answered Kostya's call. Ten laughed and then took a chance, crouching down and swooping Wilford right up off the floor. The cat stiffened and yowled but didn't try to escape.

Back in the kitchen, he gave Wilford the rest of his treat and then gently dropped him into the carrier. The cat meowed pitifully but stayed calm.

"My boys will pick you up out back," Nicky offered. "Where did you leave your vehicle?"

"The park a few blocks over." He shifted the cat carrier so he could grab the handles of the two suitcases and the canvas tote bag filled with cat gear. "I left some kids watching it."

"Carter?"

Ten nodded. "Should I be worried you knew exactly what kids I meant?"

"Nah, he's a good one. A little wild, but we all were at that age."

Ten grunted. The less said about his teenage years the better.

"If you need any help—."

"I won't hesitate to ask." Ten hefted his cargo toward the back door. "When it comes to keeping Nisha safe, I'll call in every marker and cross any line."

Even if that meant going back to prison.

CHAPTER SEVEN

I WAS FOURTEEN when I met Kiki. I was a stupid kid hanging out with older girls in places where I never should have been. At the time, I had been so desperate to belong I let myself be pressured to do things that made me uncomfortable.

Clothes that were too revealing. Smoking. Drugs. Drinking. Dancing. Staying out all night and acting foolish.

Even now, I cringed thinking of how much trouble I caused my poor grandmother. All she had ever wanted was to protect me and keep me safe, but I was convinced she wanted to control me. I didn't see her high standards for me as love. I saw them as proof that I wasn't even good enough for my own grandma. Just like I wasn't good enough to make my mother stay or to keep my father home at night instead of running the streets where he got himself killed.

And that made me vulnerable. It made me a perfect target for a predator.

Which was how Kiki found me.

Men like that, they can smell weakness. They can spot the girl from a broken home a mile away. They know how to find the girl who desperately wants to be loved. The awkward girl who feels out of place and doesn't belong. The girls who craves acceptance, who wants to be special.

I thought I was hot shit when Kiki asked if I wanted to go for a drive. The party we were at was winding down, and I didn't want to go home yet. Besides, I wanted to spite Marissa Lopez. She had been flirting with Kiki all night, but he wasn't interested. She was constantly calling me a fat ass and making nasty remarks about me. Stealing the boy she wanted right in front of her gave me a heady sense of power.

Except he wasn't a boy. He was twenty-five. A grown-ass man. And I was a child who should have been home watching *Gilmore Girls* and *Gossip Girl* and writing that terrible *Harry Potter* Dramione fanfic I kept secret.

Instead, I found myself alone with a man who didn't take no for an answer. Later, after I got home and scrubbed my face, and used half a bottle of mouthwash trying to get the bitter, salty taste of him off my tongue, I would convince myself he didn't mean to hurt me.

I would replay the way he coerced me into putting my mouth on him. I was a tease. He thought I was more mature. I owed him for the weed I had smoked and the alcohol I drank.

To this day, I could still feel his hand on the back of my head. I could feel the panic and fear of having his dick shoved down my throat. I could hear his angry warning not to puke or else he would make me clean it up with my tongue.

After it was done, he flipped a switch. Suddenly, he was all sweetness and love. I was a good girl. I was his baby. I had a mouth like an angel. He buttered me up good, and I soaked it in like the dry, empty, desperate husk I was.

Once he had his hooks into me, there was no escape. I fell for his bullshit. I believed he loved me, that he wanted the best for me, and that only he understood me. I let him separate me from my grandmother and my uncle. I relented when he wanted me to stop playing basketball and stop playing clarinet for my school's symphony. I gave up the books I loved because they were stupid. I wore what he picked out for me because it made him happy.

I learned to apologize even when I didn't understand what I had done wrong. I convinced myself that love was supposed to hurt. He was just so passionate about me that it made him do crazy things. His love for me was so big that it made his disappointment even bigger. My mother was a tramp, and if he didn't teach me how to behave, I would be just like her. He was doing this for me, for us. Didn't I see that?

Friendless, isolated, I relied on him for everything. I made excuses for all the horrible things he did to me. I deserved that slap because I asked a question I shouldn't have. I needed to be punched because I broke a rule about wearing shorts out of the house. He had to brutally sodomize me to teach me a lesson about talking to other people about what happened inside our house.

They wouldn't understand our relationship. They didn't understand that I was wild and dirty and needed discipline. Did I want them to take him away? Did I want to be alone? Did I want him in jail? Who would take care of me? Who would love me if I got my man locked up over a little tussle?

Sometimes, my courage would flare, and I would have an almost violent urge to scream, "YES! Please, take him. Lock him away. Let me be free!"

But I didn't. Whether it was fear or brainwashing or the toxic co-dependence of domestic violence—I couldn't bring myself to ask for help or leave.

Not until it was too late.

I got away finally—but it cost me something so precious. It cost me the one thing I could never replace.

Lorelai. My daughter.

CHAPTER EIGHT

"**N**ISHA? YOU OKAY?"

I glanced up from my iPad and found Ten standing in the doorway of the bathroom with only a towel around his waist. Staggered by his incredible physique, I was left speechless.

I had expected he would be muscular and strong, but the definition of his chest and abdomen stunned me. The chiseled muscles in his arms flexed as he scratched idly at his naked chest, his fingers moving across the tattoos marking him as part of the *vory v zakone*. Had he earned one of them for killing Tony?

"Nisha?"

"Uh, yeah." I glanced away and gulped. My face burned with embarrassment for the way I had been gawking at him. "I'm sorry."

"For?" He crossed the bedroom and stepped into his closet.

"Staring at you like that."

He laughed, and a drawer opened and closed. "You can stare all you like."

I caved and looked at the closet, secretly hoping for another glimpse of his body. He emerged in loose shorts and nothing else. I felt simultaneously overdressed and under-dressed at the same time. I wore zebra print sleeping shorts and a matching tee. My hair was tucked up into a satin-lined pink slap. I was more covered up than he was, but I was showing more of my legs than he had ever seen.

I could feel the heat of his gaze moving over my exposed skin as he shut his closet door. What was he thinking? Could he see the ripple of cellulite from over there? Were my love handles and belly too much? Was he wondering why I had my hair tucked up and out of the way?

In these pajamas, without any shapewear, there was no hiding my excess weight. It was all out in the open, all two hundred and seventy-plus pounds on my 5'10" frame.

"I'm sorry I took so long getting ready for bed." I self-consciously touched my ear before glancing at his alarm clock on the other side of the bed. "It's kept you up so late."

"Don't apologize for taking care of yourself. If I was that worried about getting a shower, I would have used the guest bathroom."

"And braved Wilford?" My furious fur ball had taken up residence in there and seemed less than thrilled by the cheap throwaway litter trays Ten had picked up from an all-night Walmart on the way home. Wilford was used to his pampered life and automated space-age litter box. I had anxiously expected him to go straight psycho-cat mode after the trauma of being picked up by a strange giant and carted all the way across Houston in his carrier. Wilford had hissed and yowled, but two snaps of Ten's fingers and lowly uttered Russian words had silenced my persnickety cat.

"Wilford and I have an understanding."

I glanced at his unmarked arms. "You should give lessons in cat handling to his vet's office."

"Wilford isn't much different than Vivian when she's in one of her moods."

My eyebrows rose. "I can't wait to tell her that the next time I see her."

"If she disagrees, ask her to tell you about the nursery rug."

"Do I even want to know?"

"Not unless you want me to get on the floor with a measuring tape and start hysterically crying because the pile was 2.25 inches instead of 2."

I let loose a shocked laugh. "You're joking!"

"I wish I was. Nikolai tried to send Boychenko to buy a set of sheep shearing clippers to shave the rug down so she would stop crying." Ten grimaced. "I don't think I'll survive them having a second child."

"Well, I'm sure it will be a while before she has another piroshki in the oven."

Ten smirked at my little pun. Still hovering at the foot of his bed, he asked, "Are you sure you don't want me to sleep in the other room?"

No. Please. Stay. Hold me.

But I wasn't brave enough to ask that. Instead, I tried to play it cool. "Do you snore?"

"No." He smiled mischievously. "Do you?"

"No!"

"I'm a cover hog," Ten warned.

"I run hot so I don't mind if I end up uncovered." I ran my thumb along the edge of my tablet. "I don't want to be alone tonight."

"I understand." He walked to the bedroom door and shut it nearly all the way. "I'll leave it open in case Wilford comes looking for you."

Touched by his concern for my cat, I said, "He won't. He's very particular about not having anyone near him when he sleeps."

Ten looked unconvinced. "He'll probably want to come in here later to make sure you're safe." He touched his face. "Hopefully, he won't try to sneak in a few scratches while I'm passed out next to you."

"He better not!"

"I won't hold it against him. I'd do the same thing if I walked in and found a strange man in bed with my woman."

"Ten!"

His rumbling laughter almost made me forget all about the nightmare lurking somewhere in the darkness.

"Will this light bother you?" He gestured to a night light plugged in near the door. "I don't need it," he added quickly, as if he feared I would think less of him for having it.

"I need it." I wasn't saying that just to make him feel better. "I have them all through my house. If I wake up in pitch black darkness, I panic and think I'm back in—." I abruptly stopped myself before I blurted out one of my secrets.

"Back where, Nisha?" Ten asked gently.

I held his gentle gaze for a moment before admitting, "Kiki used to punish me by locking me in a closet with…" I shuddered with repulsion. "I just need there to be some light at night, okay?"

"So do I. If I don't have light when I wake up, I forget where I am. I get confused and think maybe I'm back in prison."

I smiled sadly. "Another thing we have in common."

"Yeah." He walked over to the bed and turned off his bed-side lamp. "What are you reading?"

"I'm playing a game." I flashed him the screen of my iPad. "My therapist suggested it. There's all this new research that shows that playing games like Tetris or Candy Crush helps the brain process stressful events better."

"That's interesting." He slipped into bed next to me, and I held still, fighting that magnetic pull of his body heat. "Do you see your therapist often?"

"Once a month." I frowned. "But I suppose I'll be seeing her more often now."

"I'll drive you."

His offer startled me, and I glanced at him with surprise. "Why?"

"You know why." He moved slowly, giving me a chance to reject his advancing hand. When he gently grasped my hand and lifted it, I held my breath. He tenderly kissed the back of my hand and then dotted soft kisses atop each knuckle. "I'm in this for the long haul, Nisha."

"Why?" I asked again, unable to fathom why any man would want to buy into my fucked-up life. Those old feelings of unworthiness filtered to the surface. "Ten, you don't have to do anything else for me. Please don't feel obligated just because—."

He swooped in for a kiss before I could finish my thought. His mouth eased over mine, slow and seeking, and I surrendered to the incredible feelings he evoked. I dropped my iPad and clutched at his bare shoulder. The feel of his hot skin under mine ignited something wild within me.

Wanting more than the chaste kiss he offered, I daringly flicked my tongue against his lower lip. He groaned, and the rough sound traveled right down to the womanly heat of me. I flicked again, and he took control, cupping my face and stabbing his tongue against mine in the wickedest way. I whimpered and grasped at him, desperate for something to hold onto as he rocked my world with his talented mouth.

"Does this feel like an obligation?" he asked huskily.

"No." It was wild and dark and exciting and all the things I had craved from him. "I want you so much, Anton."

"Say it again." His voice had gone so rough and low.

"Anton." I pulled back enough to look into his eyes. The vulnerability reflected in them shook me. "Anton."

He growled like a fucking bear, and then I was on my back. My tablet was shoved aside, hitting the floor with a *thunk*. Ten's hand glided along my side to grip my hip. The other remained at the back of my neck, cupping gently as he kissed me like a man dying for love. All the fear and shame I had felt with other men I had tried to date vanished. There was no time to think all those troubling thoughts with Ten. There was only time to feel.

And, God, help me. This man knew how to use his hands and mouth. There was nothing clumsy or uncertain about the way he moved. There was an elegance to the slide of his hand and the tickle of his fingertips moving over my skin.

"Tell me how far I can go." His fingers hesitated on the pearly buttons of my top. "I'll stop whenever you want."

"Don't stop," I begged. My body was on fire, and I wanted to know. I wanted to feel what he had to offer. I wanted to be worshipped and loved and left trembling and sated. "Please, don't stop, Anton."

He held my gaze as he plucked through the buttons of my top and bared my heavy breasts to his hungry gaze. No one had ever looked at me like that. Any worries I had that I was too big, too fat, too lumpy, too much fled. There was no mistaking the way this man wanted me.

I cried out in shocked excitement when he used both massive hands to squeeze my breasts together and buried his face against them. He flicked his tongue over my dark nipples and then sucked each one. His teeth glided over the sensitive peaks, and I curled my toes into the bed. My clit ached and throbbed as he enjoyed my breasts.

"Your tits are incredible," he said, his voice thick and dark. "Fuck, Nisha. You're even more beautiful than I had imagined." He shot me a mischievous smile. "And I fucking imagined every night."

"Tell me," I urged, wanting to hear all the filthy things he had imagined about me.

His eyes sparked with amusement. "I thought about what it would feel like to slide my cock between your breasts, to hold them together like this and fuck between them until I came. I thought about my cum on your nipples, about the way I would mark you like the fucking dog I am, and then bury my face between your legs. You would make me lick your pussy until I earned forgiveness for making such a mess all over you."

"Jesus," I breathed out tremulously. I could see everything he described, and filthy as it was, I wanted to experience it.

"I dreamed about the way your thighs would feel against

my ears." He danced slow, sensual kisses along my breasts and then toward my belly. "I dreamed about gripping your waist and your ass while you rode my face. I dreamed about your pussy on my tongue, and my cock in your hand."

"Anton." I was panting now, thoroughly overwhelmed by the fantasies he shared. "You are a dirty, dirty boy."

He smirked in that devilishly sexy way. "You haven't even heard the wildest things I've dreamed about doing with you."

"Show me," I commanded, feeling suddenly bold. "Show me how much you want me, Anton."

He nodded dutifully and began to peel my shorts down my body. I lifted my hips to help him. He tossed my shorts somewhere behind him. The dim glow of the lamp on my side of the bed cast just enough light on us, and I knew he could see everything.

His brow furrowed, and he froze in place. His pained gaze lifted to mine, and I managed not to look away in shame. The pain in his eyes turned to blazing fury. His jaw worked, and he glowered at the scars carved into my body like a map of torture. "I'm going to fucking kill him."

I believed Ten when he said that. If he got his hands on Kiki, he would tear him apart, piece by piece, for all the pain and torment he had caused me.

Ten shifted until he was beside me, gazing into my eyes. He gently stroked my face and then kissed me so lovingly. He carefully caressed my body while kissing me senseless. He still wanted to fuck me—that much was evident by the rock-hard erection jutting against my belly—but he was taking his time now. He was showing me that I didn't have to fear him and that he wasn't turned off by the ugliness marking my body.

"You are the strongest person I have ever met," Ten whispered against my lips. "Do you know that? Do you know how incredible you are? To have survived all this and come out on the other side as the powerful, sexy, successful woman you are today?"

He wasn't blowing smoke at me. He was serious. The way he looked at me with that smoldering gaze did crazy things to my heart and my mind. He was telling me all the things I struggled to believe about myself. He was showing me that I was worthy and deserving of the life I had fought so hard to rebuild.

"I'm starting to believe it." I touched his jaw, the rough stubble rasping my fingertips. "You'll have to keep reminding me."

"Every day," he promised before claiming my mouth in a sensual kiss that left me dizzy with lust. He took his time kissing and touching his way back down my body. He kissed every scar he found, and I had tears in my eyes from the tender sweetness.

When he made it all the way down to my toes, he kissed right back up my legs. This time his lips were teasing and ticklish. I breathed faster as he drew closer and closer to where I ached the most. He grabbed my thighs in both giant hands and shoved them wide open. My face flared with heat as he gazed down at me.

Should I tell him? That no one had ever done what he was about to do? That I had never known the caress of a lover's tongue down there?

Another face—an ugly, twisted hateful one—flashed before my eyes, and I slapped it away, refusing to let that asshole

Kiki ruin my night with Ten. With my Anton.

"Your pussy smells so good." Ten didn't shy away from saying exactly what he thought. It affronted my modesty, made me shiver with shock, but I couldn't ignore how wanton it made me feel. "I have to taste you."

He swiped my slit with his tongue, and I cried out at the delicious contact. I arched into him, and he chuckled darkly before settling one hand on my belly and the other on my hip. His giant hands branded me with their heat, and I never wanted to forget what it felt like to be held by this powerful man.

"Fuck." He groaned and then flicked his tongue over my clit. When he sucked it gently between his lips, I nearly died. Pleasure burst behind my eyelids, and I gripped his covers in my hands. Ten nuzzled his face into me, licking and suckling and driving me crazy.

Lost in the sheer joy of it, I closed my eyes and let go. I let go of the shame, the embarrassment, the lingering traumatic pain. I let go of it all and sank into the moment. This frenzied, passionate lovemaking with the man of my dreams.

Ten found a rhythm that made me moan. He stroked my belly and hip with his hands, keeping me centered as his tongue lashed my clit. I reached down to touch him, combing my fingers through his hair and along his ears. His mouth felt so good on me, and I was torn between wanting to come right now and wanting to draw it out as long as possible.

He groaned against my clit, and the reverberations left me clenching and panting. His fingers tightened on my hip, and I hovered on the edge. I rose up on one elbow, desperate to see him. The sight of Ten, my giant protector, on his belly with his face hidden in my pussy, broke me. He looked so pleased with himself, and I understood then what all my friends meant when they talked about their men. This was a *real* man. This was what a real man did for his woman. He gave pleasure and enjoyed the simple act of it. He didn't do it out of obligation. He didn't grumble and extort other sexual favors for it. He did it because he wanted to make his woman feel good.

Ten's eyes fluttered open, and I couldn't take it. I couldn't hold back. I came so hard I couldn't make a sound. Pleasure exploded in my core, and the shockwaves shattered me. Mouth agape, I rode out the waves of my climax until I was weak and shaking.

I fell back onto the bed and panted to catch my breath. Ten pressed loving kisses to my belly and mons before grasping the backs of my thick thighs with his big hands and shoving my knees toward my chest. In the next instant, his tongue was *inside* me.

"Anton!" What was this man doing to me? "Oh, God."

He made the wickedest sounds as he fucked me with his tongue. It was unlike anything I had ever imagined. I was dripping wet after that wild orgasm, and I was certain I was making a mess of his face. He didn't care, and I decided I wouldn't either. He wanted me to feel good, and I was damn well going to feel it.

He returned my clit after a few minutes of thrusting his tongue into me, and I didn't need much to send me hurtling over the edge again. I screamed this time. I couldn't hold it back. I was at the mercy of the pleasure gripping me, and there was nothing that was going to stop me from letting Ten know how good he was at this.

Breathing hard and trembling with shuddery bursts of ec-
stasy, I barely registered Ten standing to take off his shorts. He
opened a drawer and tossed something onto the bed next to
me. A condom, I realized, after blinking the tears from my
eyes. He swiped his forearm across his mouth and then
prowled onto the bed like a jungle cat intent on snaring its
prey.

He gripped my ankles and dragged me across the bed
where he wanted me. He was careful as he did it, moving
slowly as if to give me a chance to say no or stop. He could
hurt me. It was clear from the way his muscular body rippled.
If he wanted to, Ten could break me.

But he didn't want to hurt me. He wanted to love me. He
wanted to cherish me.

"Come here," I begged, reaching up for him like a child. "I
want you."

"Not as much as I want you," he said before capturing my
lips in a possessive kiss. I could smell and taste myself on him,
and it was a heady aphrodisiac. "I've waited months for this."

I imagined him in this very bed, thinking about me and
touching himself. It rattled me to the core, and I wanted to
experience it. I wanted to feel this powerful man pounding me
into the bed. "Make love to me, Anton."

He shuddered and then kissed me again. His hands were
so gentle on my body as he stroked and caressed. I couldn't get
enough of him either. My greedy hands moved over his arms
and down his ribs to his waist. He was hard and solid everywhere, and I couldn't believe this outrageously sexy man was
all mine.

He made quick work of the condom and then stuffed a

pillow under my hips. It was a bit awkward at first, but I trusted he knew what he was doing. My gaze lingered on his cock. I clasped the huge shaft and marveled at its weight. It was long and thick, and I wanted it inside me right now.

But it had been a long, long time since anything had been inside me. He must have known because he let me set the pace. I dragged the crown of him between my labia and then down to my vagina. He was careful as he thrust forward, just a little, and then withdrew. He kissed me as he probed a little deeper each time.

I was so relaxed from the foreplay that he slid right in as if he belonged there. I was stretched and full, but it felt *good*. It felt *right*. I squeezed him with my inner muscles, and he swore a streak of Russian. "I'm not going to last if you keep doing that, *zolotse.*"

"I want you to feel as good as I do." I brushed my hands up his chest and grabbed hold of his shoulders. "There's no pressure, Anton."

He lowered his face to mine and kissed me. We exchanged sappy smiles, and then he began to thrust into me, his hips cradled perfectly between my thighs. He went slow and easy, taking time to kiss my lips and caress my body. It was the most romantic and wonderful experience, and I wished with all of my heart that I had met him first. Why hadn't our paths crossed here in Houston all those years ago? Why had the universe thrown me at Kiki's feet? Did I have to suffer to deserve this man in this moment?

Ten snapped his hips, and all those ugly thoughts fled. I was back with him, my whole focus centered on this man who was showing me what sex could be. He slipped a hand between our bodies, and his thumb settled over my clit. I wasn't sure I could come again, but I was damn willing to let him try.

He must have been some sort of sex god because he knew exactly what to do to drive me right to the edge again. His thumb swirled over my clit, and the slide of his cock in and out of me was almost too much. That coil of bliss tightened low in my belly, and I clenched him with my thighs.

"Come on, baby." His smoldering gaze burned right through me. "That's it. You can come again. I know you can. Let me feel you, Nisha. Let me feel your cunt milking me dry."

"Anton!" I came with a stunned cry. The orgasm punched the air right out of my lungs. I curled my toes and clawed at his chest and shoulder, desperate to keep hold as I reeled from the pleasure. Ten drove into me with speed and power that left me gasping and grunting. I was completely at his mercy, but I trusted him to see me through it.

And he did. He covered my body with his. One hand gripped my waist and the other was under me, holding me right where he wanted as he pounded me into the mattress. He whispered my name over and over again before finally stuttering out a Russian word I didn't know. He shuddered against me, his hips jerking as he came.

Overwhelmed, I held onto him and buried my face in his neck. Eventually, he found the strength to roll off of me and onto his side. He reached for me, drawing me across the bed and into his arms. We were both a sweaty mess, but it didn't matter.

Right then, nothing existed outside his bedroom. Our whole world was right there in that bed, and I never wanted to leave.

CHAPTER NINE

I WISH TEN *was with me.*

I was sitting with Eloise, my attorney, and Savannah in the cold, brightly lit conference room at the Houston headquarters of the Texas Rangers. The state troopers, the Rangers, Houston PD, Harris County Sheriff's Department, and a whole host of other agencies were working together on Kiki's escape. Why they seemed to think I would have any idea where that lunatic had gone befuddled me.

I had handed over my phone after arriving and informed them that Kiki had called me last night. They hadn't given it back yet, and I worried they would keep it. I kept everything backed up in the cloud, but the thought of going to get a new phone was not one I relished.

"Is that Chess?" Savannah asked and leaned back in her chair for a better look through the glass wall. "It is her!"

Through the glass, our gazes met. Chess Mendoza shot me a look of sympathy, and I mirrored her expression. Here we were, two women dragged right back into the bullshit of the men who had ruined our lives.

"Why would they bring her in?" Savannah wondered aloud.

"She was in a relationship with Kiki's partner, Adrian." I

kept everything else I had learned about Adrian from Kostya to myself. Those were details I wasn't going to share with anyone. "Adrian went missing after Kiki went to prison. They probably think she knows where Adrian is, and if he's somewhere local, they probably think he's helping Kiki."

"Do you think he is?" Eloise asked, suddenly alert.

"No."

"How can you be sure?"

"I have it on good authority." What was I supposed to say? That a Russian mafia cleaner who I was pretty sure used to be a spy had told me so while sitting in the kitchen of my boyfriend who had been convicted of killing Kiki and Adrian's partner in crime?

"Wait. Seriously?" Savannah seemed startled by that information. "Is he...? Is this Adrian guy the father of her daughter?"

"Yes." That was all I was going to say about that.

"Let's not talk about Adrian or Chess once the interview starts," Eloise coached. "This is new information to me, and I don't want us stumbling into something we aren't prepared for yet."

I appreciated her use of we when discussing this mess. It made me feel less alone and like I had a team helping me through it.

But I would have felt much better with Ten sitting right here holding my hand.

He had wanted to come, but Kostya had forbidden it. The mysterious Russian had been at Ten's door super early with updates on the search for Kiki and a set of rules about Ten's involvement. As much as I wanted Ten with me, I understood why Kostya had his rules. He wanted to keep Ten out of trouble and in the good graces of his parole officer. Ten was too close to the finish line to fuck it up now.

The door opened, and a stream of law enforcement agents entered the room. The Texas Rangers in their starched white shirts and khaki pants led the way. It seemed as if they were going to be running the show this morning.

Eloise and the lead Ranger discussed the rules of the meeting. She was more aggressive than normal, but I understood she was showing them we weren't going to be fucked around here. Even at the risk of being uncooperative, she would protect me with the full might of her bar license.

"Miss Jackson, I'm sorry to have dragged you in here today," Major Whitmore apologized. "I'm sure you don't want to be here anymore than we do."

"Not particularly," I agreed, "but I'll do what I can to help you catch Kiki and put him back in prison where he belongs."

"Do you have any idea where he might go to hide? Is there somewhere near here? A place where he used to spend time before he was arrested?"

"I've thought about that all night and all morning. The places he used to haunt are all public spots. He's not going to pop up in Houston without being spotted and reported. He's a psycho, but he's not completely stupid."

The major hummed in agreement. "And what about friends? Adrian Umansky maybe?"

"I doubt that very much."

"Why?"

"Adrian disappeared after Kiki went to prison, and as far I know, he went back to Russia."

"Yeah, that's the rumor we've heard as well," the major confirmed. "What about family?"

"No family. His mother died a few months after he was convicted." I hadn't gone to her funeral either. Not that she would have wanted me there. The last time we had been in the same room together she had slapped me across the face and called me a *puta*.

"And no friends on the outside?'

"I don't know," I answered honestly. "When he was arrested and all the details of what he had done came out, he lost all of his connections. That's why they had him in a special segregated unit when he was awaiting trial. They were worried the cartel would take him out before they could get him into a courtroom." I nervously touched my ear. "I mean, you already know that, obviously."

"Yes, but it's always good to have confirmation." The major glanced at his colleague and then back at me. "I'm going to be frank, Miss Jackson. We believe that you are in grave danger. We can't prove it yet but we feel strongly that Kiki had outside help orchestrating his escape. He may not have those old underworld ties anymore, but he has some lowlife friends helping him. It's possible that he also may have been extorting corrections officers on his unit."

"I figured," I said, the reality of my situation settling in my chest. The heavy weight of the invisible target on my back made it hard to breathe. "Do you think...?" I stopped myself. Was I really going to ask this? I could practically hear Ten shouting at me not to even think about it. But I wouldn't be able to live with myself if I didn't offer and Kiki killed more people. "Do you think using me as bait would help?"

Every eye in the room snapped to my face. I squirmed under the intense scrutiny.

"Absolutely not," Major Whitmore stated firmly. "We are not in the business of putting innocent women in danger."

"Yes, but you don't know what he's like." I hated thinking of Kiki. I hated the chill that coursed through my veins. "He's a monster, and he will hurt anyone who gets in his way. If I can help you catch him quickly, it might mean saving someone else's life."

"And it could mean you lose yours," the sheriff interjected.

"Yes, but—."

"No," the sheriff disagreed. "There are no buts to this discussion."

"Sheriff Ramirez is right," Major Whitmore agreed. "We're not using you as bait. If anything, we want to offer you the choice to go into protective custody."

"I don't need protective custody." They would separate me from Ten, and I couldn't abide that.

"Now, Nisha," Eloise cut in quietly. "We should consider this offer."

"Consider it strongly," Major Whitmore urged. "We can keep you safe."

"I'm sure you can," I agreed, "but I don't want to run and hide. He wins if I do that."

"He wins if you get killed," Sheriff Ramirez interrupted. "Don't let him win."

The sheriff's words spun around in my head as we finished the meeting. My phone was returned, and I gripped it tightly in my hands. I wanted to text Ten, but I didn't know what to say. Would he be disappointed that I had refused protective custody? I suspected he would be, especially after last night and his whispered promises to always protect me after we made love. He would happily send me into protective custody if it meant I would survive.

And if I did go? Then what? How long would I be hidden away in a safe house? A few days? A week? A month? What if Kiki was never found? What if he made it across the border and disappeared? Would I have to go into witness protection? Spend the rest of my life looking over my shoulder?

I can't live like that.

My offer to act as bait for the police wasn't an empty one. This morning, as Ten and Kostya talked quietly in his living room, I had remained curled up in bed, thinking about what awaited me. Kiki had called me last night promising to come for me. He wouldn't break that promise.

And if I let him lure me close, if I let him take me, I would have him right where I wanted him. I could turn the tables and finally give him a taste of the pain that he gave me.

I wasn't that scared little girl anymore. I was stronger. I could do anything I set my mind to—even killing that murderous piece of trash.

"Nisha." Chess called my name and caught up with us in the lobby of the DPS building where the A Company of the Texas Rangers was located. "Hey, can we talk?"

"Yeah. Of course." I stepped away with her, leaving Savannah and Eloise to chat among themselves. "How are you holding up?"

"Me? I should be asking you that." She reached out and gave my arm a friendly squeeze. "Are you okay? Are you going into protective custody?"

"I'm okay, and no."

She seemed surprised. "Really? Do you think…? I mean, is that wise?"

"I don't want to run anymore."

Chess nodded with understanding. "I get it."

"What about you? Were they asking you about Adrian?"

"And Tony," she said leveling a look at me.

Even though our men had been partners in crime, we had never talked about what we had witnessed back then. When she had come into the salon the first time, we had both exchanged anxious, panicked gazes. Neither of us had wanted to dredge up the past, not after we had worked so hard to move on and build independent lives. We had simply never spoken about Kiki, Adrian or Tony.

But now?

"You know that Ten…?" Chess asked carefully.

"Yeah, I found out last night."

"I wondered if you knew," she said apologetically. "I saw him flirting with you one day, and I was surprised that you were smiling right back at him."

"Well, it's not as if Tony was a saint." I still couldn't quite wrap my head around the man I had known as the lighthearted comedian of the group was a child molester.

"No, he wasn't." Chess grimaced. "Neither was Adrian as I found out later." She looked like she might be sick. "I didn't know until it was too late. He ran away like a fucking coward rather than face up to what he had been doing by making those videos and selling them." She glanced away and inhaled a deep breath. "I took everything to the FBI. All of it. They followed up on it and used the evidence to catch other men involved in the ring, but they never found Adrian."

I didn't want to know. I really didn't. But I had to ask. "Was Kiki on the videos?"

"I only watched a few seconds of one," she said with a shudder of revulsion. "He wasn't on it. It was just Fat Tony and Adrian behind the camera yelling at the boy." She put her hand against her mouth, and I felt so guilty for bringing up such painful memories. "I'm sorry, Nisha. I can't."

"No, it's okay. I understand." God, did I ever. "We don't have to talk about this ever again."

"I'm taking Callie and getting out of town." She glanced at the double doors of the lobby. "Artyom is so stressed out, and I know he won't rest until we're safe in a different state."

It wasn't the first time she had mentioned the three-fingered Russian who seemed to shadow her. I knew who Artyom was, of course, and I knew what he did. Back when Kiki and Adrian ran guns and drugs together, Artyom had been Adrian's street captain and boss.

"Oh, for fuck's sake!" Savannah snarled as we stepped out of the building. "Here comes that lawyer bitch from yesterday! And her annoying cameraman!"

My panicked gaze flitted toward the stairs and Robin Harris, Kiki's attorney. She was bounding toward us with the podcaster, Chad, right behind her. A few steps behind them, there was a crush of media, some of them local news crews and the rest amateur sleuth types who wanted to use me to get more views on social media.

"Nisha! Do you know where your ex is hiding?"

"Nisha! Do you think there are more bodies?"

"Chess, where is your ex hiding? Is it true he was a pedophile?"

"Chess, did he make you act in pornos?"

"Is Kiki going to kill again?"

"Does Kiki have a hit list? Are you on it?"

"Why aren't you in protective custody?"

"Chess, does your daughter know her father was a child molester?"

"Are you truly a victim or were you the secret accomplice?"

The last one got my attention, and I scanned the crowd to find the bizarre voice that had shouted it. "Who said that?"

But I never got my answer.

There was a crack and a *thwap* sound. The noise had barely registered before I saw Robin jerk forward. Blood exploded from her chest and splattered all over me. Something hit the concrete by my foot—a bullet I would realize later—and bits of the cement and metal tore into my leg.

Suddenly, everyone was screaming and running. I froze, and Savannah grabbed me by the hand. "Come on! We have to—"

Savannah lurched forward, and her eyes widened with shock. Blood erupted from her shoulder and breast, staining the shimmery coral blouse she wore. She fell into my arms, her full weight taking me to my knees.

"Savannah!" I screamed her name and pressed my hand to her chest, desperately trying to stem the blood flow. "Savvy!"

"We have to move!" Chess shouted and tugged at my arm. All around us, police were firing their weapons across the street.

"Help me!" I flinched as gunshots cracked on either side of us.

Chess grabbed one of Savannah's arms and Eloise joined at Savannah's feet. We moved her off the steps and toward a statue with a broad base we could hide behind. We were nearly there when Chess cried out in pain and stumbled forward. An expanding bloodstain blossomed on the thigh of her clover green pants.

"Chess!" I couldn't believe another person I cared about was now bleeding right in front of me. I kept one hand on Savannah's chest and pressed the other on Chess's thigh.

"Here. Use this." Eloise shrugged out of her suit jacket and handed it to me to use on Savannah's gushing wound. She moved to Chess's side and placed both hands on the gunshot wound on her thigh and pushed down with all her might. "You're going to be okay, Chess. Just stay calm."

Stay calm.

I repeated those two words as the world descended into chaos around us.

Stay calm.

Savannah's shaking hand gripped my wrist. Her eyes were wide with fear. "Don't let me die like this."

"You're not going to die." I wouldn't allow it. I refused to lose my friend. "You're going to be fine. We'll get you to the hospital and you'll be fine."

"Tell him—." Savannah's teeth began to chatter, and her face seemed pale and gray under her blush and lipstick. "Tell Gabe..."

"Savvy?" I pushed harder on her wound, desperate to keep every drop of blood in her body. "Savvy, who is Gabe? Savannah!"

Her eyelid fluttered, and she passed out cold right there on the concrete. A puddle of blood grew around her, and I began to sob hysterically as I tried to give my friend the best chance at survival.

"Just hold on, Savvy. Please hold on."

CHAPTER TEN

"WILL YOU STOP pacing? You're going to wear a hole in Vivian's rug and then I'll never hear the end of it." Nikolai scowled up at Ten from the floor where he played with his son. Lev slammed two brightly colored blocks together while his father stacked the rest of the set into neat little towers.

"*Prostite.*" Ten slumped down onto the overstuffed love seat and picked up a board book from the cushion. He made a face when his fingers encountered the gummy wetness of saliva-soaked paper. "Looks like it's time for a new copy of *Goodnight, Moon.*"

Nikolai frowned. "That's the third one." He turned his attention to Lev who was happily knocking over the towers his father had finished. Gently, he gathered the boy close and managed to coax the child to open his mouth. "Yes, there it is. Another tooth. Lev, you have a million teething toys in this house. You don't have to gnaw on books like a little mouse."

The baby laughed and chewed on his father's finger. Nikolai reacted with exaggerated pain which made Lev laugh even harder. Nikolai nuzzled Lev and began to tease him about being a little mouse.

Ten watched the pair together and tried not to think about

how much he wanted a family. It had always been a fuzzy future goal. Fall in love. Get married. Buy a house. Have kids. When he had gone to prison, that fuzzy goal had faded to near nothing. Now, he was so close to freedom that he was actually starting to think about the future and all the possibilities it held.

Possibilities he wanted to share with Nisha.

Last night had been a dream. He truly hadn't planned on even trying to kiss her again. He hadn't wanted her to feel any pressure or obligation toward him. But then she had looked at him with those big, brown eyes, and he had fallen head-first into an abyss of need and want. Once she made it clear that her consent flag was flying high, he succumbed to his desperate desire for her.

The sex had been incredible. By far, the best of his life—and he'd fucked a lot of women. But what he shared with Nisha had eclipsed those other experiences. There was just something about the way she looked at him, the way she kissed him, the way she held onto him, that left him dizzy and damn near giddy.

But those scars.

Jesus Christ, those scars.

Burns. Knife wounds. Ligature marks. Gunshot wounds. Surgical repairs. Her poor body had been battered and abused unlike any he had ever seen.

Ten's heart ached at the thought of her being so young and scared, completely alone with that fucking monster. How had Nicky allowed that sort of damage to happen to his niece? There was no way that had gone unnoticed. Not years of torment like that.

Why hadn't anyone helped her?

"Ten." Nikolai spoke his name loudly. "You okay?"

"Uh...yeah." Ten set aside the book and cleared his throat. "Yeah, I'm fine."

Nikolai regarded him with suspicion. "Tell me."

He shook his head. "It's nothing."

"It's Nisha." Nikolai knew, of course. He could read faces as easily as a book. "Tell me."

"Her body," Ten said, his gaze settling on innocent, chubby Lev who crawled toward Stasi. The Great Dane opened one eye as the baby drew near and huffed a dramatic sigh. The dog's temperament was so good around the boy, but his huge size meant that even a light smack of his paw could bruise Lev.

"Careful," Nikolai said and moved to intercept his son. "Gentle." He took Lev's hand in his own and showed him how to pet the dog. "We're gentle with Stasi, and he will be gentle back to us."

Lev repeated his father's lesson and then bonked the dog in the head with a stuffed elephant he had left right next to the dog earlier. Stasi grumbled, and Nikolai redirected Lev away from the dog and back to his pile of blocks. The boss gave the dog a scratch between the ears and then turned his attention back to Ten. "Her body?"

"The scars," Ten explained. "There are so many."

Nikolai nodded somberly. "I suspected."

"And nobody did anything to help her," Ten said, at a loss. "Not Nicky. Not her friends. No one?"

"Relationships like that are complicated for everyone, Ten. I'd like to think Nicky Jackson would have gotten involved if he had known how bad the abuse was, but maybe he figured that was her own problem to solve."

"She was a child."

"She was," Nikolai agreed.

"It's not right."

"It's not," Nikolai agreed.

"I keep going back through my memories, but I don't re-member her." As soon as Ten had learned her name, he had been trying to place her in his memories. "Why didn't we ever cross paths?"

"You're older than her. You were busy shadowing Artyom. You never handled any of the business we had that overlapped with the Fifth Ward. You were in two different orbits."

"I wish I had known her back then. I could have—."

"What?" Nikolai interjected. "You could have saved her? How?"

"I don't know, but I would have figured it out," Ten stub-bornly insisted.

"You can believe that if it makes you feel better."

"But?"

"But there's no point in torturing yourself about the past. You can't change it, and neither can she. Today, right now, you're exactly where you're supposed to be—with her."

"Except I'm not with her," Ten muttered with frustration. "I should be with her at the police station."

"She has her lawyer and Savannah with her. You would be a distraction."

Nikolai was right, of course, but that didn't mean Ten wanted to hear it.

Lev crawled over to Ten and grabbed hold of his jeans. He reached out to steady Lev as the baby hauled himself to a standing position. He wobbled a bit before leaning forward and biting Ten's knee through the denim.

"Hey!" Ten scooped up the laughing baby and plopped him down on his thigh. "I'm going to start charging hazard pay."

"You joke, but I should probably increase your pay now that Lev is mobile." Nikolai gathered up the blocks and other toys. "Or—."

"Or what?" Ten seized on the boss's strange tone.

"Your parole is nearly finished." Nikolai tossed the last block into the white organizer bin. "You paid your dues, Ten. You served the family. You proved your loyalty."

"Yeah? And?" Where was he going with this?

"And if you want out, I'll make it happen." Nikolai's serious expression matched the weight of his promise. "No strings. Clean. Done. Out."

Ten was still trying to process that offer when his phone started to buzz across the changing table where he had left it. Nikolai's phone began to ring and vibrate across the rug where he had been sitting with Lev. Ten exchanged a worried glance with the boss who snatched up both phones.

"Here." Nikolai thrust Ten's phone at him. A second later, he answered his with a gruff, "What?"

Ten swiped his thumb across the screen to answer Boychenko's call. "Boy?"

"Someone shot at Nisha," Boychenko said in a hurried rush. "They hit Savannah and killed the lawyer lady. Chess got hit in the leg. It's a shit show, Ten. You need to get down here right now."

"Where?" Ten cradled Lev against his chest and shot to his

feet. "Where am I going?"

"They're waiting for an ambulance. There's not—hang on."

"Ten." Nikolai stepped forward with his phone clamped between his ear and shoulder. He grasped his son and then said, "Go."

Ten raced from the nursery, startling Stasi who barked and followed him out into the hallway. "Roman!"

"Sorry!" Boychenko apologized. "I was waiting to see what Kostya said. Ben Taub. They're taking the women to Ben Taub."

"I'm on my way." Ten raced by Ilya in the kitchen and burst out the back door of the house. He ran straight to his Tahoe and hopped behind the wheel. Horrible images flashed before his eyes. Nisha torn open by a bullet. Nisha bleeding on the pavement. Nisha terrified and calling out for him.

I should have been with her.

I should have been beside her.

I should have been protecting her.

"Never fucking again," he swore furiously. He was never letting her out of his sight again.

Right before he reached the hospital, Ten's phone rang again. He tapped his touchscreen to accept the call via the SUV's Bluetooth. "Yeah?"

"Anton!" Nisha's agonized voice filled the vehicle. "They shot at us! Savannah is dying, and Chess is bleeding a lot. Why would they do this? Why would they do this?"

"Nisha. Baby, I'm almost there." Her sobs tore at his heart. "I'm almost there. Stay with me."

Her sobs and the sound of ambulance sirens echoed in his

ears. He gripped the steering wheel and silently cursed whoever had targeted Nisha. Murderous intent burned through his veins. He wanted to hurt someone.

"We're at the hospital," Nisha wept. "Ben Taub. We're at Ben Taub."

"I know. I'm a few blocks away. I'll be there as soon as I can."

"I have to hang up. The paramedics are taking me in now." Her voice was small and weak. "Please hurry."

"I'm coming." Ten's chest constricted so tightly he could barely breathe. How badly was Nisha hurt? Was Savannah really dying? And Chess? Fuck, Artyom was going to burn this city to the ground if Chess had been hurt.

Ten pulled into the parking garage and furiously cursed under his breath as he searched for a parking space. He found one, finally, and bailed from his Tahoe. He didn't bother with the elevator. He took the stairs, hopping down three and four at a time to get to the ground floor faster.

He jogged across the hospital campus, desperate to reach Nisha. When he reached the ER entrance, he grimaced at the number of people packed into the waiting room. Not that it surprised him, of course.

Ben Taub. The Tub. The county's main hospital took in all the patients no one else wanted. It was where the best trauma surgeons worked. Gunshots, stabbings, anything brutal or violent—Ben Taub's trauma rooms had seen them all.

He stepped inside the lobby and spotted Artyom standing near a set of double doors. Their gazes clashed, and Ten nodded somberly. He weaved his way through the sea of bodies milling around the waiting room. "Artyom."

"Ten." Artyom stepped closer so their conversation wouldn't be overheard. He slipped into Russian to add another layer of privacy. "It was a sniper on a building across the street. Savannah took a bullet to the chest. Chess took a round to the thigh. Nisha's leg was bloody, but I think she missed the worst of it. Kiki's lawyer died before she hit the ground."

"Were you there?"

Artyom's jaw clenched. "The parking lot. Chess didn't want me to come inside with her. She worried I would get hassled."

Ten heard the regret in the other man's voice. "You could have been shot if you were with her."

"I wish it was me instead." Artyom glanced at the doors. "If something happens to her, I can't even help. I'm not her family. Not legally. I can't make medical decisions for her. I can't keep Callie if—." He couldn't even finish the thought. "I should have done something sooner."

Ten regarded Artyom with surprise. He had known that Artyom had feelings for Chess that were stronger than friendship, but there were complicating factors. Namely that Artyom had been there the night Adrian had been killed and that he had actually been the one who—.

The double doors opened with a loud clunk. A nurse appeared and called out, "Anton? Artyom?"

"That's us," Ten said.

"This way." She flicked her fingers and stepped aside to let them pass through the controlled doors. As soon as they were on the other side, she shut the doors, and the automatic locks engaged. He didn't want to think about why they needed that level of security back here.

"Artyom?" She glanced at them to see who was who. When Artyom raised a hand, she said, "You're in Trauma 3." She turned her gaze. "You must be Anton?"

"Yeah."

"Exam 4." She pointed out the room on the other side of the bay.

"Thanks."

He parted ways with Artyom and strode to Nisha's room. He knocked before entering, just in case she was undressed, and entered as soon as he heard her voice. He quickly shut the door behind him and took in the scene. Nisha reclined on the exam table with her foot elevated on a pillow. She had a trauma dressing on her left calf, and it was soaked with blood.

Actually, everything she wore was soaked with blood. Her shirt. Her skirt. Her face. Her hands. There was blood everywhere.

"Savvy's," she said as if reading his mind. "She wouldn't stop bleeding, Ten. I think she's going to die."

"No, baby, she's not to die." He didn't know that, but he couldn't bring himself to confirm her worst fears. From the amount of blood that had transferred to her body, Ten wouldn't be surprised if Savannah did lose her life.

"It's all my fault," Nisha sobbed, and his heart shattered. He crossed the space between them and gathered her into his arms. She was sweat-slicked and damp, and she smelled of blood. He squeezed her tightly, pushing all the love he had for her into his embrace. She shuddered against his chest, sobbing loudly as the guilt of her friends' injuries overwhelmed her.

"It's not your fault, Nisha." He kissed her temple. "It's not your fault."

She said something, but he couldn't understand her. She was crying so hard he worried she was going to throw up. He hadn't heard anyone weep like this ever. It was like it came right from the bottom of her soul, just ripping through her heart and pouring out of her in agonizing waves. She clutched at him, her nails biting into his shoulder and arm, and soaked his shirt with her tears.

When the nurse and doctor entered the room, he shifted aside but kept one of her hands trapped in his. She still sobbed but quieter now, more controlled. He soothingly rubbed her back as the doctor and nurse peeled away the dressing to reveal a series of gashes in her leg. They irrigated and sutured the wounds and ordered a tetanus vaccine, just in case.

Nisha seemed completely out of it by the time her discharge papers arrived. She clung to his hand, and he worried about her mental well-being. She already carried so much guilt and shame over the crimes Kiki had committed. If she lost a friend because of Kiki's escape, she would never forgive herself.

There was a knock at the exam room door, and Ten answered it. A Texas Ranger and sheriff's deputy stood on the other side. He swallowed the urge to tell them both to fuck off. He warily stepped aside and let them enter. Nisha flinched at the sight of them, but then she lifted her chin and pushed back her shoulders. She wiped her face with the tips of her fingers and prepared to meet their questions head-on.

She was so torn up inside, consumed by fear that she would lose her friends and the guilt that she had been the cause of their pain. She had a crazy ex-husband on the loose, and now some lunatic taking shots at her. The police were going to make her life very uncomfortable, but she wasn't backing down or slinking away.

She was facing the ugliest possible outcome with a brave face.

And he'd never been prouder of her.

CHAPTER ELEVEN

WRUNG OUT, I curled up on my side on Ten's couch. Wilford was perched on the back of it. Every now and then, I would feel his fluffy tail swat my shoulder. He seemed to understand I was feeling poorly and anxious and kept close by. He wasn't quite an emotional support animal. He had too much dignity to ever deign to be a servant to his owner. Still, he was there when I needed him, and I appreciated it.

I appreciated Ten even more. Right now, he bustled around his kitchen making dinner for us. He had promised, after all, when asking me out on a date yesterday.

Yesterday. Lord Almighty, why did yesterday seem like it was weeks ago? How was it possible that so much had happened in the space of thirty hours or so?

"Do you want to eat at the table or are you more comfortable on the couch?" Ten appeared in the doorway between the kitchen and living room. He had a dish towel slung over one shoulder and looked impossibly sexy in his bare feet, jeans, and Markovic MMA gym tee.

"The table." I shifted, and Ten immediately moved toward me. He was at my side faster than I had expected, and his burly arms lifted me into a sitting position. "Ten, I can sit up and walk."

"I know you can." That didn't stop him from helping me stand and then sliding his arm around my waist to guide me to the table at the far end of his kitchen. I didn't bother with the crutches they had given me at the ER and hobbled along at his side.

I was taken aback by the tablescape he had prepared. There were candles and short glass vases of roses in the strangest toffee shade. He had the most beautiful stoneware plates and champagne gold flatware. "Anton!"

"I know it's not a very romantic night. Not with everything that happened," he said gently. "But I still wanted it to be special for us. If nothing else, I hope you can forget about all the stress that's eating away at you long enough to enjoy a meal with me."

I blinked rapidly, trying to clear away the tears making my vision all blurry. I wrapped my arms around him and hugged him. "Oh, Anton, you're the most wonderful man."

He embraced me and lowered his face to nuzzle at my hair. "I'll do anything for you, Nisha."

That's what scared me. He was so close to being free from his legal entanglement. Being with me put him at risk of doing something really stupid. How far would he go to protect me? What lines would he cross to keep me safe?

I can't let him go back to prison.

I have to solve this problem myself.

But I kept those thoughts to myself. There was no point in voicing them. Ten would only argue, and I didn't want to ruin his lovely dinner.

"It's nothing fancy." He brought dinner to the table in various serving dishes. "I thought comfort might be something we both needed."

"I like comfort." I smiled up at him from my seat. "This looks delicious."

It tasted even better than it looked. The brown rice was seasoned beautifully, and the steamed vegetables were fork-tender. The pork chops impressed me the most. "How did you manage to make these so crispy without drying them out?"

"Air fryer."

"No way."

"Yes, way." He picked up his glass of water and took a sip. "My toaster oven has an air fryer setting. I use it for every-thing."

"Well, don't tell Billie. She'll want you to try all those wild TikTok recipes."

"Why does that not surprise me?" Ten shook his head and speared a zucchini medallion. "She's a menace."

"She's not so bad once you get to know the girl under the spunky exterior. She's hiding something painful under it, I think."

"Yeah?"

"I haven't figured it out yet." Something—someone—hurt her. I just didn't know who or when. "But I will."

Ten smiled at that, and I was glad he didn't try to dissuade me. He must have known it would be pointless. "Speaking of Billie, she told me to make sure I provided a good dessert, but I didn't have time to make or buy anything. I have some ice cream from H-E-B in the freezer. It's the good stuff—cookie dough and Oreos mixed up in vanilla."

"A scoop of ice cream is perfect."

After dinner, I tried to help him clean up the kitchen, but

he refused and threatened to carry me back to the couch if I kept trying to load the dishwasher. I finally gave in and took my seat on the couch as he had commanded. Wilford climbed onto my lap and batted at my hand until I agreed to pet him.

As I stroked his fur, I popped into the salon's group chat to see if there were updates on Savannah. She had come out of a multi-hour surgery successfully and was in ICU. She hadn't woken up yet, and I doubted she would before morning. She had lost so much blood. It was a miracle she was still alive.

Holly was back in Houston and at the hospital. Since Savannah had no family, she had asked Holly to be her emergency contact and medical power of attorney. I wasn't quite clear on when they had come to that agreement, but I suspected it was around the time they had decided to build the salon together. It made sense that they would need to have everything worked out, just in case.

Nisha, are you okay?

Holly texted me solo, pulling our conversation out of the group chat.

I'm so worried about you.

> *I'm fine. I'm with Ten.*

I really think you should get out of town.

> *I don't think I'll be any safer out of town than it.*

This is so fucked up, Nisha. This isn't fair. It's not right.

> *Life isn't fair. I know that better than anyone.*

Promise me you'll be careful.

Please, Nisha.

We almost lost Savvy.

We can't lose you.

I'll be careful. I promise.

Oh—and Holly?

Yeah?

Savvy mentioned someone named Gabe?

Do you know who that is?

Yes. I do.

What did she want to tell him?

She didn't finish her thought.

She just said:

Tell Gabe

and then she passed out.

I'll let him know.

I swiped my thumb across the screen, closing the messaging app, and noticed I had dozens of social media notifications. My phone was set to Do Not Disturb with only select contacts able to get through to me so I hadn't heard any of the notifications. My gut twisted with anxiety as I tapped the screen.

"Oh, no." My head began to throb, and my ears grew hot as I scanned the notifications. People were brigading my Instagram and Facebook pages and even TikTok where I shared silly salon videos. Some of the comments were encouraging or defending me, but so many of them were horrific accusations against me.

Serial killer slut! Chad411 has spilled all the dirty tea.

She knew! There's no way she didn't know what he was doing!

Y'all are disgusting! Victim blaming assholes! Leave
her alone!

She's such a liar. There's no way a wife doesn't know
what her man is up to! She knew!

Gonna get her friends killed because she's too much of
a coward to tell the truth!

You people are insane! She was a kid married to a
grooming rapist psycho!

What happened to Derek Miller, Nisha?

Are y'all serious with this victim blaming nonsense? He
killed their baby! Leave her alone!

Go watch Chad411! He has ALL the details. He knows
ALL her secrets. She's a fucking liar!

Ghetto trash! She's no victim. She's just like her nasty
pimp uncle who runs the 5th ward!

Someone ask her about Marissa Lopez! Yeah, girl.
That's right. We all remember what you did!

Get a grip you nuts! She is a victim! He was beating on
her and brainwashing her!

"Nisha." Ten's deep voice broke through the panic gripping me. I glanced up at him, and my stomach flopped wildly.
He was holding his phone, and I could tell by the look on his
face he was reading the same horrible shit I was.

"It's not what you think."

"What's not what I think?" His brow furrowed, and he
crossed the living room to sit next to me. He gently took my
hand. "What's wrong, Nisha?"

"Marissa Lopez," I said, choking on her name. "It's not
what they're insinuating."

"Marissa Who? What are you talking about?'

"These comments," I said, shaking my phone in his direction.

"I know. I saw them. They're awful, and you shouldn't read them. These people are idiots."

"Yes, but Marissa—." I stopped abruptly, suddenly embarrassed to tell him how horrible I had been. "She was this older girl who wanted Kiki."

"Okay?"

"And I hated her," I confessed with a sob. "She was always so mean to me. She made cracks about my weight, and my mom running off with a man. She made jokes about my dead dad. Just constantly, constantly tearing me down."

"She sounds like a bitch."

"She was. Probably still is," I said, thinking that she didn't seem likely to ever change.

"What happened? Why are people bringing her up in the comments?"

"I cut her," I confessed, my head hung low in shame. "She slept with Kiki. I was fifteen, and I was stupid and jealous and so wrapped up in him. He slept with her to prove a point to me, that I was replaceable, and I freaked out and got so angry. She kept getting in my face about it, and I slashed her with a knife. Just swiped her right across the chest."

The memory of the violent and horrible thing I had done turned my stomach. I shot to my feet and bolted for the guest bathroom. The pain in my leg made it hard to move quickly, and I barely made it before the dinner Ten had so painstakingly cooked for us erupted from my stomach. I shoved the door closed, barring him from entering, and heaved again.

Ten wasn't about to let a little thing like a door stop him.

He pushed it open and slid behind me, gently bracing my stomach and sweeping my hair out of the way as I retched into the toilet. When I was done, he helped me rinse my mouth and face.

I couldn't understand why he was being so nice to me. He gently cradled me against his chest as I hid from him in shame. "Nisha, you were a kid who did something stupid."

"I shouldn't have done it. I shouldn't have hurt her like that."

"No, you shouldn't have," he agreed. "But you did, and there's no changing it. You have to face it and accept it." He rubbed my back, and I melted into him, loving him even more for the way he accepted me, warts and all. "How badly was she hurt?"

"Six stitches across her breast." My voice was muffled by his shirt and chest. "I got it worse, though."

"How?"

"Kiki took me to the back room of the bar where he and Adrian liked to hang out, and he locked me in the room with Marissa and six of her friends. They beat the shit out of me, and he egged them on, telling them I needed to learn my lesson." I touched my left eyebrow, remembering the pool cue that busted my forehead wide open. "It wasn't my place to question him."

Ten traced his thumb along the scar on my eyebrow. "They did this to you?"

I nodded. "Kiki wouldn't let me go to the hospital. He told me the scars would always remind me of how I misbehaved."

Ten snarled in Russian, and I was certain the words were vile. "You were fifteen years old, Nisha. You weren't even old enough to drive a car! How old was Marissa?"

"Twenty? Twenty-one?" I shrugged. "Older."

"Old enough to know better."

"I guess." I gulped as the reality of my situation soured my stomach again. "But you see what they're getting at, right? That I cut someone in a fight?"

He frowned down at me. "And?"

"Kiki cut those girls he killed. People think I must have known what he was doing. That I couldn't possibly have been in the dark about the murders. Now, they know I cut someone who slept with him."

"And it's a big leap to accuse you of being the one who attacked and killed those prostitutes for fucking your abusive husband," Ten finished with a scowl. "That's crazy, Nisha. No one would believe that."

"The people commenting do!"

"They're a bunch of internet assholes hiding behind keyboards! Who cares what they say?"

"I care! This is my life! It's my reputation! I worked hard to get where I am, and now Kiki is ruining my life all over again!"

"Hey," Ten said tenderly and gathered me back in his arms. "It's going to be okay, Nisha."

"It's not," I protested, losing hope. "It's not going to be okay."

Both of our phones started to ring. We exchanged a worried glance and returned to the living room where our phones had fallen onto the floor when I ran to the bathroom. He picked them both up and studied the screens. His jaw tightened, and my heart skipped a beat.

"What?" I wrung my hands. "Is it Savannah? Is it Chess?"

"No. It's not your friends."

"What? What is it?" I held my breath, expecting the very worst.

"A small mob vandalized Allure."

My breath rushed out of my lungs in a shocked gasp. "Vandalized?"

"Burned," he clarified. "Kostya says the fire wasn't big, but it caused damage before the fire department arrived."

"Oh, my God!" Guilt swamped me, driving me to my knees. They buckled, and I tumbled forward. Ten wasn't fast enough to catch me. He knelt and wrapped his arms around me, helping me back to my feet and speaking tender words. I couldn't bear to hear them. I wanted to suffer. I deserved to suffer.

"Nisha, it's not your fault."

"It is my fault! Everything is my fault!" Realizing that I had nearly gotten two friends killed and burned down the business my two best friends had built, I shoved him. "Get away from me, Ten!"

"What?" His eyes widened. "Why? What's wrong?"

"What's wrong? I'm a fucking curse! If you stay near me, you're going to get hurt." I glanced around in a panic. "I have to go. Right now."

"What? No!" Ten snatched my hand, holding tight and preventing me from leaving. "You're not going anywhere unless I'm right beside you."

"Anton," I pleaded. "Let me go."

He dragged me into his arms and kissed my cheek. "Never."

CHAPTER TWELVE

TEN CLASPED NISHA'S hand as he barreled down the highway and out of Houston. He wasn't giving her a chance to run away from him. She felt things so deeply, and she was raw and vulnerable right now. She would bolt if she got a chance.

Wilford yowled pitifully in the backseat, and Nisha glanced back at her cat. "Wilfy, I know you're miserable in your crate, but we'll let you out as soon as we get there."

The cat let loose a howling whine and then hissed twice.

"The feeling is mutual," Ten muttered. He eyed the angry scratches on his forearms. Wilford had been less than enthusiastic about going into his carrier for the second time in as many days.

"I'm so sorry about your arms." Nisha leaned over and kissed the closest scratch.

His gaze softened, and he lifted her hand so he could kiss her knuckles. "Never thought I'd have someone kiss my boo-boos."

She laughed. "I will happily smooch all your ouchies."

"You would have been a good mother." The words fell out of his mouth before he could stop them. He swallowed hard, realizing too late what he had said, and glanced at her. There wasn't very much light inside the SUV driving this late at night, and he couldn't get a read on her face. "Nisha, I'm sorry. I shouldn't have—."

"Her name was Lorelai."

"Lorelai," he repeated, thinking it was exactly the sort of name he would have expected her to choose. "That's a beautiful name."

"I thought so." She kept her gaze fixed on the windshield. "Kiki didn't. He hated the name, but he hated that he was having a daughter even more. I think if he'd found out early enough in the pregnancy he would have made me get another abortion."

Yet another reason to beat that asshole.

"I'm glad he didn't. I'm glad I got to carry her as long as I did."

Ten wasn't sure whether he should ask or if he should stay silent and let her talk. When she didn't say anything, he cautiously asked, "Was it the shotgun blast that killed her?"

"No, not exactly," Nisha said, and her fingers tightened around his. "He had strangled me a few times during the pregnancy. That night he had done it worse than ever before." Her voice was monotone as if she were reciting words from a page. "I thought I was going to die. I really did. He just kept squeezing and squeezing, and I felt her kicking in me, and then—nothing."

Ten's heart raced as she recounted the horrific abuse. "Nisha, I'm so sorry."

"Yeah, so am I. I failed her. I should have—." She made a gulping sound and then roughly wiped her face. "I should have left as soon as I knew I was pregnant. I should have protected her."

"Nisha—."

"I know," she interrupted. "I know what you're going to say." She exhaled roughly. "But I also know that I had a duty to my child. I was supposed to keep her safe, and I didn't. She died because I wasn't strong enough to leave."

"That's not true." He couldn't bear the thought of her carrying that immense guilt. He couldn't bear the thought of her suffering under that weight. "She died because Kiki was evil. He killed her. Not you."

"They cut her out of me, you know?" She seemed far away now. "Emergency c-section. Right there in the ER. Just hacked away at me. They call it a splash and crash or something like that." She rubbed her face. "It was awful, but I was desperate for them to save her." She inhaled a shaky breath. "But she never breathed. She never cried. She was already gone before the buckshot tore through me."

Ten almost couldn't bear the image that her words painted. How had Nisha survived? Not just physically, but mentally? Emotionally? To be battered and abused? To learn that her husband was a serial killer? To have her baby killed before she ever had a chance to live? It was too much for one woman to endure.

"I can still have kids," she said. "In case you're wondering."

"I wasn't, but that's good?" He wasn't sure if it was or not. Maybe she didn't want to ever be pregnant again after what she experienced with Lorelai. "If you want to have more children?"

"Yes, I want to have more children." Nisha turned her attention from the windshield to him. "Do you want to have kids?"

"With you?" he asked, glancing away from the road to meet her gaze in the dim light from the dashboard. "Yes."

She seemed startled. "Just like that? Yes?"

"Nisha, I'll give you as many babies as you want. Fuck, I'll even stay home and be a full-time dad if that's what makes you happy." He lifted her hand and kissed the back of it again. "I'll do anything you want. Whatever makes you happy, you ask me, and it's yours."

"Why?" she asked, sounding completely bewildered.

"Why?" he echoed. "Because I love you, Nisha Jackson." He swallowed the ball of emotion blocking his throat. "I think I fell in love with you the first time you scowled and rolled your eyes at me."

"Anton!" she scolded.

"What? It's true! I fumbled through my attempt to flirt with you, and you made that face and rolled your big, brown eyes. I was done. That was it. You fucking owned me from that moment."

"You're serious." She seemed to have finally grasped he was telling the truth. "You've loved me this whole time?"

"Yes." Knowing she was under so much emotional strain, he said, "But you don't have to love me back. Not yet. I can wait."

"Anton."

"Yes?"

"I love you."

His heart pounded against this sternum. "Yeah?"

"Yes."

"Okay. Good. That's…good."

"Yes, it is."

They settled into a comfortable silence. She shifted his hand between both of hers and stroked his tattooed, scarred knuckles. He felt impossibly young and carefree after that confession. *She loves me.*

He wasn't stupid or naïve. He knew that it wouldn't be that simple. Even if they got through this nightmare with Kiki and the lunatic who had taken shots at Nisha earlier that day, their relationship would not be a cakewalk. He was a felon, and that stain would follow him everywhere. She was the niece of a Houston underworld boss. He worked for a rival boss. He was part of the Russian mafia, and even if Nikolai offered to set him free, it was hard to ever really break free.

Sergei, Ivan, and Alexei were proof enough of that. All three men had fought their way out of the life, but circumstances had dragged them right back into it. Once the underworld imprinted on you, there was no way to wash that mark clean. It lingered.

"Is that it?" Nisha asked as they approached a gate on a secluded FM road in Brazos County.

"I think so." He glanced at his iPhone mounted on the dash. The directions Kostya had given to one of his nearby hideouts were very thorough, and they had managed the drive without any wrong turns.

"It's not what I expected," she remarked. "When he said cabin, I was picturing something rustic. More off-grid."

"So was I," Ten admitted. He had been expecting to pull up to a hut with an outhouse and no running water.

The limestone and wood cabin sat back from the main road, giving a good view of any cars coming and going. There were plenty of trees for privacy, but there were a number of strategically placed lights around the perimeter of the house to make it difficult for someone to sneak up unnoticed. There was an ultra-high-tech security system waiting for them, and knowing Kostya, the whole house was probably rigged with defensive explosives.

He drew to a stop at the gate keypad and punched in the code Kostya had given him before they left Houston in one of the Suburbans stored as part of Nikolai's backup fleet. Kostya had also exchanged their phones and other devices for clean ones, just in case. There were envelopes of cash, emergency escape routes, and numbers to call and text if they ran into trouble. As usual, Kostya had shit covered.

Ten pulled around to the back of the cabin to park, making sure his vehicle was hidden from view. He asked Nisha to stay in the SUV while he checked the cabin, and she waited impatiently for him to return. When he did, he grabbed Wilford's carrier and then helped Nisha out of the Suburban. She used her crutches to move down the sidewalk to the back door of the cabin. Wilford meowed and whined the whole time, clearly desperate to get out of his travel crate.

"Let me get our bags." Ten couldn't shake the feeling that he needed to stay right next to Nisha. She didn't seem like she wanted to try to run and hide to save him anymore, but he worried that he might have missed a tail. What if someone was lurking out there? Waiting for him to be out of the picture just long enough to snatch her?

"I'll be fine, Ten." It was as if she could read his mind. "I'll wait right here."

"Okay." He hurried to gather their suitcases and lock up the Suburban. When he entered the cabin, he locked the door behind him and armed the security system.

"Did he tell you that he had the fridge stocked for us?" Nisha called out from the refrigerator. The main floor of the cabin was open space, and he was glad that he could keep an eye on her. "I mean, it's completely jam-packed with fresh food!"

"He said he had it prepared so I'm not surprised. He's very thorough in everything he does."

"That explains the smile on Holly's face and the pep in her step when he's in town."

"I don't doubt it." Ten didn't particularly want to think about Holly or Kostya in that way. "There's a main bedroom on the first floor, but we can take one of the two upstairs if you'd rather."

"No, my leg is actually starting to hurt," she admitted. "I think I'd rather stay down here."

He set up their suitcases and checked the bedroom closet and the bathroom for any hint of an intruder. There wasn't.

Back out in the living area, he found Nisha coaxing Wilford out of his carrier. When the bushy beast finally emerged, he hissed and swatted at her before racing off to hide somewhere.

"Are you okay?" Ten rushed to her side. "Did he get you?"

"No. He just batted at me with his paw." She rolled her eyes. "He's such a drama queen."

"He must get it from his mother," Ten teased.

"Hey!" She playfully swatted his chest.

"See?" Ten gestured to her hand. "He learned that from you."

"You're impossible."

"Impossibly in love with you? Yes." Ten slipped his arm around her waist and hauled her close. He swept the bouncy curls from her eyes and leaned down to capture her lips in a sensual kiss. He was dog-ass tired, and he was certain she was, too. He didn't expect the kiss to lead anywhere. He simply wanted to taste her mouth, to remind himself of how good it felt to claim his woman.

She smiled up at him, her eyes glimmering with emotion. He could read all the words she wanted to say in her dreamy expression. Happy enough with that, he kissed her again. "Bed?"

She nodded, and he handed her the crutches she had left propped against the kitchen counter. She was moving easier with them the more she practiced. He hoped she wouldn't be on them too much longer, but keeping her weight off her leg and letting those wounds close was the most important thing.

Nisha picked through her suitcase, and Ten had a sudden feeling they were being watched. Kostya had video surveillance on all of his properties. Which made him wonder...

Are you watching us?

Maybe.

Kostya.

Cameras are off in the downstairs bathroom and bedroom.

Thank you.

I'm not trying to be a pervert. I'm trying to keep you safe.

I know.

Stay in the cabin.

Don't make contact with anyone.

Do exactly as I told you.

Until?

Until we flush out this motherfucking rat and finish him.

Ten wished it would be that easy.

CHAPTER THIRTEEN

I WAS FIFTEEN the first time I got pregnant.

I hadn't even realized how many risks I was taking until it was too late. No one ever sat me down and gave me a proper sex talk. When I started my period at eleven, Mimi June handed me some too bulky pads, told me a story about keeping an aspirin between my knees, and then sent me back out to ride my bike with my neighborhood friends.

I had a vague idea about how conception worked, but it was based on that nonsense about twenty-eight-day cycles. Like—what the fuck? Why didn't anyone ever tell us that was average? Why didn't someone sit us down in a health class or biology and explain that sperm could live for five days after ejaculation? That we could get pregnant any time during those five days if we ovulated? It wasn't just day fourteen that was dangerous. It was a whole bunch of them right there in the middle of the cycle.

But I didn't know.

And, frankly, even if I had, Kiki wouldn't have stopped anyway. I learned very quickly that I wasn't allowed to say no. I mean, I could, but it was going to cost me. It was easier to acquiesce and let him do what he wanted. The faster he finished, the sooner it was over, the less it hurt.

That was another thing I didn't know.

Sex was supposed to feel good for both partners, not only the man. It had only ever been painful for me. Too rough, too hard, too fast. Kiki liked to hit and bite, and I didn't have the experience or maturity to understand that wasn't normal. He told me it was, and I believed him because I didn't know any better.

I really was a sweet summer child.

Naïve.

Trusting.

Gullible.

Vulnerable.

Desperate to be loved.

I convinced myself what Kiki felt for me was love. It wasn't. It was possession. It was ownership. I was lower than a stray dog to him, and if I didn't do exactly what he said, I was going to catch a boot to the backside—or worse.

So, when my period was late for two weeks, I got nervous. When it was late for three, I got really nervous. When it was missing for four? I panicked. I ran to my Uncle Nicky's girlfriend and begged her for help. One positive, cheap Walmart pregnancy test later and I was in the front seat of her car, racing down the highway to visit her "auntie" for some pills from Mexico.

I got lucky, and they worked exactly as advertised. The cramping and bleeding were horrific. I hadn't realized my uterus could feel that way, like it was being turned inside out and wrung dry. The whole experience was traumatic, and I had been alone, handling something that was far more serious than any fifteen-year-old child should have to face.

When it was done, I promised myself I would be more careful. I started sneaking away to get the Depo shot from Planned Parenthood. That was still a thing back then, back before Abbott and his cronies went wild and decided to drag all Texas women back to the Stone Ages by forcing pregnancies on us. I had been able to access the care I needed to stay safe, to stay healthy.

Until, one day, Kiki found out where I was going. A whackjob protester had taken photos of women going in and out of the clinic and shared them on flyers posted around the town. Someone recognized me and took the flyer to Kiki.

And, my God, the beating he doled out for that transgression.

Never in my wildest dreams had I imagined an extension cord could hurt like that. It had never even crossed my mind to think someone would hit me with one.

But he did. He beat me until I couldn't stand. He called me all sorts of degrading names. He accused me of being one of my uncle's whores out walking the Track. Why else would I need birth control? Didn't I want to give him a baby? Didn't I love him? Didn't I trust him to take care of me? Why did I want to kill his babies?

That messed me up mentally and physically. Looking back, that was the beating that broke me. That was the one that left me too exposed to ever recover. My protective shell had been shattered.

I was seventeen the second time I conceived. I thought he would be happy, but he had been furious. Suddenly, I was trying to baby-trap him. I was trying to keep him locked down and on the line for child support. He wasn't even sure the baby was his. Maybe I was having an affair with Nero Robles, a boy on the pick-up basketball team I played with on the weekends. Maybe I was trying to leave him for another man.

He had been the one to bring me the pills that time. I hadn't wanted to take them. I had been afraid of complications. I had already felt a connection to the tiny life growing inside me. It was my body, wasn't it? Why couldn't I make that decision for myself?

But he stood over me with that sawed-off Mossberg until I swallowed everything. He even checked my cheeks and under my tongue. Then he locked me in the bathroom and told me I couldn't come out until I had proof that it was over.

The degrading humiliation of that gut-wrenching ordeal had turned my heart cold. I had finally understood that nothing I would ever do would be good enough for him. Nothing I would ever do would be right.

And I was stuck. I couldn't get out.

It had struck me quite suddenly that I, like Maya Angelou, knew why that caged bird sings. I was that stuck starling Maria Bertram mentioned in *Mansfield Park*.

But those feelings of self-loathing and hatred turned the soft, wounded exposed parts of me as hard as steel. I developed emotional armor. I withdrew into myself, protected inside my mind from the constant torment of the man who supposedly loved me.

And I promised myself that one day I would leave my cage.

One day, I would fly.

CHAPTER FOURTEEN

T HE WARM GLOW of sunlight illuminated the bedroom we were sharing. Off in the distance, I heard the jingle of Wilford's bell as he chased something, hopefully, one of his many toys and not a bug or something worse. He seemed to think I enjoyed the little pest presents he brought me. I acted as if I did so I wouldn't hurt his feelings, but honestly, it squicked me right out to have to deal with dead scorpions and spiders.

Ignoring Wilford's mischief, I snuggled back against Ten's hot body. His broad chest was pressed to my back, and one of his heavy arms was draped over my waist. I was a tall woman, but he was so much bigger. My heels barely touched his calves, and I felt unnaturally small in his arms. He made me feel feminine and elegant, and I wondered if maybe I had always been waiting for a man just like him.

I could tell the moment he woke up because his breathing shifted. A moment later, his lips ghosted across my bare shoulder. I wore a nightgown with thin straps, and it became clear very quickly that he would have preferred I come to bed naked.

I closed my eyes and enjoyed the ticklish touch of his lips along the curve of my neck and clavicle. He nuzzled against the scarf I had hastily wrapped around my hair before bed and then nibbled at my earlobe. "How do you always smell so fucking good?"

His hand slipped under the hem of my nightgown, and he stroked my thigh. "Can I…?"

"Yes." If he stopped, I was going to be a frustrated mess.

He chuckled against my neck. His caresses were slow and teasing. He swept his big hands over my belly and up between my breasts. He palmed one and then the other, squeezing and brushing his thumb over my nipples.

I could feel his erection growing against my back. Harder. Longer. Thicker. Memories of his dick thrusting in and out of me made my pussy throb. Slick heat dripped out of me, my body responding to the promise of incredible sex.

I reached back to stroke him. My hand followed the outline of his cock through his shorts, and he groaned against my ear. I liked those animalistic sounds he made, and when my hand slipped into his shorts, I was rewarded with a grunt. His rock-hard penis filled my hand, and I had the wildest urge to feel him inside my mouth.

I rolled over, careful not to bang my wounded leg, and pressed his shoulder until he was flat on his back. His gaze darkened as I lowered my head to his chest. I began to kiss the tattoos marking his skin. I didn't know what they meant. Part of me never wanted to know. Someday, I would ask him. Not today.

Right now, I wanted to escape reality. I wanted to slip into a fantasy bubble where only the two of us existed. I wanted to pretend nothing else mattered outside the walls of this cabin. It was just me and Ten, wrapped up in our love nest.

I dragged his shorts down his hips, and he lifted up to help me slide them out of the way. They were kicked aside somewhere under the covers. His massive cock sprang straight up, and I marveled at how mean it looked. Thick. Throbbing. Drops of precum slipped from the tip, and I ran my thumb along them, gathering and tasting them with a swipe of my thumb. Ten growled at the sight, and I wondered what other sounds I could draw from him.

He wasn't cut, and I had only ever seen one other penis this close. It was something of a novelty to explore him with my hands and tongue. He tasted good—clean with a slight hint of salt. It made me crave more of him. Could I take him? Could I swallow all of him?

"Don't put your hands on my head or my face," I said, unable to meet his gaze. "I don't like that."

"I won't," he promised. And then, as if to prove he wouldn't do anything to trigger a panic response, he slid both of his hands under his backside, trapping them between the bed and his body.

"You're so good," I praised him. "Thank you."

I let a little saliva pool on my tongue and then swiped a stripe straight from his balls to the tip of his cock. He growled and grunted and then swore a nasty streak in Russian and English when I wrapped my lips around his dick and sucked.

There was a moment of panic as his shaft filled my mouth. I couldn't help it. My brain flashed back to uglier times, meaner times, but I pushed those intrusive thoughts away. I wasn't going to let Kiki ruin this for me.

This isn't Kiki. This is Ten. This is my Anton.

He held perfectly still as I used my tongue to discover every inch of his erection. My lips were stretched wide around him, and I used one of my hands to stroke his shaft while my mouth concentrated on the top. I hadn't ever done this by choice, and it had been years since I was forced to do it.

Somehow, I managed to find the right rhythm. I wasn't very good at it, but Ten didn't seem to mind. His breaths were shuddery and short, and I could feel his thighs tensing under me. I hungrily lapped and sucked and stroked until he was gasping and begging me not to stop.

"Baby. Don't stop. Fuck. Fuck. *Zolotse!*" He made a pained sound and then hurriedly exclaimed, "Pull off. I'm going to come."

I did the opposite. I slipped down his dick, sucking him deep and stroking faster with my hand. He shouted my name and his cum spilled onto my tongue in short bursts. I drank him down, my mind reeling at the sensation of power I had at that moment. Ten, with his hands trapped under his body, begging me to keep sucking and then begging me to stop.

I eased off his cock and cleaned him with my tongue. The flush of his orgasm had stained his skin a dark shade of pink, and I enjoyed the way my darker hand looked gliding over his lean belly. I clasped one wrist and then the other and dragged each hand free. He cupped my face, and I crawled over him, careful not to hit my leg on his body, and let him kiss me until I was breathless and shaking.

"I want to make you come." Ten gripped my ass in his big hand. "Do you want me to use my mouth or my fingers?"

I felt suddenly shy and ducked my head, pressing my cheek to his chest. Should I tell him? Should I ask?

"Nisha? Baby, we don't have to—"

"No, I want it," I said a bit too quickly. "I just…"

"What?"

"You're the only man who has ever…"

"Ever what?" When I didn't answer, he guessed, "Made you come? Or ate your pussy?"

He spoke the words so easily, as if we were discussing the weather instead of such an intimate act. Of course, he had obviously had much more experience than me. He was very comfortable with all things sexual, and I wanted more than anything to learn to be the same.

"Yes. Both."

"I see." Ten gave my ass a playful pat. "Well, I better get to work."

"What?" I gasped as Ten shifted so quickly that it stunned me. He had me on my side with my hurt leg propped out of the way in a flash and then he dove between my legs. He attacked me with enthusiasm, cupping my ass in both hands and nuzzling his face into my labia. He used that magic tongue to trace every last inch of me, and when he finally suckled my throbbing clit, pulling it between his lips, I saw stars.

"That's it, baby. You scream all you want." He flicked his tongue over me again and again. "I like to hear you make noise."

Well, that was a good thing because he was drawing all sorts of sounds from me. His tongue was incredible, but when he added two fingers, stroking deep inside and hitting all the spots that made me moan, I tumbled over the edge. My orgasm hit me fast and without warning. I clutched at his head, my fingernails scraping against his scalp, and rocked my pussy against his face. "Anton!"

He growled like an animal and used his brute strength to flip me onto my stomach. I barely had a moment to register the movement before he dragged me up on my knees and shoved my thighs apart with his strong hands. I blushed with embarrassment, fully aware that he could see the most intimate parts of me.

And then his tongue snaked through my folds.

He stabbed it into my vagina, fucking me with it. His tongue moved higher, fluttering over a place where I had only ever experienced pain. I tensed, and Ten eased off, silently giving me a chance to decide if I wanted him to keep doing such a wicked, naughty thing.

"Anton, you don't have to do that." My face was on fire.

"I know I don't have to," he assured me. "I want to."

"Why?" It was such a taboo thing.

"Because every part of you turns me on and giving you pleasure makes my dick hard," he said matter-of-factly. "I want to taste and tongue fuck every single last inch of your body."

I thought I was going to pass out. My body throbbed, and my head pounded. Ten's willingness to explore all erotic avenues emboldened me. Deciding I wanted to know if I could find pleasure this way, I relaxed and let him show me.

All the memes and hip-hop lyrics about eating ass had never made much sense to me. All of my experiences with anal sex had been painful and degrading. I didn't have any other way to frame the subject.

But now?

Oh, fuck me. The things Ten was doing, the way he lapped and explored without a hint of shame, awakened something needy and wanton inside me. I let go of all those shameful ideas I had been harboring. I trusted Ten to lead me through this. I closed my eyes—and felt joy.

Ten slipped a single finger into my ass, and I groaned with unanticipated desire. It was a gentle probing, nothing too rough or fast, and it felt *good*. It felt even better when his tongue returned to my clit. He hooked his thumb into my pussy, and his fingers thrust in and out of me, lighting up my nerve endings until my heart was racing.

Pleasure swirled low in my belly, spinning and tightening. I fisted the covers in my hands and rocked my hips, grinding myself against Ten. The erotic exploration of my body with this man who loved me, who accepted me as I was and found me wildly desirable, turned my brain to mush. I came with a scream of his name, drenching him with my slick heat and making him groan with appreciation.

I collapsed onto the bed in a boneless heap. I barely even noticed the slight throb in my leg. Later, I would realize I had popped a stitch, and Ten would worry over me like an anxious mother, dabbing and cleaning and repairing the area with Steri-Strips from Kostya's first aid kit.

But right then? I didn't care about anything except for the feel of Ten's hands stroking my back and his lips pressing loving kisses along my spine.

I didn't even try to hide the tears running down my face when he moved onto his side next to me. He seemed to understand that I didn't want to talk. Instead, he gathered me into his arms and held me, letting me cry healing tears, purging myself of the ugly parts of Kiki that were still inside me.

For the first time in years, I didn't feel broken. I didn't feel diminished. I felt free. I felt as if the whole world was open before me, filled with endless possibilities.

And then Ten's phone rang.

CHAPTER FIFTEEN

HALF-HARD AND READY to go again, Ten scowled at his phone. He wanted to ignore it, but that wasn't a good idea right now. Not with Kiki still on the loose and a madman taking shots at Nisha and a podcaster riling up the whole fucking city of Houston against her.

Irritated, he rolled over and reached for the phone he had left on the bedside table. One of Kostya's spiders had set up some type of forwarding system that sent calls from his old phone to this one. He didn't understand the ins and outs of it and hadn't really been paying attention when Fox had tried to explain it.

He glanced at the screen and swore. Sitting up, he cast a quick apologetic glance at Nisha. "I have to take this."

She nodded and gestured to the bathroom. As she climbed out of bed, her nightgown rode up around her hips, baring her plump ass to his appreciative gaze. He tore his attention away from her and back to his phone. "Hello?"

"Mr. Vasiliev." Pete, his parole officer, greeted him much too cheerfully. "Do you know what today is?"

"My lucky day?" Ten guessed.

"Bingo! Come on down, Ten. You've been selected for a random piss test."

"Listen, Pete, it's not a good time for me." He had never asked his parole officer for an inch of leeway. Not once in the twenty months he had been on the hook and working his program. "I'm dealing with some personal and family issues."

"I'm sorry to hear that, Ten, but you know the rules."

"Yeah." Ten gritted his teeth, hating that he was under the thumb of another man. Pete had never been anything but fair. He wasn't doing this to be an asshole or to play games.

"Listen, Ten, you have until 3 p.m. to take the test. If you miss it, we're going to have a problem. You're four months away from completing your program. Don't fuck it up now."

He ended the call and rubbed his face between both hands. "*Blyad*. Fuck. Shit."

"Anton?" Nisha stood in the doorway of the bathroom, looking sexy as hell in her nightgown with her hair let loose from her scarf and falling around her shoulders. "What's wrong?"

"Nothing."

She didn't buy it. Narrowing her eyes, she demanded, "Tell me the truth."

He sighed and scratched the top of his head. "My parole officer called me in for a random piss test."

"Oh. Well—you have to go."

"I can't leave you here."

"I'll be fine."

"You don't know that."

"You cannot skip a drug test and mess up your parole because of me."

"You come before my parole officer. You're my priority."

"And if you get picked up? If they revoke your parole and

send you back to prison? Then what? Huh?" Nisha crossed her arms, and he couldn't help but gaze longingly at her tits framed so beautifully on top of them. She suddenly snapped her fingers. "Eyes up here, Anton."

"Yes, ma'am." *Fuck me.* Those snapping fingers and that commanding tone made his dick ache. "Do you have a pencil skirt?"

"What?"

"Not here with you, obviously, but like back home in your closet?"

Nisha huffed. "Are you seriously asking me to dress up for you?"

"Okay, hear me out." He slipped off the bed and prowled toward her. "You in a sexy librarian or boss bitch outfit. Fake glasses. A ruler. Snapping those fingers. Barking orders at me."

"Ten," she warned with a poke of her finger. "You better behave yourself. You are not going to distract me with your fantasies."

"Not even a little bit?" He eased his hand along her hip. "I'll be a very good boy for you."

"I'm sure you would." She patted his chest with her elegant hand. "Anton, you have to go."

"I'm not leaving you here."

"I'll go with you."

"You're not leaving this cabin."

She rolled her eyes. "Well, then we have a problem."

"Yes, we're at an impasse."

"Big word." She drew the letters on his chest. "What if I call Eric?"

Ten didn't like that suggestion one bit. "No."

"Why not?" She poked his chest. "Eric has always been a good friend to me. He offered to help."

"He's a cop."

"Yes, and a damn good one."

Ten hated that she was right. Eric was a good choice. "I'll call Kostya first, and if he can't send Ilya or one of the other boys, we'll reach out to Eric."

"It's that or I call the Texas Rangers and accept their offer for protective custody."

He liked that idea even less. "Fine."

"I'm not trying to make trouble." She traced her finger along the star adorning the right side of his chest. "I don't want you to go back to prison, not when you're so close to being done with your sentence."

He had been wondering since Kostya spent the evening with her whether or not she was going to ask him about Tony. He wanted to tell her the truth. He wanted to tell her all about that night, if for no other reason than to raise himself in her eyes. He wanted her to know what kind of man he really was.

But he couldn't. He couldn't break the vow of silence he had made to his blood brothers. Nikolai had softened since marrying, but he didn't abide by rule-breaking. A promise was a promise, and he would have Ten's blood if he broke it.

"I didn't know it was Tony," she said finally. "I didn't realize that's why you went to prison."

"No?" He was surprised. "I always assumed you knew."

She shook her head. "I wasn't really with it during that time. You know what I mean? The trauma and the trial and postpartum depression. I was on all sorts of medications and going to intense therapy in Dallas. There's a place there that does inpatient psych treatment in a sort of resort setting. I was in an apartment basically."

"I see." He had wondered whether she had been in a mental hospital after all the horrible shit she survived. It seemed like the safest place for someone in her predicament to go.

"I didn't have access to the internet or newspapers. Uncle Nicky kept my flow of information tightly controlled to protect me. I didn't mind," she assured him. "It was nice to be in that safe little bubble."

"But you didn't know about Tony or me," he said. "And you never wanted to look online? After I started flirting with you?"

She shook her head. "Definitely not."

"Why?"

"I didn't want to learn something that would change my feelings toward you," she admitted. "I knew you were dangerous, and I knew you were wrong for me, but I liked the attention. I liked the way you made me feel. I wanted to live in that fantasy a little while longer." She bit her lower lip. "And, now, it's reality and I know the truth."

"And?" He wasn't sure he wanted to hear her answer.

"And I don't care," she confessed. "I don't care that you killed Tony. If he was really involved in molesting kids? He deserved it."

"He was truly involved in it." That was one part of that night that wasn't a lie. "He and Adrian were up to no good. They were fucking monsters, and I wish I had been able to get my hands on Adrian, too."

"Was there…? I mean, the way Kostya described the situation, it sounded as if there was a boy there."

"There had been," he confirmed. "He was a friend of Danny's. Younger kid. His mom worked at Samovar. She was a good lady. Worked hard. Tried to keep her kid off the streets." Ten's jaw clenched. "That was how Tony picked them. He was this big, dumb friendly guy, right? Everyone liked him. Everyone trusted him. He would find these kids from broken homes, the ones who saw their moms working two jobs, who were alone all the time. He would offer them money for work. You know—mowing the yard, helping move boxes. Stuff a kid would think was normal."

"And then he'd hurt them," she guessed.

"He and Adrian would get them drunk or drug them first." Ten inhaled sharply. "And that's all I'm saying about that."

"I don't want to hear anymore," she assured him. Then, cautiously, she asked, "Was Kiki in their videos? Was he involved?"

Ten didn't want to tell her. He really didn't. "Yeah. From what I heard, Kiki was in very special videos that Adrian sold to specific collectors of that sort of horrific shit."

She took a moment to digest that news. Eventually, she said, "It doesn't surprise me. Not knowing what I do of Kiki. Although, I am surprised he wasn't tried for those crimes."

"They probably figured they had nailed him dead to rights on the murder charges and it wasn't worth going to trial again for the videos."

"Or maybe they had another case going? Maybe it's still going." She glanced toward the window and shuddered. "Maybe the sicko fans of those videos helped him break out of prison."

"It wouldn't surprise me," Ten agreed, thinking that was as good a possibility as any other. Feeling dirty after talking about Kiki, Adrian, and Tony, he said, "Let me make some phone calls and then we'll shower. Yeah?"

"Sure. I'm going to feed Wilford."

Unsurprisingly, Kostya was one step ahead of Ten. It occurred to him as they discussed the situation with his PO that Ten's spiders must have been listening in on his call. It was a gross invasion of his privacy, but he understood that it was to keep Nisha safe. He let it slide.

"Ilya will be there in…" Kostya's voice faded out as if he were checking his watch. "Eighty-three minutes."

"Right." Ten hated how precise Kostya always had to be. "Nisha wants Eric here."

"It's not a bad idea."

"It's not a bad idea to have Eric fucking Santos in your hideout?"

"Well, it's not a hideout anymore, is it? Maybe I'll let Holly put it on Airbnb when you're done with it."

"Yeah, I'm sure there's a big market for cabins with more security than a prison," Ten grumbled.

"Hey, even criminals need a vacation," Kostya reasoned.

Ten let loose a rough laugh.

"Listen, call Eric. Have him come sit with her. He and Ilya get along fine. I'll meet you after you're finished with your PO. We'll get you a clean car and another phone, just in case."

"Yeah. Okay." Ten didn't like the way this day was turning out, but he didn't have a choice. He didn't want to go back to prison or be separated from Nisha. He would drive to Houston, take the test, meet with Kostya, switch out his vehicle and phone, and drive back to the cabin.

Piece of cake.

Right?

CHAPTER SIXTEEN

Holly, I don't even know what to say about the salon.

It's not your fault.

These people are lunatics.

She sent four rows of angry emojis. As much as she insisted it wasn't my fault, we both knew that wasn't true. I might not have broken the windows or spray painted the exterior or tossed a Molotov cocktail, but those vandals only attacked the salon because I worked there and was part-owner.

Savvy woke up a little bit ago.

Sort of.

Sort of?

She's still intubated. Lots of drugs.

She's improving?

Yes. And still stable.

Good

You hear anything about Chess?

Ten spoke to Artyom this morning.

She's doing well.

Surgery was successful.

Bullet missed her femoral artery by a few millimeters.

Holy shit! She's insanely lucky.

Or the shooter wasn't trying to kill her.

Holly's comment mirrored my thoughts.

Savvy's wound is bad, but I wonder if it's because she moved in front of you.

Your height difference?

Maybe?

Billie is going to sit with Savvy for a while.

Im going to the salon.

I'll give you an update once I know more about the damage.

I set aside my phone and watched my new babysitter as he methodically checked the view from the cabin's front-facing windows. He had been here for a little more than an hour, and already I could tell he was a very regimented person. Exacting. Reliant on routines.

Ilya was nothing like I had expected. He looked like a literature professor from a private liberal arts college. Scruffy golden blond beard. Grass-green eyes. Brown tortoiseshell glasses. Dark jeans with turned-up cuffs. A charcoal vest and matching tie layered over a smoky gray pinstripe shirt. Brown lace-up boots.

"What?" he asked with an amused smile as my gaze followed him around the living room of the cabin.

"You don't strike me as a mafioso."

"That's the point, sweetheart." His accent was strange, and I thought I heard a bit of British in it. As he shucked his navy blazer, he revealed a leather shoulder holster and two guns.

"Is that a SIG P365?" I asked, pretty sure I was correct.

He reacted with surprise and then grinned. "You know your guns."

"Our salon has a monthly night at the shooting range," I

explained. "Holly rents out the whole place so we can practice. Not all of us go, but most of us do."

"Does that pre-date Kostya?" Ilya wondered.

I laughed. "It does. Holly's always been big on self-defense."

"She's not wrong. The world is a dangerous place for women."

Something in his voice told me there was a story there. Maybe Ten would tell me later.

Wilford crept across the living room to investigate our visitor. Ilya's eyes lit up at the sight of my surly cat. He crouched down and clicked his teeth before saying, "*Ksksksks.*"

I started to warn him about the murder mittens situation, but Wilford pranced right over to Ilya and let this literal stranger sweep him right up off the floor and into his arms. "I thought this cat was a demon?"

I snorted. "Is that how Ten described him?"

"Pretty much." Ilya scratched between Wilford's ears and praised him in Russian. Switching to English, he said, "You're not a demon, are you?"

I could hear Wilford purring from across the room. I rolled my eyes and muttered, "Traitor."

Ilya laughed and set Wilford back down on the floor. Wilford rubbed against Ilya's legs, begging for more pets or treats. Ilya glanced at me, and I pointed to the bag on the counter. "Treats are in there."

As Ilya fetched some crunch treats for Wilford, his phone chirped. He gave the treats to my cat and then glanced at his phone. He tapped at the screen, and his tense expression relaxed. "It's Detective Santos."

"Eric is here?" I clambered to my feet with the help of my crutches. My leg wound had been freshly bandaged by Ten after he repaired the broken stitch. It still hurt though, more than yesterday actually. I suspected that was the swelling and inflammation. Although with my luck lately, it was probably the start of a raging skin-eating infection.

"Wait, please," Ilya instructed.

He asked so nicely I happily obliged. He waited at the door with a gun drawn, making sure it was actually Eric. When he confirmed the detective's identity, he deactivated the alarm to let Eric enter and then tapped the touchpad to rearm.

"Nisha!" Eric rushed across the cabin and crushed me in a bear hug. "God, I was so worried! When I saw the footage from the shooting, I was down in Corpus on a case. I couldn't get back to the city fast enough."

"I'm fine, Eric." I patted his back. "Really."

"Your leg doesn't look fine." He pulled back enough to look me over thoroughly. "Why didn't you take police protection?"

"Not to be a jerk, but law enforcement let Kiki escape so I'm not sure I would have been any safer with them."

"There's a big difference between DPS and the Rangers and the corrections officers who were in charge of Kiki when he escaped," Eric argued. "Please, let me call my contact and get you some real protection." He glanced back at Ilya. "No offense."

"Offense taken," Ilya replied.

"Eric, I made my choice."

He exhaled in frustration. "Fine. I tried."

"And I appreciate it." Wanting to steer him away from a

continuing disagreement, I asked, "Are you hungry? Thirsty?"

"I ate on the drive." He glanced at the farmhouse table. "Can we sit and talk?"

"Sure." I let him get settled in while I made a PB&J with the freshly baked bread and locally made jam that was waiting in the kitchen. "Do you want one?"

Ilya shook his head. "I'm allergic to peanut butter."

"Oh." I looked at my sandwich as if it were a loaded weapon. "Let me get rid of this."

"You're fine." Ilya waved his hand. "I'm used to being careful in other people's spaces. Just try not to kiss me, and we'll be okay."

"If that happens, finding an Epipen will be the least of your worries." I was only halfway joking. Ten would blow a gasket if I was swapping peanut particles with anyone but him.

"Who needs an Epipen?" Eric returned to the kitchen.

"Me." Ilya held his gaze as if daring him to say something else. "Peanuts."

"No shit?" Eric sat across from me. "A friend of mine with the Marshals knows we're close friends, Nisha."

"Okay."

"He gave me a heads-up about some leads they're following."

"And?"

"They suspect two guards were in on the escape. One of them went on a trip to the Florida Keys. Chartered a boat. Hasn't been seen since and is probably in Cuba."

"Oh, well, that's nice," I grumbled. "And the other?"

Eric hesitated. "He was found dead at a motel in Clute. Throat slit."

"Like that Dancing Bear guy," I murmured.

"Exactly."

"Sounds like someone is tying up loose ends," Ilya remarked, now holding Wilford in his arms.

I gawked at the sight of my cat cuddling with Ilya and doubled down on my earlier remark. "Traitor."

Ilya smiled and stroked Wilford's fur as he murmured to him in Russian.

Ignoring Wilford choosing Ilya as his new best friend, I turned back to Eric and asked, "But why would anyone help Kiki?"

"Money," Eric said as if it were the most obvious thing in the world.

"From where? He was flat broke when we were together, and I'd be surprised if he had even two nickels in his commissary account."

"Both of the guards had come into money over the last few months. Marshals and Rangers interviewed family, friends, coworkers, and neighbors. A boat, vacations, and new vehicles. Their credit reports showed discharged debts. The one who retired? His granddaughter had her face repaired by a high-end plastic surgeon in Dallas. She was mauled by a dog as a little kid. She's walked around with scars ever since."

"Until Grandpa suddenly had money to burn." I peeled the thick crust away from my sandwich and nibbled on it. "So who paid all this money to orchestrate his escape? The cartel? A friend?" I glanced at Ilya. "Adrian? Maybe he's back from wherever he ran off to after Tony was killed?"

Eric's face registered surprise. "Adrian? Umansky?"

"Yes. What other Adrian would I be asking about, Eric?"

Eric glanced at Ilya, and I suddenly had the feeling there was something important I didn't know. "What is it?"

"The rumor I've heard," Eric said, staring at Ilya with laser focus, "is that Adrian didn't run anywhere."

"Well, I mean, if he didn't run…" My voice trailed off as I finally understood what he meant. "Oh." I looked at Ilya who seemed very interested in Wilford's handmade collar. "Ilya?"

"You can't possibly expect me to answer that." He flicked his finger against the bell on Wilford's collar.

"No answer is an answer," I reasoned. Adrian was dead. There was no doubt about it. Which led to more questions. Where was his body? Why hadn't anyone told Chess?

"What about the lawyer?" Ilya bent down to let Wilford scuttle off to chase dust in sunbeams. "Who was paying her bills?"

"I don't know. I wasn't given that information." Eric leveled a stare in Ilya's direction. "But I bet you know someone who could find it."

Ilya chuckled. "I bet I do."

"What about Chad? How did he get mixed into this?" I had been thinking about that nosy bastard all morning. I didn't dare look at my social media accounts, but I was certain they were filled with ugly comments.

"The podcaster?" Eric asked. "I don't know."

"He's a leech," Ilya interjected from his new position by a window overlooking the front of the property. "He's desperate to be the next **Grizzy's Hood News**, but he's too slow, too fake, and too fucking annoying to ever be her."

"If she was on the case, she and her followers would have already solved the whole damn thing," Eric grumbled.

"In twelve hours or less," Ilya remarked, his gaze still focused out the window.

As the two of them talked about notable crimes she had helped solve around Houston, I picked up the phone Kostya had given me and used it to Google Chad and Kiki's dead lawyer. There had to be some missing links. It probably wouldn't be obvious. Law enforcement would have seized upon that.

Who would have the kind of money that was needed to set up Kiki's escape? Why would someone help him? Was Chad trying to build his career on this? I could only imagine what sort of views he would get if he followed a serial killer's escape and capture, right up close and personal. He probably had dreams of a Netflix docuseries in his eyes.

I ate some more of my sandwich while falling down the rabbit hole of Chad's history. He was a failure at everything he tried. He'd self-published a *Game of Thrones* knockoff that had seventeen one- and two-star reviews on Amazon. He'd switched to thrillers, but their reviews were just as savage.

He'd moved on to true crime podcasting and a YouTube channel, but he hadn't managed more than a few thousand views on any video. He seemed to be always one step behind everyone else, chasing stale stories and regurgitating case details without anything new or fresh to entice followers.

Except now, his social media accounts were on fire. Kiki's escape, the shooting, the fire at Allure—his new followers were eating it up. There was a deep dive video that I couldn't bear to watch, even on mute, where he delved into Kiki's crimes.

Scrolling through it, I found trial photos of my injuries from the night Kiki tried to kill me. The prick had a snapshot of Lorelai's grave, and my heart skipped in my chest, the painful memories twisting my gut and making my lungs hurt.

I didn't even bother looking at the comments. My heart was beating so fast, and my ears were getting hot as I swiped to his next video. This one was a breakdown of Kiki's connections to Adrian and Tony. He had included images of the house where Tony was killed as well as redacted case documents regarding the child sexual assault videos and images found near his body.

When Chad began to discuss Adrian, images of Chess and Callie, photos that must have been taken very recently, lingered on the screen. There were short clips of Callie waiting in line with her mother at Chick-fil-a, flapping her hands and making the jerky neck motions that happened when she was overstimulated. She spun around a few times, and Chess gently redirected her away from the next closest person in line, making sure her daughter was free to move without bothering anyone else.

Chad flashed an image of a crying Chess, probably no more than sixteen years old, after she had been arrested in a car that was moving drugs. I always thought those types of juvenile photos were locked down tight, but apparently not. She seemed humiliated and ashamed in the photo, and I could only imagine how scared she must have been to be arrested.

The subtitles on the screen infuriated me. Chad insinuated Callie's autism and heart defects were caused by Chess using drugs while pregnant. Nothing could have been further from the truth. It was cruel and disgusting, and if I ever saw this piece of trash again, I was going to kick him square in the nuts.

"What's wrong?" Eric asked. "You look like you're about

to set someone's house on fire."

"Look at this shit!" I flashed the phone at him. "Look at what he's saying about Callie and Chess!"

Ilya moved closer to see what was on the phone. He grimaced and immediately reached for his phone. "I need to make a call."

"Why?" I asked, but he didn't stick around to answer.

"He's probably calling Nikolai or Kostya to warn them."

"About?"

"Artyom seeing that video," Eric replied. "Imagine what he'll do to Chad if he finds out what's being said."

"Nothing good," I figured. "Did you know about her arrest?"

"Yeah, but it was a long time ago. She was a kid, and it didn't even stick. I don't even think she got probation for it." He glared at my phone. "She sure as shit was no dope fiend or whatever nonsense that asshole is peddling."

"They all think we knew." I made the mistake of scrolling accidentally on the screen. There were more comments like the ones from last night. "They think Chess and I must have known our men were monsters."

"Yeah, well, tell that to BTK's wife and kids or any of the women Ted Bundy dated." Eric took my phone and closed the app. "Don't read any more of this shit. It's going to give you anxiety."

"Too late," I said, taking my phone back. "I've been anxious since I saw Chad and Robin Harris in the lobby at Allure with Tiara."

"I have to admit I'm surprised you two get along as well as you do." Eric rose from his seat and crossed to the refrigerator.

"Why? She's a nice person. Maybe a bit too pink and glittery for my taste," I said, thinking of her station and the glammed-out décor she had. "But we get along fine."

"I didn't mean her bubbly personality," Eric corrected, his head now hidden behind the refrigerator door as he perused its contents. "I meant because of her brother."

I frowned. "She doesn't have a brother. Or any family," I added. "She was a foster kid. Aged out and went to cosmetology school."

With a carton of orange juice in hand, Eric straightened and shut the refrigerator door. Now he was the one frowning. "I meant Derek."

"Derek?"

"Derek Miller," Eric said slowly. "Her foster brother. Back in Carrizo Springs."

My whole world suddenly tilted, and I would have fallen out of the chair if I hadn't been pushed up close to the table. "What?"

Eric seemed taken aback. "You didn't know?"

"Do I fucking look like I knew?" My mind raced as I thought of every conversation I had ever had with Tiara. Had she ever mentioned Derek? Had she ever mentioned Carrizo Springs? "Why wouldn't she tell me that?"

"That's something you'll have to ask her," Eric said, his brow furrowed. "Damned odd thing to keep to yourself. There's no way I could work with someone related to a person who was suspected of murdering my brother."

"Not unless you wanted to fly under the radar and set them up," Ilya interjected as he returned to the kitchen. He pulled out a chair at the table and sat down. "Tell me everything you know about this Tiara girl."

Clearly, not enough.

CHAPTER SEVENTEEN

PARKING AT HIS PO was dog shit as usual. He had to circle the block twice before giving up and traveling farther down the street. He found a lot with open spots and queued up to turn into it.

"$45 for the day," a college-aged kid manning the entrance said.

"For a weekday? Fuck off. This lot never costs more than $25 on a weekday."

"Supply and demand, friend," the dickhead kid replied with a shit-eating grin.

For a split-second, Ten thought about grabbing the kid by the front of the shirt and teaching him some manners. Then he spotted a familiar face walking down the main row of vehicles. Sticking his head out the window, he called out, "Hey, Pelon! Tell this *pendejo* to stop trying to gouge me with this $45 bullshit!"

The kid stiffened. Ten smirked at him. "Next time you want to pull a scam, make sure your mark isn't friends with your boss."

Pelon sauntered over and told the kid off in rapid-fire Spanish. "My wife's nephew," he said as the kid hurried away. "*Pinche culero.*"

"I figured." Ten handed Pelon a twenty and a five. "I won't be long."

"PO?" Pelon guessed.

"Yeah."

"There's a spot in the back row, left."

"Thanks." Ten found the spot, locked up, and walked away from the lot. It was miserably hot, and he wished he was back at the cabin, naked and rolling around in bed with Nisha. If he had to be hot and sweaty, he'd rather it be from something he enjoyed.

The building was blissfully cold. For once, he wasn't going to complain about the waste of tax dollars. He made his way to the correct floor and noticed a familiar face as he waited to check in at the desk.

"Ruby," he greeted after finishing with the receptionist. Ivan's sister-in-law had her head bent toward her phone and one AirPod in place.

Surprised, she glanced up from the video she was watching on her phone. "Ten! I heard you were out of town."

"I was." His face lingered on the fresh shiner she sported. "That better be from training."

"Boychenko." She huffed. "When we were grappling, I figure out he was ticklish under his armpits. I should have left it alone, but he embarrassed me with a stupid crack about my period. I saw him stretching and grabbed him under the arms. He flipped out laughing, threw back his elbow, and cracked me right in the face."

Ten made a face. "You know how Ivan feels about horse-play and fucking around in his gym."

She huffed again. "My arms and legs are still wobbly like

Jell-O after all the bear crawls and running lines."

"You're lucky he didn't make you throw tires out back."

"Bro." She gestured to her body. "Do I look like I can flip tires?"

"Yes."

She sat up a bit straighter. "Well—thanks."

Ten glanced at his watch. This was taking forever.

"I'm sorry about what's happening with your girlfriend."

Word really got around fast. He and Nisha hadn't even had a legitimate date, and people were already calling her his girlfriend. "So am I."

"She cut my hair once." Ruby touched the ends of her ponytail. "Right after I got out of jail. She was really nice to me, and she didn't have to be."

"She doesn't judge people for their mistakes."

"Obviously," Ruby said, glancing pointedly in his direction.

"Ten." Pete appeared in the doorway and beckoned him back.

"Good luck." Ruby smiled encouragingly.

"Yeah. You, too." Ten nodded at Pete when he reached the doorway. "I came."

"I see." Pete turned and led him down the hallway to his cramped office. "Take a seat."

Ten did as instructed. The uncomfortable chair squeaked in protest at his weight, and he wondered how many more asses it would bear before it cracked. Pete tapped away on his faded keyboard glancing over the tops of his smudged bifocals to read his computer screen.

Ten shoved down the rising ire threatening to erupt. He

wanted to shout at Pete to hurry the fuck up so he could get back to Nisha, but the months of mandated anger management courses helped him keep his worse impulses under control.

"I know you have somewhere better to be," Pete said, still squinting at his screen. "I'll try to make this quick."

"I'd appreciate that." Ten stretched out his legs and flexed his fingers atop the denim covering his thighs.

Pete worked methodically through the questionnaire required for each visit. Even though he had been here less than a week ago and none of his answers had changed, he had to calmly respond to each one. Address. Place of employment. Meetings. Alcohol? Drugs? On and on and on.

"Well, you know the drill, Mr. Vasiliev." Pete opened a drawer and retrieved a piss cup. "Let's go."

"Yeah," he grumbled, not looking forward to the invasion of his privacy.

When they reached the bathroom, Pete handed him the cup with a rainbow band of tests fixed on the inside. "I gotta see it go in the cup."

"Yeah." Ten unscrewed the blue lid and placed the cup on the metal ledge by the urinal. He unzipped his pants, whipped out his dick, and then grabbed the cup. Even though Pete didn't hover, it was still awkward as fuck to have another person staring at him while he tried to take a leak.

Finally, he managed to start a steady stream. He filled the cup to the line and then finished in the urinal. He screwed the lid back on the cup and handed it back to Pete who had put on a disposable exam glove. As he buttoned up and washed his hands, he kept an eye on Pete in the mirror.

His PO checked his watch and the cup a few times. "Negative across the board."

"Can I go now?"

"Not yet." Pete disposed of the urine and cup. He peeled off the glove and washed his hands at the sink. "I don't get involved in the personal lives of my clients. When I was younger, I made the mistake of caring too much. I'm not getting burned like that ever again."

"Okay?" Where the hell was he going with this? Pete had never been one to wax philosophical during their meetings.

"I know you're with Nicky Jackson's niece," Pete said, catching his eye in the reflection. "The whole city knows it. It's burning through the streets like wildfire. Nisha Jackson and the man who killed her serial killer ex-husband's child molesting partner."

"When you put it like that," Ten muttered distastefully.

"How else would I put it?" Pete turned to face him. "That girl has been through too much, Ten. She's been through more than any person should, and I won't have you fucking her life up with your bullshit."

"I don't need your permission to date, and I certainly don't need you lecturing me on how to take care of the woman I love."

Pete studied him for an agonizing moment. "All right, son."

"All right?"

"Yeah. Come on. I need to show you something."

Confused and apprehensive, Ten shadowed Pete back into the office. His PO shut and locked the door and then gestured for Ten to take a seat. He walked over to one of the dented filing cabinets lining the far wall and opened the third drawer. He yanked out a fat, stained, and faded file. "Here."

"What is this?" Ten accepted the file and realized it held information on two men—Adrian Umansky and Tony Guerrero.

"I worked on the probation side before I moved to parole. Those two idiots were in and out of my office as soon as they were old enough to be tried as adults. Can't tell you how many times I had to chase down those two for violations and revocations." Pete leaned back against his desk. "I keep detailed notes."

"So I see," Ten replied, flipping through the pages in the files. "What am I looking for?"

"I'm not sure," Pete admitted, "but if there's something that will help Nisha in there, you can have it."

Ten wasn't exactly sure this was legal, but far be it from him to turn down an offer of help, no matter how shady it might be. "Thank you."

"Get that back to me when you have a chance."

"Will do."

"Go on. Get out of my office."

Ten grabbed one of the red tote bags that was given out to newly paroled ex-cons from the basket by the door. He stuffed the file inside between the pamphlets for AA and accessing food banks. Out in the waiting room, he scanned the space for Ruby, but she was either with her PO or already on her way back to the Warehouse.

He left the building with the tote bag dangling from his fingers. What would he find in Pete's notes? The possibilities rattled around his brain as he walked to the parking lot. He used the remote start to cool down the interior of the SUV so he didn't roast. At least Kostya didn't skimp out when he made arrangements for the getaway fleet.

Ten spotted the kid who had tried to fleece him. Apparently, he had been demoted to picking up trash and directing traffic after his stunt. Ten didn't mind the kid trying to make a quick buck. That was the name of the game on the streets, but there were rules. The kid was stupid to try something like that right under his uncle's nose.

Refusing to think about the stupid scams he had tried when hustling as a kid, Ten unlocked the door of the Suburban, tossed the tote bag onto the passenger seat, and slid behind the wheel. He hit the lock button out of habit and reached over to adjust the flow from the A/C vents. As he did, he suddenly smelled something out of place.

Sweat. Mint. Suavitel fabric softener.

The steely bite of a pistol jammed into the side of his neck. The lethally sharp tip of a knife nicked just below his ear.

Ten held perfectly still. This wasn't the time to try to fight back. Not yet. He was one twitchy finger away from a cold slab at the morgue.

His gaze flicked to the rear-view mirror. A strange man crouched behind his seat, his face mostly hidden. He gripped a matte black FN Five-seveN. Belgian gun. Used by the Mexican military.

Military tracked. Whoever had taken shots at Nisha and her friends was clearly skilled with a rifle.

"You're going to drive. Slowly. Cautiously. If you try anything stupid, I will kill you." The heavily accented voice instructed. "Do you understand?"

"Yes." Ten noticed the parking lot kid staring. The kid took a step toward his SUV, and Ten mouthed the word NO while reaching for his seatbelt. "Where am I going?"

"Take a right onto the street. Three blocks. A left."

Ten watched the kid carefully walk away toward his uncle. Hoping the man behind him hadn't seen, Ten asked, "And then?"

"Drive."

"Yeah." Ten gripped the steering wheel and worked through his options. He could try to bail—but he would get shot or stabbed before he made it out the door. He could purposely wreck, but the outcome would likely be the same.

"I don't intend to kill you or Nisha."

"Then why did you try to shoot her?"

"I didn't."

"So you're just a really bad shot? You put two innocent women in the hospital. One of them is a mother—."

"To a monster's child," he snapped.

"Fucking watch it," Ten warned. There were a lot of things he could abide but digs at Callie weren't among them.

"I didn't shoot them." The man pressed the knife point deeper into Ten's skin, and he could feel blood trickling down his neck. "Keep driving."

"Where are we going?"

"You're taking me to Nisha."

"The fuck I am!"

"I need her."

"Why?"

"She's the only way I can lure that piece of shit out of hiding."

"If you think I'm going to let you use Nisha as bait—."

"She's already suggested it herself."

"What?" His stomach dropped. He wanted to argue that she would never do anything so reckless, but she would do anything to stop Kiki. "When?"

"Don't worry about that."

"I'm worrying about all of it."

"You should be worrying about what happens when the truth comes out," the carjacker warned.

"The truth about what?"

"About why you lied about being the one who killed Tony Guerrero…"

CHAPTER EIGHTEEN

CROUCHED LOW, KOSTYA dragged his fingertips through the soot and water pooling on the scorched floor of Holly's salon. The stink of accelerant and burned plastic irritated his nose. From his position, he painted a mental image of how the fire had started and spread.

The big windows at the front of the salon were easy targets for vandalism. A brick had been thrown through the window, bouncing off the gray oak floor and taking a chunk out of the wood. Glass shattered, sending shards into the lobby. The security alarms were triggered and the countdown to HFD and the police showing up began.

Cheap liquor bottles filled with a poor man's version of napalm had been thrown into the building. Soap, gasoline, Styrofoam, motor oil, and a tampon for the wick. The bottles shattered, splattering the thick, flammable liquid. The flaming tampon ignited the mess.

Kostya rose slowly, his gaze following the scorched trails across the floor and up the walls, over the furniture in the lobby to the stacks of ruined magazines. The fire suppression system had done a good job of keeping the flames from growing into a full conflagration.

All of the fire damage was confined to the lobby, but the

smoke and water damage from the firehoses was extensive.

Holly had put on a brave face when she walked through the ruined lobby earlier. She was being strong for her employees. First, Nisha was threatened by the escape of her lunatic husband. Then, Savannah was shot. Now this attack on their business.

It was too much, but she bore it without complaint. She had a smile and comforting hug for her weepy stylists and support staff. Billie, for all her faults—and Kostya had a list a mile long for that girl—, hadn't shown a flicker of panic or sadness.

She was waiting at the front door even before Holly arrived and immediately got to work after the fire marshal and arson investigator finished with the scene. She presented Holly with a list of services that specialized in fire damage and pulled the salon's insurance policies from the cloud so Holly wouldn't have to dig around for them.

Now, she was on the phone, calling each and every client to explain the situation and offer alternatives for their services. Holly had been offered space at various salons around the city. The Allure stylists would operate out of those other salon booths until this place was back up and running.

With Billie at her side, Holly would have no problem working out the logistics. Savannah, the business manager of the salon, would be out for a very long time.

If she lived.

He didn't like thinking that way, but there were so many things that could go wrong. Infection, blood clots, catching COVID or the flu, or some other respiratory virus while she tried to recover. It could go bad in a heartbeat.

Which explained why he had received a call from Gabe late last night.

Kostya wasn't quite sure what the score was between Savannah and the hitman. From what Holly had told him, there was an instant spark between the two when Gabe rescued them from that abandoned warehouse in Mexico.

Apparently, he had kept in touch with Savannah through texts. After Holly told him that Nisha had mentioned Savannah wanting Gabe as she lay bleeding on the ground, Kostya tried to reach out to Gabe.

But the calls and messages had never been answered. Kostya realized later it was because Gabe had ditched his usual means of communication before sneaking across the border. Technically, he was still a wanted man in the US. Holly's mother had been working with her contacts to free him of the warrant and charges, but it would take time. These types of things always did.

Not that Gabe was going to let that stop him from seeing Savannah. Kostya only hoped he would be smart about it and not get himself in real trouble. Spread thin by all the recent bullshit, Kostya had very few resources left for Gabe.

One of the ruined shelves finally gave way and crashed to the floor, taking bottles of destroyed shampoo. conditioner, and hair products with it. He didn't even want to think about how many hundreds of dollars of inventory that was. Dollar signs flashed before him everywhere he looked, and all of it came out of Holly's pocket.

With insurance payouts, the business would survive. He wasn't so sure about the assholes who had dared to attack his woman's place of business.

"Don't even think about it," Holly said as if reading the dark thoughts shadowing his mind. She had appeared from somewhere behind him and slipped her arms around his waist. No one ever touched him the way she did, freely and without hesitation. She leaned her cheek against his chest, and he embraced her right back. "No one died, Kostya. Everything can be replaced."

"It's the principle of the matter." He tenderly kissed the top of her head and then her temple. "I'm sorry this happened."

"So you said about twenty-seven different times since we got the call about the fire," she replied and nuzzled into him. "It's not your fault." She lifted her head long enough to meet his gaze. "It's not Nisha's either."

He frowned down at her. "When did I say it was?"

"You didn't, but I can see the wheels turning in your head."

"The wheels in my head might be rusty, but they don't assign blame to innocent women." He hated that Nisha couldn't catch a break. Ten choosing to get involved with her was a point of contention he had abandoned. If Ten wanted her, he was going to have her, and no one would be able to stop him.

"Are you any closer to finding that asshole she was married to?" Holly asked quietly.

"Why does that feel like a judgment on my tracking skills?" He was pretending to be affronted, but deep down inside, he was worried about his inability to find Kiki. It shouldn't have been this difficult. Kiki was a killer, but he was also a fucking idiot. There was no way Kiki had been able to escape and evade law enforcement without help from someone with the sort of skills Kostya usually provided.

"You're still my favorite spy-turned-mafia-fixer," she assured him with a kiss to his jaw. "Even if you are moving a bit slower these days."

"Slower?" He scowled down at her. "What are you saying?"

"Listen, we all get older and lose some of our stamina."

"Stamina?" He noticed the gleam in her eye and finally realized what game she was playing. After all the stress of the last few days, she desperately needed to blow off some steam. Locking her office door, bending her over her soaking wet desk, and fucking her like a rutting beast would be a good way to accomplish that.

"Stamina," she echoed coyly.

"You'll get your pants wet," he warned, thinking of how much water was pooled in the back areas of the salon.

"I'm planning on it." The mischievous glint turned to a lusty haze of need. Far be it from him to refuse the woman he intended to marry a goddamn thing.

Kostya grasped her hand and tugged her in the right direction. They had taken four steps before Billie said, "What the hell is wrong with Tiara?"

"What? Is she here finally?" Holly stopped and spun around to see what Billie meant. "She didn't answer my texts or calls."

"Mine either."

When Tiara appeared, his irritation with Billie's ill-timed interruption faded. Face streaked with tears, Tiara sobbed hysterically. Her nose was swollen and pink, and her dark eyes were bloodshot. Her rumpled TEXANS shirt and torn leggings spoke volumes about the type of morning she had had.

"Tiara!" Holly dropped his hand and rushed across the broken glass and water. "Oh, my God! What's wrong?"

Tiara gripped onto Holly and sobbed. "I'm sorry. I'm so sorry."

"What? What is it?"

Kostya moved closer, wondering if Tiara was about to reveal she had inadvertently helped the vandals in some way. What came out of her mouth next rocked him to the core.

"I fucked up," Tiara wept. "I fucked up real, real bad—and now Nisha and Ten are going to die."

CHAPTER NINETEEN

W HEN HE THOUGHT back to the night his life changed forever, Ten always pictured Danny's young face first. He had been a kid back then, not quite at that gangly, awkward puberty stage. Danny still had a bit of chubbiness to him, all soft and innocent and not yet fucked over by life.

That would soon change.

Back then, Danny had been adjusting to life with Artyom. His mother had died, and his father had fucked off back to Russia, probably to drink or snort himself to death. Artyom had stepped up to be the father his nephew needed. Not that the kid appreciated that sacrifice. He fought Artyom at every turn, ignoring curfews, sneaking out with his shithead friends, and failing his classes.

He had realized too late to stop that it was Artyom's nephew crying on the sidewalk and had circled back to see if the kid needed a ride. The sight of Danny crying worried him. No boy that age cried like that unless something truly fucked up had just happened.

It was the little brother of a friend. He had gone missing on the way to school. Danny and the older brother were supposed to walk the younger boy to the bus stop. They had ditched him a block from the bench to chase after some girls who were too old for them. The little boy never made it to school, and Danny was drowning in the guilt of it.

The disappearance of another young boy had riled up Ten's suspicions. There seemed to be a young boy missing every five or six weeks, always the same kind of kid from the same kind of home. Single, overworked mom or grandmother. Poor. Alone. At risk.

Ten kept quiet and out of the rumors that spread along the underworld circuit, but he hadn't been able to miss the gossip about the peculiar tastes that Fat Tony Guerrero and Adrian Umansky were purported to enjoy. After Kiki Acevedo's arrest, the streets had been on fire with wild tales. Suddenly, everyone knew what a vicious freak he was and everyone knew he had been a serial killer.

It was annoying to hear people say shit like that. When he'd ask them why they hadn't gone to the cops and saved some lives, they got really quiet. All that bluster and bravado disappeared. They were all liars.

But there was something strange about that trio. It was a gut feeling he'd had the few times he'd been around the three of them, usually offloading cargo or picking up cash. Some men had bad energy around them. It was like an invisible field of discomfort that made the skin on the back of his neck prickle.

After that night, after he had discovered things he could never unsee, Ten would learn to trust that prickling sensation, that slow churn of his guts, as a warning. In prison, he would read a book by Gavin de Becker, *The Gift of Fear*, and he would finally understand why he had felt that way.

But, at that moment, when he had picked up Danny to

take him to Artyom, he hadn't known. He couldn't have even imagined.

It was after eleven that night when Kostya tracked down the little boy. Ten never asked how Kostya had found the location of that shit-hole house. He hadn't wanted to know. He had only wanted to wash the vile stink of it off him and forget about the whole thing.

Ten had never been to that stretch of boggy, heavily forested area between Mont Belvieu and Dayton. There was no reason for anyone to go out there which was probably why Tony and Adrian had bought that piece of property. Barely an acre carved off the side of a much larger tract. Perfectly isolated the way a pair of child molesting psychos would want.

Hidden behind trees, there was a ramshackle house. The wind had been blowing that night, and it looked as if the house was breathing with every gust. There had been a strange smell in the air, one he didn't recognize but Kostya had. It was the smell of charred flesh, that greasy, foul stink of death.

After, a long time after, Ten would follow Kostya and that scent to a burn pit located at the back part of the property. The bones they uncovered there would help investigators close a number of missing persons cases, all of them young boys. The sight of that pit would haunt Ten until the day he died. It was a horrific reminder of cruelty and inhumanity.

The door had been unlocked. Ten had been shocked by that. What sort of idiots didn't lock the door of their murder house? Were they truly so arrogant? Did they think no one would ever dare to come inside?

Not that a locked door would have stopped Artyom. He had stormed into that house like a bull, raging and furious.

Artyom had always been slow to anger and never one to resort to violence. Not that night. No, Ten had seen a side of the three-fingered captain he never wanted to witness again.

Adrian had been in the back room of the house. It had been converted into a torture chamber, like something out of the *SAW* franchise. Chains, padlocks, chairs, exam tables, a bed, a dog kennel, and a wall of torture implements straight from the Middle Ages. The biting burn of bleach had saturated the whole space. A putrid stench from the drain in the center of the room had turned his stomach.

But it was the sight of that little boy asleep on the stained mattress that had nearly driven him to his knees.

The two fucking idiots had gotten the sedation dose wrong, and the kid was knocked out cold. Being so skinny and small had saved him from the horrors that others had experienced in that space. Adrian and Tony couldn't do anything with him if he was asleep so Tony had gone back to Houston for food and equipment.

What happened in that room to Adrian, Ten would never know. Kostya and Artyom had given him the little boy and charged him with returning the child to his mother and then finding Tony Guerrero. All Ten knew for sure was that Adrian had not enjoyed the last few hours of his life.

Returning the child to his mother had been the easy part. She had been overjoyed and wept as she took him in her arms. He had left as quickly as possible, not wanting to be any part of the police or EMS response that was soon to come. The mother, an employee at Samovar, had understood how these things worked. She had kept quiet about the involvement of Kostya, Artyom, and Ten.

Finding Tony had proven more difficult than he had expected. He had gone to the usual haunts including Tony's mother's house and the place Tony shared with his older brother. Ten had driven through the Hermanos-controlled streets and visited the cheap strip clubs Tony liked to frequent. They were the sort of club where the girls were long in the tooth, hooked on drugs, and didn't mind Tony touching them if he gave them a few dollars.

He had driven by Adrian's house twice but had decided to go back a third time before contacting Kostya to let him know he couldn't find Tony. That third time, he had seen Tony's car parked in the driveway. He had pulled in behind the car, blocking Tony from a quick escape. As fat as the man was, he wouldn't get very far on foot if he tried to bolt out the back door.

When he stepped inside the house, there had been a strange, eerie feeling. There was a stillness, oppressive and dark, and Ten had crept through the house, alert and ready to find the worst.

Someone had taken a hammer or something heavy to a padlocked door, busting it right off the wall where it had been mounted. When he pushed the door open with the toe of his shoe, he'd discovered Tony, flat on his back by an open safe.

Whatever had been in the safe was gone, but it seemed as if there had been a scuffle of some kind. Computer monitors and towers had been knocked over, and the numerous routers and cords and other electronic equipment he couldn't name had been ripped out of the wall.

Tony was right in the middle of it, his mouth open, face a battered mask of blood. Ten had crouched down next to the body and reached out to check for a pulse. There had been one, faint and thready, and the soft puff of air from Tony's ruined mouth was the only indication the man was still trying to breathe.

Knowing what a monster he was, Ten hadn't been in a hurry to call for an ambulance. Instead, he had checked the safe, finding only a single missed flash drive. Back next to Tony, he'd picked up a router, the front of it dented all to hell and cracked. It was coated in blood, and he'd realized that someone had used it to beat Tony.

Before he could put much thought into who had battered Tony, the man began to wheeze and make agonal sounds. Remembering what he had seen back at the torture house and the way Adrian had blubbered and blabbed about Tony being the one who actually hurt the kids, Ten had made a life-changing decision.

If he let Tony live, there would be an investigation. There would be questions. The police would use Adrian's involvement in whatever this nightmare molestation situation was to dig into the family's business. They would use RICO or some other bullshit to crack open the outer shell of Nikolai's organization.

If Tony lived, he might tell stories that were better unspoken. He might open his fat mouth to get a deal. Considering what he had done, Tony wouldn't last long in prison unless he had serious protections in place before he went inside. Even then, he wasn't likely to make it a full year, not with the cartel and Nikolai trying to silence him.

No, if Tony lived, it would cause more problems than it solved.

So, Ten had made a choice. He placed his big hand over Tony's mouth and nose and pressed down hard, sealing off the mushy, bloody openings that let him breathe. He put his knee on Tony's chest, holding him in place until Tony stopped twitching for breath. He held on a little longer, keeping his hand in place until he was absolutely certain Tony was dead.

And that was how the two police officers responding to a 9-1-1 call from a suspicious neighbor had found him.

Leaning over Tony, his knee on the other man's chest, his hand covering the other man's battered face.

By sunrise, Ten sat in a jail cell, accused of murder. Eventually, it would be pleaded down to a manslaughter charge, and he would get actual fucking pats on the back from police officers and prison guards for taking care of a child molester.

Of course, that wasn't quite the whole story. Yes, Ten had finished off Tony, but someone else had beaten him nearly to death.

Thirteen months into his sentence, Ten had received an unexpected visitor. When he had stepped into the room to sit at his assigned place, he had assumed it would be Kostya or Artyom coming to tell him something in a coded message.

As soon as he had seen her sitting there on that stool, nervously twirling her dark hair around her finger, Ten's steps had faltered.

It was Chess.

When he picked up the phone so he could hear her voice, he had thought for sure that she was going to tell him something had happened to Artyom.

But that was not the case.

"Ten," she had said, her voice breaking as she wept. "I'm

so sorry. This is all my fault."

"Stop," he had commanded roughly, finally understanding. "You shut your fucking mouth and go."

"But, I have to tell—."

"You don't say another fucking word to anyone. *Anyone*," he had emphasized coldly. "You carry this to your grave."

"Why?" Chess had asked.

"Because you're a mother now, and your baby needs you. Now get up and go."

She had gripped the phone a moment longer, obviously torn between following his orders and telling the truth. Eventually, she hung up the phone, turned and left.

Back in his cell, Ten had replayed their short conversation over and over again. Of course, it made sense.

Had Chess been suspicious of Adrian and Tony before Kiki's arrest?

Something had triggered her that day. Something had forced her hand, making her break that lock and get into that safe.

Had Tony found her rifling through the safe? Had he attacked her? Hurt her? Had she battered him in self-defense?

Or had it been something else? Had she found him in there going through the safe? Had she realized what he was? What Adrian was? Had she been so enraged she had snapped and attacked Tony?

After Chess came to see him, Ten had settled into his bid. The anger and frustration he had been feeling for his predicament faded right away. His loyalty to the family, to Nikolai, had forced his hand. He had taken full responsibility for killing Tony to protect their *bratva*.

Once he knew that he was also protecting Chess, giving her a chance to be a mother to her baby girl, to live a life of happiness, he accepted his plight. Six years in prison to keep a single teen mom safe was a small price indeed.

CHAPTER TWENTY

FEELING CONFUSED AND betrayed, I sat on the patio behind the cabin. Ilya wasn't happy about it, but he agreed I could sit out there for a short while if I stayed in a specific chair. He stood directly in front of me, blocking anything that might come my way. Eric was somewhere out front, walking the perimeter.

I had spent more than an hour going through everything I could find online about Tiara. There wasn't much. No photos of her childhood. No photos of family. No links to her high school. She had never been cagey or secretive with us. She and Savannah had bonded over their experiences in foster care. It had never been something hidden.

But why hadn't she ever mentioned Derek? Why hadn't she mentioned that my ex-husband was suspected of killing her foster brother? Why had she kept that from me?

Did she want to hurt me? Was she setting me up as Ilya believed? Did she hate me? Did she blame me?

Was I so stupid that I had been fooled by our friendship? All this time, I had believed she was genuine. I had believed she was my friend just as I was hers.

I chewed on my acrylic thumbnail. Solange, my nail tech, was going to flip the next time she saw me. All her hard work was destroyed by my teeth as I anxiously gnawed at the once perfectly shaped acrylic. I would get an earful from her about disrespecting her art and skill.

My thoughts turned back to Chad and Robin Harris at Allure. What had Tiara said? You shouldn't be here? Or something like that?

At the time, it hadn't seemed the least bit suspicious. Now, it left me wondering if she was in cahoots with that asshole and the lawyer.

"It's late." Ilya startled me out of my troubled thoughts.

"What?"

"Ten should have been on his way back by now. Has he messaged you?"

I picked up my phone from the ceramic garden stool I had been using as a small table to hold my iced tea. "There's nothing from him. Maybe he was worried about someone tracking him?"

"Possible." Ilya seemed unconvinced. "Let's go inside."

"Okay." As much as I enjoyed my time on the patio, the humid heat and the chatter of cicadas were less than relaxing. I grabbed my glass of tea and phone and returned to the blessedly cool cabin. "Should we be worried, Ilya?"

"No." Ilya hid his gaze as he swiped his thumb across the screen of his phone. "Ten is no amateur. If he's not contacting us, there's a good reason for it."

Considering where he had been, another terrible thought struck me. "What if they revoked his parole?"

"For what?" Ilya paused his typing. "Did Ten break one of his conditions?"

"No."

"Was he cleared to travel here?"

"He's been cleared for in-state travel as long as he notifies his parole officer before leaving—and he did by email and phone. I was sitting right beside him when he did it."

"If he hasn't broken any of his conditions, he didn't get revoked." Ilya returned his attention to his phone.

"What if he had an accident? What if he's been hurt?" My anxiety spiraled out of control as I imagined all the horrible outcomes.

"Who had an accident?" Eric asked as he entered through the front door. "Perimeter is clear, by the way."

"Ten hasn't made contact," Ilya explained.

"He might be in a long meeting with his PO."

"Not this long," I protested. "Surely?"

Eric checked his watch. "No, you're right. Not this long." He lifted his gaze to Ilya's. "An accident? Or maybe he got pulled into a side job by your boss?"

"I'm waiting for Kostya's answer." Ilya stared at his phone as if willing a message to appear.

Wilford rubbed against my good leg, and I crouched down to pick him up. He allowed me to cuddle and love on him as I stood there listening to Eric and Ilya toss ideas back and forth. They were right, of course. Ten was street-smart and battle-hardened.

Ilya's phone rang. I didn't even try to hide that I was eavesdropping as I stroked Wilford's fur. Not that I could understand a word he said. I glanced at Eric and noticed he seemed to be following along just fine. Apparently, my old friend had learned Russian at some point.

When Ilya ended his call, I asked, "What's wrong? Was

that Ten?"

"It was Kostya." Ilya's expression was hard to read, and I had to bite back the urge to yell at him to tell me what was happening. "Tiara showed up at the salon. She was a mess and crying. She told him that she had made a mistake that was going to get you and Ten killed."

"Where is she now?"

"He didn't say."

"What else?" Eric knew the answer.

Ilya seemed to realize that Eric had understood the conversation. "Well, why don't you tell Nisha since you were being so fucking nosy?"

"I think it's better coming from you."

"Ten was seen driving away from his appointment with a gun to his head and a knife to his throat," Ilya said without even a moment's warning.

The words hit me like a truck. I lost my grip on Wilford, and he reacted by scrambling for purchase, clawing at my arms and chest before flinging himself onto the nearby counter where he yowled angrily at me.

As he scuttled off, I stared at Ilya in shock. My body felt suddenly cold, and my knees wobbled. "What?"

"That's all I know, Nisha. I'm sorry," Ilya apologized. "The tracking device that Kostya has in every vehicle was disabled, and Ten's phone was found a few blocks away from the parking lot."

"And?" I asked, desperate for Ilya to tell me that Kostya had the whole Kalasnikov crime family scouring the streets looking for him.

"And that's all I know." Ilya speared me with a warning

look. "You are not to leave my sight until Ten is returned."

"Oh, so this is my prison now?" I gestured around the cabin. "And you're my warden?"

"Don't be dramatic, Nisha." Ilya frowned at me. "I'm charged with keeping you safe until Ten returns. I'd rather not get the ass beating of my life if he comes back and finds you gone."

"I'm not going anywhere." The last thing I wanted to do was cause any more problems. Savannah and Chess and Robin Harris. She might have been rude to me and accused me of something terrible, but she didn't deserve to die. The fire at the salon. Ten taken hostage.

What was next? Who else would get hurt because of me? Ilya? Eric?

"I need to be alone for a while." I held up both hands to prevent the men from trying to stop me. "In our room. I'll even leave the door open so you can peek in on me."

"Fine." Ilya nodded. "Leave the door ajar, please."

Once I made it to the bedroom, I left the door open a few inches. I walked to the side of the bed where Ten had slept last night and slipped under the quilt and top sheet. His scent lingered there, and I closed my eyes as I breathed deeply.

Anton.

An invisible vise squeezed my chest so hard. I wanted to cry, but I couldn't make any tears come. I was frozen in fear, my mind racing as I thought of all the ways this could end. A knife? A gun? Either one could end Ten in a heartbeat.

No. That's not going to happen.

I had lost too much. I had endured too much. I had been to hell and back, and now I finally had a taste of real happiness with my Anton. He loved me, and I loved him. We both deserved a life together.

Ten had survived prison. He was quick-witted and tough. He was a fighter, and he would do whatever it took to come back to me.

CHAPTER TWENTY-ONE

"**W**HY DO YOU think I lied about killing Tony?" Ten eyed his captor in the rearview mirror. The man had taken a more comfortable position on the seat directly behind him but kept his gun and knife at the ready.

"Your booking photos," the man said as if it were the most obvious answer in the world. "You had bruises on your hands, but they were old. You were a fighter. You trained with Ivan Markovic. I know you fought underground in the bare-knuckle circuit."

"And?"

"And I saw Tony's autopsy photos. Hands didn't cause that damage, and if you had beaten him with a piece of computer equipment, you would have caved his entire skull in," the man reasoned. "So, no, you didn't kill him."

"Well, you're wrong," Ten replied. "I did kill him. The cops walked in on me with my hand over his mouth, smothering him."

The man regarded him a moment. "You didn't do it alone."

"There was no one else there but me."

"Maybe," the man allowed, "but there was someone else there before you. They found a partial fingerprint at the scene, and it was much smaller than yours. There was also a DNA profile. Female."

"So?" Ten shrugged. "Adrian and Tony probably had girls in and out of that place all the time."

The man shook his head. "You must care about the person you're protecting."

"I don't know what you're talking about." Tired of dredging up the past, he said, "You know what's going to happen when Kostya finds us."

"I don't plan to be alive that long."

"What does that mean?" Ten kept his focus on the traffic in front of him. Houston drivers were the worst he had ever experienced. Everyone slamming the accelerator over 80. Swerving in and out of lanes like they were driving in a fucking NASCAR race. Paper plates everywhere he looked.

"It means exactly what I said."

"Who the fuck are you?" Ten switched lanes to avoid a Subaru weaving across the line. "What do you even want with me or Nisha?"

"I don't want you or Nisha. I want Kiki."

"Get in line." Ten eyed him again in the mirror. "He killed someone you loved."

The man nodded stiffly. "My daughter. JoJo."

Ten felt bad for not knowing which victim that was. "I'm sorry."

"It was my fault. I didn't understand her. I was too busy with my work, chasing after the Zetas and trying to make our home safer. I sent her to live with my mother across the border. I thought she would be better off there."

"You couldn't have possibly known what would happen."

"I should have." He was looking right at the back of Ten's head, but his gaze was far away, someplace in the past. "She wasn't like other kids. Even when she was little."

Ten wasn't sure what to say to that so he stayed quiet and kept driving. After he refused to take the asshole to Nisha, the man ordered him to get on the loop. They were circling aimlessly, and he had to piss.

"My wife thought she would grow out of it. The wearing dresses and wanting to wear her shoes and the makeup. Then she accepted it and decided that JoJo was gay. She could handle that. She was comfortable with that." He clicked his teeth. "But when JoJo told us she was supposed to be a girl? Adelina couldn't accept that."

"Oh." Ten finally understood. JoJo had been born a girl in the wrong male body.

"JoJo ran away. I was in the field, trying to track down a cartel kill squad. When I finally got the call, JoJo had been missing for twenty-six days. Do you know what can happen to a lost little girl without anyone to protect her?"

"Yeah, I do."

"I bet you do." The man shifted behind him, and Ten tensed briefly. "I heard you were the man who brought that little boy back to his mother."

There was no hiding the shock on his face. "Who told you that?"

"The little boy. Not so little anymore," his captor corrected. "He's a good kid, in case you were wondering. He's in school in Waco. Varsity baseball. First chair trumpet in the band. Lives a perfectly normal life because you and your *bratva* saved him."

"He got lucky because those two assholes couldn't calculate the correct dosage of sedatives to keep him quiet when they kidnapped him." Ten regarded him in the mirror. "Why would you chase that kid down? He has nothing to do with any of this."

"He has everything to do with this. It's not only Kiki that I want to kill. It's all of them."

"Them?"

"The ones who were paying Adrian Umansky and Tony Guerrero to make those disgusting movies."

That got Ten's attention. "Do you know who they were?"

"I'm getting there."

"Which is why you need Kiki?"

The man nodded. "He's going to tell me what I want to know."

"Do you know who broke him out of prison?"

"The lawyer," the man said. "Working for the traffickers and pedophile ring that financed Adrian and Tony, I suspect."

"And the podcaster? Chad that's causing all these problems for Nisha?"

"A leech," the man spat. "He trolls online support groups looking for families of victims to interview. He used my daughter's name to get into a closed group for Kiki's known or suspected victims. I keep tabs on everything to do with Kiki's crimes."

"Did you set up the group?"

"Of course, I did."

"To help the other families who had suffered like you?"

"No, to make sure I could control online spaces where Kiki's crimes and those of his friends were discussed. I figured the people involved in financing the videos might also be interested in those spaces."

"Your daughter...?" Ten hesitated. "Was she on one of the videos?"

"She was." He spoke so softly Ten barely heard him over the air conditioner blasting. "If you could see how many thousands of times that video has been downloaded by degenerates..."

"I can't even imagine what that's like for you." Ten swallowed the ball of emotion clogging his throat. To lose a child, but to be victimized again and again and again by sick freaks downloading and watching her violent end?

"I found JoJo staying with a group of kids like her. Transgender," he clarified for the first time. "All of them kicked out of their homes or running away from abuse. I felt like such a failure as a father. I had been spending so much time worried about the wrong things."

"You were doing your job." Ten knew the type. Loyal, honorable, committed. This man had been fighting Zetas and cartel-hit squads. He had been trying to save his country from the ravages of narco-violence. "You were doing the best you could."

The man regarded him strangely. "Are you in therapy?"

Ten snorted. "Is it that obvious?"

"Yes." The man's mouth twitched with a smile. "Your parole?"

Ten nodded. "You?"

"Self-help books mostly. I was sent to a counselor after JoJo's death, but she wasn't much help."

"You should try knitting or crochet." As soon as he said it,

Ten realized how ridiculous that sounded. Here he was, held at gunpoint, telling his captor to take up yarn arts as a means of emotional regulation. *Fuck, I'm losing it.*

"I think I won't."

"Listen, you don't have to keep that gun on me. I'm not going to wreck or try to escape. I'll help you find Kiki."

The man narrowed his eyes. "Why?"

"Because I want to find him, too. Nisha will never be safe as long as he's alive." He switched his turn signal on and began to move toward the upcoming exit. His captor said nothing as he left the loop and pulled into a gas station, out back by the dumpsters. He turned in his seat so he could look the man in the eye. "Did you kill that lawyer? Did you take shots at Nisha? Shoot Savannah and Chess?"

"No." No equivocation. No protests. Eyes clear. Not a hint of dishonesty.

"Do you have a plan for catching Kiki? You've had me driving in circles like an asshole."

The man winced before admitting, "I don't. I had been focused on the others—."

"The financial backers?"

His captor nodded. "When I heard Kiki had escaped, I acted impulsively. I seem to be five steps behind."

Ten regarded him a moment and accepted his answer as truth. "All right. Get up here and sit in the front seat and quit hiding behind me like a fucking ghoul."

The man hesitated but eventually did as Ten asked. After tucking away his gun and knife, he climbed out of the back seat, walked around the front of the Suburban, and then sat in the passenger seat. "My name is Alejandro."

"Okay, Alejandro. Do you have a phone?"

"Yeah."

"I need to make a call."

"And then?"

"And then I'm going to take a piss and get something to eat." Ten tapped Kostya's dedicated emergency phone number and waited for an answer from one of his so-called spiders.

"Hen House Security. This is the Fox speaking."

"It's Ten. I need Kostya."

"As in, you're, like, actively dying and need help right-now-right-now or you need an address for a meetup?"

"Meetup." He frowned and wondered, not for the first time, where Kostya found these women.

"Is this number good?"

"Yes."

"The main storage facility. Red door. Do you require medical attention?"

"No." He ended the call and tossed the phone back to Alejandro. "You can wait for me, and I'll take you to my people."

"Or?"

"Or you can run," Ten offered. "No hard feelings."

Alejandro considered his options. "I'll stay."

Ten climbed out of the SUV and walked toward the convenience store without a backward glance. If Alejandro was there when he got back? Fine. If he fled? Also fine.

After taking a leak and grabbing two bottles of water and two protein bars, he walked up to the counter to pay. The old man behind the counter had rheumy eyes but a friendly smile. "You having a good day, hoss?"

"Not really." Ten almost wished he had taken up smoking as a kid so he would have some way of soothing his nerves.

"You want a lottery ticket? Drawing tonight is a big 'un." The old man pointed to the sign behind him. "Maybe your luck is gonna change, son."

"Yeah. Sure. Why not?" Ten handed over the cash.

"You win, you come back and see me!" The old man called out as Ten walked to the double doors with his purchases.

"If I win, I'm coming back here to tell you it's time to re-tire," Ten promised and tucked his ticket into the back pocket of his jeans.

"I'll be waitin' for ya!" The old man's laughter morphed into a hacking cough.

Alejandro seemed surprised when Ten tossed him a bottle of water and a protein bar. "*Gracias.*"

Ten waved him off and slipped on his seatbelt. Before working for Vivian, he had never bothered with one, but she had ingrained the safety measure into him. He felt naked not wearing it now.

As he pulled onto the road alongside the gas station, Ten said, "Tell me about your daughter."

Alejandro lowered his water bottle. "Why?"

"You're risking everything to avenge her. I want to know what she was like." Ten suspected few people ever asked Alejandro about JoJo. People didn't want to make things awkward or uncomfortable. It was easier not to ask than to risk upsetting the parent of a dead child, but that meant those parents never had a chance to talk about all the good memo-ries. "Look, we have a forty-five-minute drive in front of us. We can sit in silence or—."

"She loved manga. *Sailor Moon, Peach Girl, One Piece, Sgt. Frog, Naruto, Bleach.*" Alejandro paused. "*JoJo's Bizarre Adventure* was her favorite. Have you ever read it?"

"No. I've never—I'm not really a manga reader."

"I wasn't either. Not until she..." He cleared his throat. "And then it was too late to share it with her."

"I'm sorry."

"So am I." Alejandro tore into his protein bar. "She wanted to be a doctor. She wanted to help kids like her. She loved music, and she was fascinated by Texas high school football games and cheerleaders and marching bands. She was so excited to go to her first homecoming. My mother had been working on one of those big, fluffy mums, you know?"

"Yeah, I know." Ten had been fascinated by the strange pageantry of Texas high schools. The giant mums bigger than most teenage girls' heads with ribbons and bells and charms looked ridiculous to him, but they were an important part of the high school experience here.

"She never got to wear it."

Ten's stomach twisted.

"It's still hanging in JoJo's bedroom in my mother's house. She dusts it every single day. Just ribbon by ribbon, petal by petal. Some days I think we should have buried JoJo with it. I think she would have liked that."

Christ, Ten thought sadly. How much pain had Kiki caused for these families?

"Do you have kids?"

"No." Ten decided not to let his mind wander on that subject. It wouldn't do him any good to get distracted by what-ifs.

"Do you want kids?"

"Yes." With Nisha. As many as she wanted. Four? Five? Ten? He'd make it happen.

"Be smarter than I was."

Ten glanced at Alejandro who wore the saddest, most regretful expression. The pain carved into that man's face was gut-wrenching. "I will."

CHAPTER TWENTY-TWO

WHEN I WOKE up in the hospital after Kiki tried to kill me, I thought I was dead. My ears were ringing from the gunshot blasts, and my vision was blurry and unfocused. The lights above me were so bright. My addled brain decided I was in heaven.

The sudden searing pain informed me I was in hell.

Amid the ringing in my ears, I picked out voices—men and women, all of them tense and taut. I couldn't make sense of their words. Everything was garbled and sounded as if it were coming from inside a tin can.

The pain was so bad. It was killing me. I tried to get their attention, but no one noticed my lips moving. I lifted a hand, and smacked at the plastic mask covering my nose and mouth. A nurse gently grabbed my wrist and pulled my hand down, leaned over, and spoke loudly and clearly, "Nisha, you've been shot. You're in the emergency room."

"My baby," I said, my mouth dry and my lips sticking together. "My baby."

If she heard me, the nurse didn't confirm it. No one seemed to care what I thought or what I needed. Once I was recovered and undergoing intense therapy, I would feel so much anger and frustration toward the medical staff. I had gone from being completely controlled by Kiki to completely controlled by strangers who thought they knew what was best for me.

They *did* know what was best for me. They saved my life. They gave me a chance to heal and recover and live a life so good it seemed like a dream.

But that night, writhing on that exam table, strapped down when I became combative, I hated them. I hated everyone.

The pain of the crash c-section knocked me unconscious. The anesthesiologist had been furiously attempting to get me sedated, but there wasn't enough time. The first cut happened before I got a full dose of pain medication. Years later, that ungodly burning, tearing pain would wake me up in the middle of the night, leaving me clutching my belly as phantom surgeons hacked into me.

When I woke the next time, I was in the ICU. My memories were fuzzy still, and my head throbbed. My stomach felt strange, and the realization that my baby was gone left me in a panic. I shouted for help, desperate to find her. Had they taken her to the NICU? Had CPS come and taken her away because I was unfit?

No, it was worse than that. So much worse.

The nurses who came in to help me and the doctor on shift that day were so kind to me. They didn't blame or lecture me. They weren't rough or nasty. They were gentle in their care and reminded me again and again how strong I was to have survived what I did.

I would hear that so much over the next few months. I didn't believe it. I wasn't strong. I was weak. I was stupid. I was useless. I was worthless. I deserved all the bad things that had happened to me.

It would take a long while to forgive myself. Therapy, so many group meetings, and hundreds of Sundays in a church pew listening to sermons on love and forgiveness. It came upon me slowly and finally arrived the morning I sat in the front pew at Mimi June's funeral service. She had known her end was coming, and had planned out her funeral right down to the last detail including the readings.

Mark 11:25.

The pastor began reading, and it was as if I finally understood the words. It was my grandmother's last piece of advice, chosen before her death and given to me after she was gone. The tears began to fall, and I wept, purging and cleansing myself of all the guilt and shame.

But I couldn't bring myself to forgive Kiki. After everything he had done to me and to others, it was impossible. Maybe that made me a bad person. Maybe it meant that I hadn't learned a damned thing in therapy. Maybe it meant I hadn't actually received the full grace of forgiveness my grandmother had wanted for me.

I could live with that. The same way I had to live with the loss of my daughter.

Lorelai was a beautiful baby. There was nothing of Kiki in her face. She was all me, all chubby cheeked and little nose. They let me hold her as long as I wanted. She was bundled up tight in a receiving blanket, and one of the nurses had put a tiny bow right on top of her dark hair. It was easy to imagine she was sleeping as I rocked her in my arms.

Mimi June was with me when it was time to let Lorelai go. I cried so hard, so violently overcome with mourning, that I popped my staples. I was in a gaping, raw, endless chasm of grief, and I didn't know if anything would assuage that pain.

In time, that pain faded and morphed into a sense of longing and emptiness. It would spring to life sometimes, reminding me of what I had lost. The sight of a little girl in Target. A little girl making faces at her brother in the church pew in front of me. A little girl in my cousin Willa's living room having her hair braided. The air would rush out of my lungs, and I would be overtaken by visions of what could have been.

I never gave up hope. Someday, I would find a man who wanted to be my partner, who wanted to have children and raise a family. I would find a man worthy of my love.

Only I never could have imagined that man would be a nearly seven-foot-tall Russian ex-con who cooked delicious meals and collected old books and even tolerated my grumpy, persnickety cat.

CHAPTER TWENTY-THREE

T EN PULLED IN and parked behind the row of storage units where Kostya conducted his less-than-savory business. "Stay quiet. Don't make any stupid moves."

"I understand." Alejandro sighed. "Let's get it over with."

As much as Ten hoped it wasn't going to get bloody in there, he knew that it was likely. There were rules in the underworld and consequences for breaking them. Alejandro had taken a made man hostage with a gun and knife. Back in the gas station bathroom, Ten had wiped away the trickle of dried blood on his neck, but Kostya would zero in on that cut with his eagle-eyed stare.

When they reached the door of the storage unit, he knocked three times and stood back, making sure he could be seen fully in the camera mounted above him. The door swung open, and he spotted Nikolai in the center of the retrofitted container, arms crossed and leaning back against a rolling toolbox that Ten was fairly certain held not one single wrench.

"You're alive." Nikolai looked him over like a mother duck would a lost duckling.

"*Da*." Ten noticed Boychenko on the left side of the room. A flick of the kid's eyes and Ten realized he had missed Kostya while walking through the door.

Alejandro inhaled sharply as Kostya put a gun to the man's temple as he entered the storage unit. Stas appeared from wherever he had been lurking outside, cutting off Alejandro's only means of escape. Stas shut and locked the door, and Ten gritted his teeth as he waited for the violence to come.

Alejandro lifted both hands and held still as Boychenko stepped forward and frisked him. The kid plucked all the weapons he found and carried them to a different toolbox on the other side of the unit. He placed them in the top drawer and then picked up a folding metal chair that he opened and set down in the center of the room.

Kostya grabbed Alejandro's hand and bent the man's wrist into a painful position. He pinned it to the small of Alejandro's back and perp-walked him to the chair. He shoved him down and warned, "You move and I'll have you tied to it."

"Understood," Alejandro replied, his voice calm and steady.

"You made my wife cry." Nikolai touched his wedding band, sliding it around his finger. "Ten is more than her bodyguard. He's a brother to her, and you tried to kill him. She's been upset since we got the call." Nikolai lowered his hands, the slow movement deceptively relaxed. "When my wife cries, our son doesn't understand. It makes him anxious and sad."

"I'm sorry that I upset your wife and son," Alejandro apologized. "That was never my intent." He glanced at Kostya and then exhaled hard. "Do whatever you need to do to make things square between us, but do it fast. I don't know how much longer they'll keep Kiki in the US or alive."

Nikolai exchanged a meaningful look with Kostya who had holstered his weapon after putting Alejandro in the chair. Suddenly, and so quickly it rattled Ten, Kostya produced a scalpel, tugged hard on Alejandro's right ear, and struck it free with one masterful swipe. The ear separated from the man's head, and he cried out in pain before slamming his hand against the bloody, gaping wound left behind.

Ten swore under his breath and stormed over to a rolling cart with cleaning supplies on it. He grabbed a handful of heavy-duty paper towels and brought them back to Alejandro who smashed them against his ear to stem the bleeding. Ten glanced at Nikolai who silently dared him to protest. There would be a time to discuss this, but it wasn't now, not in front of an outsider.

Ne vynosi sor iz izby.

Don't argue outside the shack.

"Explain," Nikolai demanded.

Alejandro gave a shortened version of his story to the boss. Nikolai listened intently, asking questions when he had them. "So, you think the financiers behind Adrian and Tony are responsible for breaking Kiki out of prison?"

"I do." Alejandro eyed Kostya who stood at a sink washing his hands. "I kidnapped your man over here because I wanted him to take me to Kiki's ex-wife. I interviewed inmates and guards who had contact with Kiki. I read letters he wrote to the fucked-up serial killer groupies who love him. I saw and heard the same thing again and again. He fucking hates that woman, and he'll do anything to see her one last time."

Ten curled his fingers into fists. The idea of Kiki sitting and daydreaming about torturing and murdering Nisha infuriated him. That sick freak had to go. Period. Full stop.

"I don't have to tell you how big and nasty a stain Adrian's connection to that filth left on us." Nikolai shifted his weight and pushed off the toolbox. He crossed the unit and took a good look at Alejandro's ear before calling out to Kostya in Russian. "It was a clean cut. Some of your better work."

"I try." Kostya approached with a sealed medical kit from a cabinet. Boychenko trailed behind, pushing a rolling metal tray like the ones used in emergency and operating rooms. Alejandro looked at the tray and flinched when Boychenko slipped on a pair of gloves. Kostya chortled. "What? I'm not going to cut on you again."

"You sure?" Alejandro nervously eyed the kit that Boychenko was opening.

"We're not animals," Kostya remarked. "I'm going to sew you up."

"Why?"

"We're going to need you, and I'd rather you not bleed all over my vehicles." He glanced at the kid who meticulously placed each piece from the kit onto the cloth-draped tray. "Besides, the kid hasn't mastered the art of properly cleaning upholstery yet."

Boychenko met Ten's gaze with a lopsided smile. "It's true."

Of all the men Kostya might have picked to train as a cleaner, Ten never would have chosen Roman Boychenko. He was young and kind and too nice for his own good. Yet, here he was, preparing for surgery on a man his mentor had just mutilated.

"How far did you get tracing the financiers?" Kostya wondered as he pulled on surgical gloves. Behind him, Boychenko stabbed a needle into a bottle of anesthetic and drew up a good amount into the syringe. He handed it over to Kostya who wasted no time jabbing the medication into Alejandro's head.

"All the way to Eastern Europe." Alejandro winced as Kostya moved the needle around the gaping wound where his ear used to be. "Romania."

"What happened in Romania?" Nikolai asked, stepping aside to get a better view of the man's face as they spoke.

"I tracked the IP address that was used to upload and sell the videos and photos of my daughter to a house there." Alejandro hissed as Kostya poked around his wound. "It was abandoned, and whoever had been there was gone. I could tell they had been running a fairly high-end operation."

"How?" Kostya asked and handed the empty syringe back to Boychenko.

"The wiring and the equipment left behind," Alejandro clarified. "Servers, meters of co-ax cable, fans, and overrides to the air conditioning units to keep the rooms cool. It was obvious someone had been spending big money to keep the equipment running around the clock."

"Fucking animals," Nikolai swore. "The ones selling it, and the ones buying it."

Kostya spoke softly to Boychenko in Russian. He gave the kid pointers on suturing, and Ten tuned it out. It wasn't that it made him squeamish, but he didn't want to hear it. He had enough nightmare fuel for a lifetime. Kostya talking about skin flaps was a phrase he didn't need in that pile.

"If we use Nisha as bait, you think Kiki will show himself?"

Ten snapped his attention to Nikolai. "Boss, I don't—."

Nikolai held up a hand, stalling him. "I asked Alejandro a question."

Neatly put in his place, Ten clenched his jaw. Alejandro answered honestly, "Yes, but the problem will be his handlers."

"If he's still with them," Kostya interjected. "Might be that Kiki has escaped them."

"Might be," Nikolai agreed.

"In which case, Nisha would be a very good lure to draw Kiki back to his handlers," Kostya continued. "Nothing like the promise of revenge to entice a man right back into danger."

"Even if we find Kiki, we might not find the financiers." Nikolai gestured to Alejandro who sat perfectly still as Kostya sutured his head. "And that means this man just lost an ear for nothing."

Kostya's phone began to ring on the far side of the unit. Stas lumbered over and answered it. "It's Ilya."

"What does he want?" Kostya asked, his focus on the suture he was tying.

"He says he found something in a tree outside Nisha's cabin."

"What do you mean?" Ten stalked toward Stas and snatched the phone from his hand. "Ilya? What the fuck is going on back there? Is Nisha okay? Are you with her?"

"Calm down," Ilya said in that annoying laid-back way of his. "She's making dinner. Eric is walking the perimeter."

"What do you mean you found something in a tree? What does that mean?" Ten gripped the phone and waited to hear the worst.

"Eric noticed it first. A glint of sunlight on a piece of metal or glass. It's a shooter, but he's not taking shots at us."

"He's watching?"

"Yeah."

"Bring me the phone," Kostya commanded. When Ten pressed it to Kostya's ear, the cleaner gave Ilya clear instructions to catch the intruder, if possible, but kill him if not. "And let the girl know Ten is safe."

Before Ten could give Ilya his own instructions, the call ended. Irritated, he glared at Kostya. "And then what? Ilya catches him and manages not to get shot and?"

"Wea have someone to interrogate," Kostya replied.

"And if that doesn't work? If he doesn't talk? If Ilya has to kill him?"

"There's always Chad411," Boychenko interrupted. He had been preparing a bandage for the wound and looked up as soon as he realized everyone was looking at him. "What?"

"Take Stas and go get him," Nikolai decided. "We'll arrange a rendezvous."

"Okay, boss." Boychenko looked entirely too excited to be sent on this errand.

Nikolai must have had second thoughts because he said, "Have Kir meet you before you make a move. You might need the extra set of hands."

Stas nodded. Boychenko wasn't the least bit deflated to have another older, bigger street soldier sent with him.

As soon as the kid was out the door and it clanged shut behind him, Nikolai shook his head and sighed. "He's like a fucking golden retriever…"

CHAPTER TWENTY-FOUR

*Y*OU'VE REALLY STEPPED *in the shit this time.*

Eric slowly walked the perimeter of the cabin for the third time in the last two hours. He didn't want to think about all the laws and rules he was breaking. Left and right, he was trampling them to keep his friend safe. He was risking his job and his reputation as a stand-up lawman, but he wouldn't have it any other way.

In all his years on the job, he had seen too many innocent people hurt because law enforcement was too slow to move. It wasn't incompetence or apathy on the part of his colleagues. It was the red tape and the bullshit laws that made it impossible to protect victims.

What good was a restraining order against a psycho with a gun who was pissed off because his wife finally had enough and wanted to leave? It wouldn't stop a bullet. It wouldn't stop angry fists.

Sometimes, Eric found himself fantasizing about taking the vigilante's way. Just pounding the absolute shit out of some dirtbag's face or pulling the trigger on a child rapist. Some people were unworthy of life, and it sickened him to see them walking free among good people, sniffing out their next bit of prey.

Nikolai's crew didn't have restrictions. They didn't have lawyers and judges tying up their hands behind their backs. They lived by their own code, and that code was going to keep Nisha alive.

For the second time in the last ten minutes, Eric detected the faintest shimmer of metal in the distance. He pretended not to see it and kept walking. It was someone with a weapon. Rifle probably. Aimed right at him as he moved.

But they hadn't taken a shot yet and didn't seem inclined to either.

They're watching us.

More and more, Eric believed there was something much bigger at play here. Kiki escaping his prison escort was the tip of the iceberg. The shooting that had killed Robin Harris and nearly ended Savannah and Chess began to feel like a distraction.

For a shooter to be able to pick the exact place and time where Nisha and the other women would be entering and exiting? To pick a vantage point and set up his equipment? That wasn't dumb luck. That was someone who had been tipped off by a leak inside law enforcement.

But who? Why?

The questions swirled around in his tangled thoughts as Eric finished his perimeter check. His keen investigative mind kept going back to Tony and Adrian. What Kiki had done was vile and sick, but it had clearly been something he did for his own benefit. He tortured and killed those women because it made him feel good.

Tony and Adrian kidnapped and molested those kids because it made them money. They were motivated by greed.

Mostly. Tony did seem to have a nasty taste for children. He was getting something other than money from it, but not Adrian. For Adrian, it was money and power.

When Vivian had been kidnapped by traffickers, Eric had gotten his first real look into that world. Walking around the warehouse and touring the shipping containers where those women had been kept was horrifying. He had known that world existed, but until he smelled it, felt the grit under his fingertips, he didn't *know*.

There was a whole other level to that hellish world beneath even that. Children. More than one of his colleagues had burned out in the sex crimes unit from being exposed to the trauma of child sexual abuse. Those were nightmares you couldn't unsee, and no amount of therapy was going to wipe their brains clean of those vomit-inducing photos and videos.

Someone had been paying Adrian for his work. As far as Eric knew from a mentor who worked that case, the FBI swooped in, grabbed all the evidence, and took jurisdiction. No one ever followed up locally, and the financiers and buyers of that filth were never caught.

Did Kiki know who they were? Was that his ace in the hole? His final bargaining chip? Did he want to trade that information to escape the needle?

What if he had been busted out by the traffickers? Not to rescue him and give him a new life in exchange for his silence, but to kill him and silence him completely?

Which made Nisha incredibly valuable.

If there was one thing in the whole wide world that would draw Kiki out of hiding, it was her. The woman he had groomed from childhood, beaten into submission and abused as a plaything. The woman who had reclaimed her power, told the world about his crimes and fought to have him put on death row where he belonged.

Yeah, Kiki would risk anything to get his hands on her.

When Eric stepped inside the cabin, he smelled something delicious. He found Nisha tending something on the stove. "Smells good."

"It's almost ready," she called back with a smile.

Ilya pocketed his phone and approached him. "Well?"

Eric nodded. "Still there."

"Well, if he wanted to kill you, he would have taken the shot by now."

"Yes." Eric glanced at Nisha who was far enough away she couldn't hear them talking in low voices over the stove's exhaust fan.

"Do you want to kill him or do you want me to do the honors?"

Eric snapped his attention right back to Ilya. "Are you insane? I may not be wearing my badge right now, but I'm still a fucking cop."

Ilya lifted both hands to placate him. "Say no more, friend. I'll handle it."

"Do you really think it needs to be handled this way?" Killing someone after they took a shot was one thing, but preemptively killing a man? That was something entirely different.

"Well, I could walk over and invite him in for dinner," Ilya suggested.

Eric scowled at him. "Fine. Go."

"I wasn't asking your permission, but thanks." Ilya gestured toward Nisha. "Keep her away from the windows. Keep her inside. If I'm not back—"

"Yeah, I know what to do," Eric assured him.

Ilya nodded and pivoted on his heel, striding toward the front door and out of the cabin. Eric followed, locked the door and set the alarm. He used the remote on the console table behind the couch to activate the blinds, drawing them down with a press of a button.

"Where did Ilya go?" Nisha asked, two plates in her hands.

"For a walk." Eric took one of the plates from her. "Thanks for dinner."

"Will he be back soon? I don't want his dinner to get cold."

"I'm sure he knows how to use a microwave."

She frowned at him. "That's not the point."

"He'll be back when he's back."

"All right. Fine. You don't have to be snippy." She joined him at the table. "You're worse than Wilford before he's had his breakfast."

Eric eyed the mean cat sitting on the back of the couch. The evil thing had swiped him at least six times today and tried to trip him on the stairs. "He looks like he could stand to skip a few breakfasts."

"He is not fat! He's just fluffy."

"If you say so."

"I do say so." She picked up her phone and checked it. "Still nothing from Ten."

"You know he's safe with his crew."

"I know he's safe, but why isn't he back here with me?" She toyed with her fork. "I don't like it. They're hiding something from me."

"Of course, they are. They're Russian mafia, Nisha. Everything they do is one big, dark secret." He studied her for a moment. "You understand that, right? That if you stay with Ten, you're going to be living on the fringes of that world. He'll never belong to you. He'll always be Nikolai's man first and yours second."

Nisha scowled. "I'm not stupid, Eric."

"Did I say you were?"

"Why are you talking down to me like I'm a child? I know what Ten is. I know what he does. I know who Nikolai is. I know all of this. I don't need you patronizing me like I'm some stupid little girl."

"I'm not trying to be condescending. I'm sorry if I came across that way." He reached for her hand and gave it a friendly squeeze. "I don't want to see you get hurt again."

"Ten would never hurt me that way."

"No, he wouldn't," Eric agreed, "but there are other ways to get hurt."

"I know," she said sadly. "But I love him."

Eric remembered another conversation, another time, when he heard Nisha profess her love for a man unworthy of her. Looking at her now, seeing the depth of her love for Ten reflected in her gaze, he understood that this time was different. What she felt for Kiki wasn't actually love. It was childish infatuation and then later abusive coercion. *This* was real, true love.

"Then I'll be happy for you, and I won't say another word about it." Eric squeezed her hand again before letting go and picking up his fork. He had learned his lesson with Vivian and the awful things he had said to her when she announced her engagement to Nikolai. He wasn't going to cause that same type of pain twice.

"Thank you, Eric."

They finished eating in companionable silence. Nisha picked up her phone every few minutes to check for a message, and he tried not to think about Ilya out there stalking the watcher. He kept his ears trained for the sound of a gunshot and tried not to rouse Nisha's suspicions when he surreptitiously checked his watch.

The sun was setting which meant Ilya was running out of daylight. What if the watcher got the drop on him? What if there was more than one man out there? What if Ilya was already dead?

He shuddered to think what Kostya would do to him. Eric didn't scare easily, but he knew better than anyone what that man had in his black bag. He knew all about the storage containers modified as interrogation chambers. He had zero interest in getting up close and personal with Kostya's dental tools.

The alarm beeped, and Eric jumped to his feet. He drew his weapon and quietly motioned for Nisha to crouch down and hide behind the kitchen counter. Carefully, he crept toward the door. The screen mounted above the alarm system control pad showed a clear view of the sensor that had been tripped. A black Suburban rolled down the road toward the cabin, still far enough away that he could grab Nisha and make a break for it.

His phone vibrated on the table, and he rushed back to grab it, figuring Kostya had also received notice of the tripped sensors.

It's us. Don't fucking shoot.

Eric huffed and typed his reply.

A phone call would have been nice.

"What's wrong?" Nisha asked, barely peeking her head over the top of the counter. "Should I get my gun from my luggage?"

"It's the cavalry." He pocketed his phone. "But, yeah, it probably wouldn't be a bad idea to have your weapon at hand. Criminals incoming and all that."

"Eric!" she chastised and shot to her feet. "Don't start trouble."

"Me?" He strode to the door to welcome their guests. "I wouldn't dream of it."

CHAPTER TWENTY-FIVE

WHEN TEN STORMED through the door, I nearly fainted. My legs got all wobbly, and I gripped the counter for support. He scanned for me, and as soon as he spotted me, he ate up the distance between us with powerful strides. "Anton!"

He wrapped both burly arms around me, crushing me in his embrace. "I'm here."

I gripped his shoulder and waist, refusing to let go. "I was so worried."

"I know." He kissed my cheek and my jaw. "I'm so sorry."

"It's okay." I leaned back enough to gaze up into his handsome face. "You're not hurt?"

"No, I'm not hurt." He dipped low and claimed my lips in a tender kiss. When he pulled back, he sighed. "You're going to be mad at me."

"Why?" I searched his face.

"I brought the man who kidnapped me." Ten's gaze shifted back to the front door where a man stood between Kostya and Eric. The man had dried blood on his neck and cheek, and a bandage over his ear. I didn't want to ask how he had been injured.

"Why?" I searched Ten's face, hoping against everything that he hadn't brought this man back here to kill him.

"Because he wants the same thing we do." Ten slid his hand along the curve of my back to settle just above my hip. "His name is Alejandro, and his daughter was JoJo Ochoa."

The mention of her name rattled me. I felt suddenly embarrassed standing there in front of a man who had lost his child to my psycho ex-husband. Unsure what to say or do, I took a few tentative steps toward him. "Alejandro, I'm so sorry."

"You don't have anything to apologize for," he said, his Mexican accent rolling over the syllables in a way that was smooth and lyrical. "You were also a victim."

"Yes, but not anymore." My gaze shifted to Kostya. His presence didn't bode well. "How is Holly? Tiara?"

"Holly is at the hospital with Savannah. She's still intubated and unconscious," Kostya said. "Tiara is with people I trust to keep her safe."

"I don't want her hurt."

Kostya actually looked affronted. "She won't be."

"Do you promise?" It was dangerous to push a man like Kostya, but I had to know for sure.

"I already promised Holly." Kostya leveled a stare, and I understood what he was saying. A promise to Holly was sacrosanct. "Tiara will be safe until we've finished this."

"And how are we going to finish this?" I looked at the men in the room. "Do I even want to know what the brain trust in front of me has planned?"

"You're not gonna like it," Eric remarked dryly. Whatever they planned, they must have informed Eric when he went outside to meet them. "I, for one, think it's a batshit crazy idea and too dangerous."

"She already suggested it," Alejandro interjected.

"Which you still haven't told us how you know that," Ten interrupted from behind me. I did a double-take at the sight of Wilford purring in his arms.

"I worked on a task force with the Rangers a few years ago," Alejandro explained. "I made good friends. One of those friends gave me a heads-up about what happened during her interview and the one with Francesca Mendoza."

Eric sneered. "Oh, that's fucking great. Law enforcement leaking information like a sieve!"

"Yes, but what's new?" Kostya ignored Eric's outburst. "Nisha, how far are you willing to go?'

I held his questioning gaze. He meant Kiki. "To the very end."

Wilford made a noise behind me, and Ten lowered him to the ground. The back door suddenly opened, and Ilya appeared with a bruised and bloodied man with hands zip-tied behind him. He shoved the man across the living room. "Look what I found!"

"Take him upstairs to the second bedroom," Kostya ordered. "I'll need to get my bag from the car."

The man Ilya had captured started to plead and cry, and I stood there absolutely shocked. I glared at Eric. Had he known? Is that why he had been so tetchy at dinner? He didn't want me to find out that Ilya was outside hunting a man. A man who probably wanted to kill me.

"Come on." Ten grabbed my hand, brooking no refusal, and tugged me toward him. "We need to talk."

As he led me across the cabin, I suspected there wasn't going to be much talking happening at all. When I stepped into the bedroom we had claimed as ours, he shut and locked the door behind us. He walked to the faux vintage radio on the dresser and flicked it on, turning up the volume. Otis Redding began to croon *I've Been Loving You Too Long*, and I couldn't help but think that was fate.

Ten's mouth crashed down on mine. Whimpering, I clutched at his arms, desperate for purchase as I tried not to fall. He slid one arm around my waist, hauling me up tight against him. The other cupped the back of my neck, holding me right where he wanted me as he plundered my mouth.

The smell of him, the taste of him, intoxicated me. My head spun, and I wondered if this was what Beyoncé meant when she sang about being drunk in love. "Anton."

"Do you want me to stop?" He kissed my cheek and my neck, and I gasped at the sensation of his teeth scraping over my pulse point.

"No. Don't."

"I need you." He walked me back toward the bed. "I need to be inside you."

There was something primal in the air. Ten exuded raw sexual lust, and I wanted him to take me, to ravish me, to find satisfaction in my body. Even though his hands were gentle, he wasn't careful with my clothing. He tugged and jerked and yanked until I was naked from the waist down, wearing only my faded and well-loved Alicia Keys tee.

"On your knees," he urged, and I scrambled to comply. My pussy throbbed, and my breasts ached as Ten stroked my bare ass and ran his hands along my thighs and hips. His fingers skimmed along my slit, and he groaned at the wetness he encountered there. "Look at how ready you are for me, Nisha."

I hit back a cry of pleasure as two of his thick fingers thrust into me. He worked them slowly in and out while the fingers of his other hand played with my clit.

"I promise when this is over, and we have more time, I'll make this up to you. You can sit on my face and drown me with your pussy juice." He gave my ass a playful slap. "But I can't wait anymore."

My face burned. The way he said such filthy things, the dirty compliments he gave me, made my pulse pound. He was wild and wicked, and he wanted me. He craved me. He needed me.

"Touch your clit for me." Ten unbuckled his belt and lowered his zipper. "Be a good girl and get yourself close."

I managed to shift my weight to one knee and rubbed my fingers over the pearl hidden there. It was so sensitive, and I knew without a doubt that Ten was going to make me lose my damned mind once he got inside me.

He dragged the head of his cock through my folds, slicking his skin with my arousal. He pressed into me, and I buried my face in the covers, refusing to let anyone else in the cabin know what we were doing in there.

But Ten didn't want quiet. He wanted me to make noise. He wanted everyone to know he was laying claim to me and that he could satisfy me like no one else.

His first thrust drew a soft cry from my lips, the second a gasp, and the third a keening wail. I didn't know how, but he felt bigger inside me, thicker and longer than this morning. Maybe he was more excited, more amped up, or maybe he just really got turned on by the sight of my bare ass slamming against his thighs.

I couldn't hold myself up with one hand and rub my clit with the other. His thrusts were too powerful, and it took every bit of my weight to push back and meet them. Otherwise, I was going to slide across the bed.

He gripped my hip in one big band and used the other to caress my back and shoulders. He set a pace that rocked me to the core, plunging in and out of me so fast I saw stars. I could feel his hands tightening on my body as he chased his climax. It wasn't a mean touch or an intimidating one. It was the grip of a man on the verge of losing control.

"Nisha!" He thrust deep, spilling into me, filling me with his cum. He rocked back and forth, milking the last bursts of joy, and then draped himself over me. He shoved my shirt up and out of the way, and kissed a line down my spine.

He withdrew slowly, carefully, and then pressed on my hip until I rolled onto my back. My pussy ached, and my clit pulsed. I wanted to come so bad.

Before I could vocalize my need, Ten was on his knees, pushing my thighs apart. I cried out in shock as he descended on my pussy. His tongue lashed my clit, suckling and fluttering until I thought my heart was going to explode.

"Anton." I gripped a handful of his hair. "Anton!"

He growled like a starving man and devoured my cunt, showing me with his tongue how much my pleasure meant to him. I climaxed with a moan, shoving my pussy against his mouth in a desperate bid to make it last.

When it was over, I covered my face with both hands and tried to catch my breath. Ten kissed my inner thighs and my belly before rising to his full height and striding into the bathroom to tidy his face and fix his clothing. I didn't even try to move. I stayed there, basking in the afterglow of being reclaimed by him.

"Get dressed when you can." He leaned over me and kissed me tenderly. His face and beard smelled of hand soap which made me blush when I considered why. "Stay in here until I come to get you."

"I will." I had no desire to overhear whatever was happening with the man Ilya had caught. The reminder of that situation killed what was left of my afterglow. The ugly reality hit me hard, and I forced myself to get up and take care of the mess between my legs.

He came inside me.

The realization didn't upset me. In the throes of passion, neither of us had been thinking about slowing down and being careful. I was nearing the end of my cycle. My period tracking app had alerted me Aunt Flo was due in four days. My cycles were like clockwork, and the risk of pregnancy was basically zero.

There were other concerns, obviously, and we would have to discuss that as soon as possible. Not that I didn't trust Ten to keep me safe, but I had to be clear that this could not happen again until I had his test results right in front of me.

After I tidied up and slipped back into my clothes, I noticed that even though the sex had been aggressive I didn't hurt. I felt relaxed and languid. With Kiki, it had never been that way. It had always been painful. With Ten, it was nothing but pleasure.

I reached over to straighten the covers on the bed, but something outside caught my eye. The blinds in the bedroom had been pulled down earlier by Eric with the remote, but I could see a strange red glow outside.

Curious but with trepidation, I slowly walked over to the French doors that opened onto a private patio. Otis Redding continued to croon, this time *My Lover's Prayer*, and I wondered if I should turn it down. The thought of hearing whatever was happening with the man Ilya had dragged into the cabin stopped me.

At the door, I gently pulled aside the gauzy drape and parted two wooden blind slats. The red glow came into focus, and I couldn't quite make sense of it at first.

Was it a bird? No. Not a bird. It hovered not far from the cabin, just under a tree, and the red glow of what looked like three eyes was fixed on my window.

It was a drone.

I opened my mouth to shout Ten's name, but it was too late. Gunshots erupted. I couldn't tell if they started inside the cabin or outside. I screamed and flung myself to the floor, scrambling for a place to hide. It was like being in the middle of a war zone. Glass shattered. Men shouted. Rapid gunfire left my ears ringing.

I crawled toward the bed, away from the French doors, but I wasn't fast enough. There was a sudden explosion of glass and wood. I turned my head and screamed at the sight of two men in black SWAT-type uniforms on the other side of the now gaping hole in the room. One of them had a sledgehammer, and he slammed it into the remaining fragments of the glass panes and wooden supports.

He dropped the hammer, picked up the rifle hanging from his shoulder, and began to rapidly fire at the door to the bedroom. No one could make it through that suppressing gunfire. I was caught and at their mercy.

His partner rushed into the room, grabbed me by the back of my hair, and painfully hauled me to my feet. I shrieked in agony, certain I was being scalped, and tried to fight him off. He popped me right in the mouth, and I stumbled back a step. Blood poured from my busted lips, and my vision danced from the blow.

He curled his gloved fingers tighter into my hair and shoved me down until I was bent at the waist. He marched me through the broken glass and wooden splinters, and my bare feet took the brunt of the punishment. I didn't dare slow down or try to escape. The hand that wasn't in my hair had a gun pressed to my temple. He would blow my head off if I so much as twitched.

A loud *thwapping* sound echoed in the night. A helicopter. Louder than the gunfire. Louder than the shouts from the cabin behind me. More men jumped out of the helicopter and began to fire their powerful rifles at the cabin. I was hustled up into the helicopter, shoved into a seat, and quickly belted into place.

The men scrambled back inside the helicopter, all the while firing at the cabin. Through the haze of tears and blood, I stared at the cabin, now aglow with fire. Ten! Wilford! Eric! Ilya! Kosyta!

How many of them had been shot? All of them? Were they badly injured? Were they dead?

Oh, God. No. No. Not again. Not again. Please.

Death and destruction followed me wherever I went. Savannah. Chess. Robin Harris. The salon. Ten kidnapped. The cabin shot to hell and now engulfed in flames.

This is all my fault.

I'm a curse.

Maybe it would be better for everyone if I didn't survive the night.

CHAPTER TWENTY-SIX

SHOULDER BURNING, TEN groaned and reached over to touch the wound. A through-and-through, he realized, as he probed the injury. *I'll survive.*

As he clambered to his feet, he coughed. Smoke was heavy in the air, and it irritated his lungs. He spotted Kostya at a window, trading gunfire with someone outside the cabin. The cleaner glanced at him and then kicked one of the M4 Carbine rifles toward him. "*Davai!*"

Ignoring the pain in his shoulder, Ten picked up the rifle, checked that it was loaded, and then used the butt of it to knock out the glass in the window on the far end of the room. He used the wall for cover, sighted a man firing at the cabin, and squeezed the trigger. He missed the first shot but hit the second.

As he continued to fire, the only thing on his mind was Nisha. She was downstairs, probably still in the bedroom, terrified and unprotected. He needed to get to her, but he couldn't abandon Kostya or this vantage point.

"Get down to the ground floor. Get Nisha!" Kostya shouted over the hail of gunfire.

Ten didn't stick around to argue. He fired three more rounds before rushing to the door, hopping over the dead body in the center of the room. The man Ilya had captured hadn't been killed by them. A stray bullet through the window, when the gunfire erupted, had gone right through his brain.

He snatched another magazine from the ammo box Kostya had produced from a cabinet at the first gunshot. He crept down the floating stringer stairs and found Ilya firing out the sliding glass door that faced the rear of the property where the attack stemmed. Ilya noticed him and gave a series of hand signals.

Ten nodded and moved toward the bedroom where he had left Nisha. The smoke was thicker here and caustic. He heard coughing and gagging, but he couldn't see through the oily black cloud. This wasn't a normal fire. This had been started by the attackers to keep them away from the bedroom.

His heart stuttered, and it hurt to breathe. Was she already dead on the other side of the door? Shot? Left to bleed alone in a haze of smoke as flames licked at her skin? Was she crying out for him? Terrified?

He nearly tripped over Eric Santos and Alejandro. The detective had taken a nasty bullet to the gut and another to the chest. Alejandro had taken a blast to the face, killing him instantly. He had fallen against the door, his blood and brains smeared down the wood.

Through the burning smoke, Ten could see the men had been trying to get to Nisha, to save her. Ten's failure to protect the woman he loved had caused Alejandro his life. It was a debt he could never repay.

"Eric?" Ten carefully shifted the man upright. "Eric? Can you hear me?"

"Took her," Eric groaned. "Took Nisha."

Ten's stomach dropped. He swallowed down the bile that threatened to erupt from his throat. "She was alive?"

"Think...yes?" Eric's head lolled, and Ten wasn't sure how much time the detective had left. If the blood loss didn't kill him, the smoke sure as hell would.

As he lifted Eric from the floor, he gritted his teeth against the tearing pain in his shoulder. Awash in agony, he heard the unmistakable chop of helicopter blades. From the living room, Ilya shouted, "They've got Nisha. They're putting her in a helicopter."

Ten couldn't believe this was happening. It was a nightmare he couldn't escape. With Eric in his arms, he kicked the locked bedroom door, shattering what was left of the wood pocked with bullet holes. He stepped into the bedroom, took in the gaping hole where the French doors had been, and roared with fury and anguish.

There, far in the distance, he could just make out the shape of a helicopter. Men spilled out of it, all of them armed to the teeth. He couldn't chase after her, not with Eric in his arms bleeding to death and all those rifles pointed at him.

The hardest thing he ever did was turn away from the hole and dart back into the hallway with Eric.

Gunfire tore through the cabin, and he flinched as bullets snapped and pinged all around him. He rushed down the hallway and met Kostya who had called Ilya back from the sliding door.

Grabbing his shirt, Kostya forced Ten to look at him. "We'll get her back."

"We fucking better," Ten warned, his temper hanging by a thread.

"We will." Kostya let go of the fistful of the shirt he held and checked Eric. "Ilya, call 9-1-1. Get the police here immediately. Drive toward the main highway so EMS can intercept you."

"And then?" Ilya asked, clearly not enjoying the thought of being the focus of an investigation.

"Fucking lie," Kostya said as if it was the most obvious thing in the world. "You and Eric were out here with Nisha. Ten is still in Houston. He went to see his PO. He didn't come back. The man upstairs broke into the house first and then the others attacked."

"That's not going to explain all the shots fired from inside the cabin," Ilya warned.

"I guess they'll have to work overtime figuring it out," Kostya remarked coldly. He seemed to finally realize they were short one man. "Where is the Mexican?"

"Dead," Ten said. "Bullet to the brain. Outside the bedroom."

Kostya nodded and glanced at Ilya. "He can be an attacker or a friend. Your choice."

"A friend," Ten insisted, refusing to allow Alejandro's memory to be tarnished.

"Sure." Ilya's mouth settled into a grim line. "Can we go now? Before we all die from smoke inhalation and Eric bleeds out?"

Ten situated Eric in the front seat of Ilya's vehicle. Kostya grabbed his first aid kit and jammed trauma dressings against the wounds while Ilya called 9-1-1. Ten had never heard Ilya pretend to be afraid, but the man had the makings of an Oscar-winning actor.

"Let's go." Kostya grabbed Ten by the back of the shirt and hauled him away from the scene. "We need to move."

Ten climbed into the front seat of Kostya's vehicle. The fire raged through the cabin, lighting up the inky black sky. He didn't know if the police would believe a word Ilya said. If Eric woke up and told them something different, it would cause problems.

Problems I can't worry about right now.

Ten braced himself on the door as Kostya took a turn like a stunt driver from the *Fast & the Furious* franchise. "Fuck! Kostya!"

"Calm down." Kostya pointed at the glove box. "Grab the phone with the red tape on the back. Find Fox in the contacts. Tell her I want all the real-time FAA data and heliport traffic within a 500-mile radius of Houston. She needs to find the helicopter that was in Brazos County fifteen minutes ago. I want our men waiting for me at the warehouse. Stage the spiders at Sunny's. Get the word on the street that we're paying good money for intel on Kiki or Nisha."

Ten did as Kostya instructed, talking to the same woman he had spoken to earlier that day. It felt like a lifetime ago now. She didn't have any witty questions tonight. She took the message and ended the call without a single word.

"Send a text to Boychenko. I want an update on Chad. Then call Nikolai. Let him know what's happened."

Ten didn't relish that thought. After he sent Boychenko a text, he dialed the boss on his private line.

"Kostya."

"No, it's Ten."

"Ten?" There was rustling in the background. Nikolai's

tone grew concerned. "What's wrong?"

"We were attacked at the cabin. It's on fire. Eric is badly hurt. Ilya is taking him to the hospital. The Mexican is dead. I don't know how many we killed firing back. At least one," Ten said, thinking of the man upstairs. "And they took Nisha."

Nikolai muttered a string of profanity. "That's it. We're finishing this my way."

"Kostya has Fox gathering everyone at the warehouse."

"Fine. I'm going to see Nickel Jackson after I call Besian and Diego."

The call ended, and Ten almost felt bad for the idiots behind the attack and kidnapping of Nisha. Nikolai didn't only have pull locally. He had pull internationally, and the long tentacles of Maksim Prokhorov's criminal family could reach out and strangle anyone.

"He's going to see Nicky Jackson after he calls Besian and Diego."

"Good." Kostya took another hairpin turn, and Ten pushed his foot against the floorboard to keep himself from sliding. Kostya glanced back and frowned. "Do you hear that?"

"Hear what?" Ten shifted in his seat to see if they were being followed. He listened intently but heard nothing.

"I keep hearing something scratching back behind us."

Ten frowned. "Scratching?"

"I know I'm losing my mind now because I thought I heard meowing while you were talking to Nikolai."

Ten's pulse spiked. "Wilford! Oh, shit. I forgot him. I left him. Nisha will never forgive me if—."

Rowowowoww.

Ten froze. "I heard that."

"See? I'm not crazy!"

"Wilford? Wilford!" Ten called for the cat, hoping and praying the mean fluffball had stowed away in Kostya's SUV when the cargo door had been open. It would have been easy for the cat to jump into the back while Kostya was ferrying first aid supplies between vehicles. "Wilford!"

The white beast yowled pitifully and poked his head up over the back seat. He howled and whined as Ten cajoled him to come closer. Eventually, the cat decided he could trust Ten and scampered across the seats.

"Oh, you crazy fucking cat." Ten cuddled the fluffy demon in his arms, earning a quick bite in the process. "Asshole," he grumbled and stroked the cat's dirty fur. "I'm going to forgive and forget about that bite because of what you just survived."

The cat turned its gaze upon Kostya. His hackles rose, and he hissed and spit.

"Keep that thing away from me," Kostya warned. "I can't stand cats."

"Yeah, well, he clearly doesn't like you either." Ten scratched between Wilford's ears. "We're going to get your mom back. I promise."

"Okay, that's it." Kostya shook his head. "You have to stop working for Vivian. Look at you? Cuddling a cat and talking to it like it's a baby. It's disgusting."

Ten ignored Kostya's barbs, fully aware the cleaner was trying to rile him up and keep him from getting maudlin as they prepared for what was sure to be a bloody night. "I'll remember that when you're holding your first baby with Holly."

Kostya's gaze jerked away from the road. "Do I look like

father material to you?"

"You've taken care of your spiders like a father."

"Yeah, and what a dysfunctional mess our little family cobweb is!"

"Holly's mother was far worse than you." He was one of the few who knew the full score with regard to Holly and her parents. "Frances," he clarified, "and Holly turned out fine."

"Okay. We're done talking about this." Kostya slashed his hand through the air, and Wilford followed it with his predatory gaze. "You just sit there and hold your cat while I drive."

Ten smirked and glanced out the window as the Texas countryside blew by in a blur. Somewhere out there, Nisha was scared and helpless.

Did she know he would move heaven and earth to find her? Did she believe that he would do anything to save her?

Does she know how much I love her?

CHAPTER TWENTY-SEVEN

TEN RUBBED HIS aching head. *This is pointless.*

A dozen feet away, Podcaster Chad was tied to a chair, blubbering and bawling like a baby. Boychenko, Kir, and Stas had encountered zero problems obtaining him from his house and bringing him here to answer questions. He had already pissed himself, and he hadn't experienced anything more than a couple of slaps from Stas.

Kostya pinched the bridge of his nose. "Chad, if I have to open my black bag, you're really, really not going to like it."

"Please," Chad begged, snot running down his face. "Please. I'm sorry."

"Yeah, we've heard the apologies." Kostya sighed. "We don't care about any of that. We want to know what you know about Nisha Jackson, Kiki Acevedo, Chess Mendoza, Tony Guerrero, or Adrian Umansky. This is a give-and-take. Okay? You give me information, and I don't take pieces off of you."

Chad wailed. "I'll tell you anything you want."

"He already told you what he wants!" Stas shouted right in Chad's ear, and the idiot started to sob even louder.

Ten hated this side of their world. It was messy and violent and successful maybe six out of ten times. Kostya would say that was still better than half, but he wasn't so sure it was worth all the trouble. And, anyway, where the hell was the boss?

Fox had given Kostya information, but it wasn't as helpful as they had hoped. She managed to locate the helicopter, but it had dipped below the radar for a while. When it appeared again, it was headed in a different direction. Kostya figured they had set down in a field somewhere, handed off Nisha, and taken flight again. They were no closer to finding her, and nothing in the file he had received from Pete was useful either.

Fox was now back at Chad's place, going through his computer and external hard drives looking for clues. They hadn't heard from her yet, and Ten wasn't sure she would find anything that could point them in the right direction.

"I didn't know it would go like this." Chad finally started to offer something useful. "I was only supposed to be the go-between for the lawyer and the guards she wanted to be paid off to get Kiki out of prison."

"Why?"

"I didn't ask why she wanted him out of prison."

"That's not what—." Kostya huffed. "Why did *they* pick *you* to be the intermediary?"

"I don't know."

"Maybe they knew he was a greedy prick who wanted to make a name for himself from other people's pain," Stas suggested. "Running around, shoving cameras in people's faces when they're in the worst moment of their lives. Chasing down families in front of hospitals. Live-streaming women bleeding to death in front of a goddamned police station to get views."

"It's just a job," Chad weakly defended himself. "It's how I pay my bills."

"Do you?" Kostya wondered. "Can you pay your bills with what you earn?"

"Yes."

"So, if I have my spiders look through your financial records, I'm not going to find anything interesting?"

"Well, look," Chad hurriedly clarified, "they paid me. A lot."

"Uh-huh." Kostya reached for his black bag. "Okay. Time for the taking part since you're not giving anything useful."

"Wait! Please! Don't! Please! I know where they're located! The men who paid me!"

Kostya paused with his hand inside his bag. "Where?"

"Dubai!"

Kostya narrowed his eyes. "Your money came from there?"

"No, the money came from Switzerland. It went into a bank account in the Bahamas."

"So, why do you say they're in Dubai?"

"I…" Chad turned his weasel eyes toward the floor. He was caught in a lie, and he didn't know how to get himself out of it.

Ten glanced at Kostya who clearly had the same thought. What was he hiding? What was worse than taking money to break a serial killer out of prison?

Kostya's phone buzzed and vibrated across the table next to his bag. He picked it up and answered, "Yeah? I see. I see. I'm sorry. I would never have asked you to look if I thought—. No, no, that's fine. Please. Do whatever you need to do. I'm sorry."

Ten furrowed his brow. What was that about?

Kostya set aside his phone. His gaze had turned steely and cold. He glowered with disgust. "Fox found your secret, Chad."

The man sobbed, a hacking, agonized wail of shame and fear. Whatever that secret was, he must have known it would cost him his life. "I can't help it. I'm sorry. I've tried. I really have. I went to therapy, but I can't stop. I can't."

"You haven't tried our brand of therapy yet." Kostya started to take off his watch, likely because he didn't want to have to clean the blood off the expensive face later. "I bet we can cure you." He placed his watch next to his phone. "*Pederast.*"

Ten went rigid. He sneered at the filthy sack of shit tied to that chair. Kostya's one-sided conversation with Fox made sense. She had found evidence, videos of children being sexually abused, on Chad's home computers. Of course, that was how they had blackmailed him.

Before Kostya could start in on Chad, someone forcefully banged on the rolling metal door at the far end of the warehouse. Ten gestured for Boychenko and Kir to answer. The kid pulled the long chain, raising the door slowly, and revealing Nikolai in jeans which he typically only wore when he was forced to get up after settling in for the night with his wife and child. There was a man standing next to the boss in tactical pants and a black T-shirt.

"Gabe!" Kostya forgot his business with Chad. "Boss?"

Gabe? Ten was taken aback when he realized the man standing there was none other than Gabe Reyes, the older brother of Diego and Nate who had been a highly decorated Marine. There had been trouble in Houston when the other boys were younger, and Gabe had been forced to flee south of the border.

When he was in prison, Ten had heard whispers of an American hitman working off a debt down there. He'd heard Gabe's name in those same rumors. Now he believed them.

"I told you I was going to do things my way." Nikolai crossed the warehouse as Boychenko closed the rolling door. "I called in a favor from Moscow, and now Gabe has a contract."

Gabe walked close to Nikolai's side, his practiced gaze scanning the room. Ten caught and held the other man's gaze. Gabe approached him and held out his scarred, rough hand. "I'm sorry about your girl, man."

"Yours, too." Nisha had mentioned Savannah begging her to tell Gabe, and here he was, in the flesh. "How is she?"

"Not well." Gabe turned his murderous gaze toward Chad. "Is this the worm that filmed Savannah bleeding out on the steps?"

Kostya nodded. "He's also a client who likes the sort of movies that Adrian Umansky and Tony Guerrero filmed."

"That so?" Gabe leaned down to look Chad in the eye. "You know my little sister lost a friend to those two dirtbags. They found his bones in that pile out behind their shack. She still cries about it, and it makes her terrified for her son, my nephew."

"Please," Chad pleaded. "Please, I didn't hurt any of those kids."

"They wouldn't make that shit if it wasn't for animals like you." Gabe punched Chad, burying his fist in the man's stomach. He rose slowly. "Make sure to save a piece of this for me."

"I will." Kostya reached for his watch and draped it back over his wrist. "Boychenko, you're staying here with Kir."

"Stas," Nikolai addressed the grizzled fighter who had joined their ranks all the way from Brighton Beach. "I'd appreciate it if you would go back to my house and keep an eye on my wife and son."

Stas nodded. "Yes, boss."

"Don't let her do anything silly like try to drive to College Station to see Eric," Nikolai warned. "Sergei is with her right now, but he's a soft touch when it comes to Vivian."

"I understand."

As Stas left on his mission, Gabe said, "We move in two minutes. I'll brief on the drive."

"How far?" Ten wondered, hating that he still had no idea how long it would be until he saw Nisha again.

"Sour Lake. An hour if we push it."

"Then we better push it." Ten walked to the cabinet where Kostya kept gear and grabbed the only bulletproof vest that would fit him.

"Anton." Nikolai's use of his real name startled Ten.

"Yeah?" He stared at the boss, wondering what was so important.

"If you go and you get caught," he warned.

"I know."

"It's a big risk."

"I know."

"Two years from your original sentence and probably more for the weapons charge," Nikolai continued. "And that's if they don't catch you on a scene surrounded by dead bodies."

"I know."

Nikolai studied him and then nodded. "As long as you know."

"Don't worry, boss." Ten reached for a high-powered rifle from the rack. "My grandmother said I was born lucky."

"*V sorochkeh roditsa*," Nikolai guessed.

"Yeah. That's me. Born in a shirt." He thought of her, back in her apartment in Moscow, enjoying her afternoon tea. If he made it through this, he was going to find a way to get the two women he loved most together. Baba Olya would adore Nisha.

"Let's hope that luck holds out." Nikolai clapped him on the back. "If you don't come back in one piece, I'll never hear the end of it from Vivian. Don't consign me to that fate."

Ten grinned. "You tell Vivian I'll be on your doorstep, bright and early on Monday."

As he grabbed the rest of his gear, Ten vowed that was a promise he would keep.

CHAPTER TWENTY-EIGHT

M Y FIRST HELICOPTER ride was nothing like I had expected. It had always been on my bucket list of things to do. Usually right under LOSE ONE HUNDRED POUNDS and GO TO HAWAII. I had seen plenty of videos on social media of tourists riding helicopters around Hawaii or other tropical locales. I wanted to do that someday.

If I survive tonight...

That seemed less and less likely as the helicopter stayed in the air. Wherever we were going, it wasn't nearby. Even if Ten and the others had survived the shootout and the fire, they were so far behind I wasn't sure they could catch up in time. If they did manage it, then what? Another shootout? More death?

Please be alive, Anton. Please be okay.

I had the same thoughts for Ilya and Eric and even scary old Kostya who Holly loved more than anything.

Holly.

Did she know? Was she sitting next to Savannah, scared out of her mind that Kostya was dead? Would she blame me? Could she ever forgive me for being the cause of so much hurt? I was the reason the salon had been vandalized and burned. Now, I was the reason her man was hurt—or worse.

The tears on my face felt cool with the rush of night air swirling in the cabin of the helicopter. My feet hurt so badly. They throbbed and stung, and a pool of blood had gathered beneath my injured soles. I desperately wanted to bend down and pick out the glass and splinters, but I worried that one move would earn a slap.

The men surrounding me ignored me completely, their faces hidden behind their tactical masks. Their efficiency with their weapons convinced me they were professionals. These men would kill me and move right on with their lives as if I was nothing more than a bug in their way to be crushed.

Where are we going? Why did they take me?

This wasn't about Kiki. There was something else at play, something I couldn't even fathom. Whatever it was, if I didn't figure out what they wanted and quickly, I wasn't going to see the sunrise. As much as I wanted to get lost in self-pity and call myself a curse, I didn't actually want to die.

I have to fight.

I want to live.

I wanted to cuddle up on Ten's couch and listen to him read one of his favorite books while Wilford sat behind us, flicking his tail and purring.

Wilford.

Of everyone who had been in the house when the attack started, Wilford seemed the most likely to have survived without a scratch. I had watched him stalk enough frogs and crickets and run from a loose dog in our neighborhood to know he could book it when necessary. He was a villainously smart cat, and he would have gone straight outside the first chance he got. Hopefully, he was hiding up a tree somewhere, waiting out the danger.

The helicopter made a sudden turn, and I clutched at the hard metal seat where I had been installed. We swooped left and then right before the helicopter dipped down and leveled off. My stomach pitched wildly, and I was sure I would be sick if the pilot did any crazier maneuvers.

Slowly, the helicopter lost altitude in a controlled descent. We touched down finally in the middle of a pasture. The rotors were still spinning fast as the men spilled out of the contraption. Two of them hauled me up by my arms and forced me to jump. I landed awkwardly on my bloody, injured feet and cried out in pain.

"Hush!" A man snarled in my face. He grabbed the back of my hair, and I knew from his grasp it was the same man who had captured me in the cabin. I scurried to keep up with his quick pace as he rushed me across the pasture to a waiting SUV. I was shoved inside, a hand slapping my ass in the meanest way, and I fell forward onto the middle seat.

Hissing in pain, I lifted my throbbing feet off the floor-board. I could feel the jagged bits of glass and splinters poking from the bottoms. Desperate and ready to accept whatever punishment was doled out, I lifted my left foot onto my right knee. All those Pilates classes finally came in handy, and I was limber enough despite my size to do what needed to be done.

Carefully, I picked out the glass and splinters I could feel. There were smaller ones embedded too deeply, but I managed to get the worst ones. I switched feet, hissing and biting back whimpers with each chunk of glass or wood I pulled from my skin. I had two pieces to go when the doors to the vehicle opened again and men started to climb on either side of me. I hurriedly plucked those last two shards of glass and tossed them behind me with the others.

Gingerly, I lowered my bloody feet to the floorboard and placed my dirty, grimy hands on my knees. Squashed between the two intimidating men, I tried not to move or even breathe too loudly. I wanted to sink into the upholstery and disappear.

I wasn't that lucky or magically gifted.

The man who seemed to like pulling my hair now sat on my right. He kept his fingers curled in my hair, winding the strands around his fingers. I clenched my teeth, refusing to cry out and show him how much he was hurting me. I blocked out the nasty, racist shit he said to his friends about my hair.

I hope Ten beats the dog piss out of you.

I glanced surreptitiously in the man's direction, using the flash of light from the driver opening and closing his door to memorize details about my tormentor's uniform. His exposed forearms revealed tattoos, one of them a set of lightning bolts and the other a strange skeleton head that gave me big white supremacist vibes.

Of course.

I sank inside myself, going into a calm, quiet place where I was safe. I remembered all the mantras and affirmations my therapist had taught me over the years.

I am strong.

I am brave.

I am worthy.

I have a purpose.

I own my power, and no man can take it from me.

I repeated those silent affirmations again and again. The vehicle carrying me left the field and turned onto a darkened highway. I didn't recognize anything outside the windshield. Wherever we were, it wasn't a place I had ever visited. We were still in Texas. Of that much, I was sure. The road signs were all TxDOT-issued.

We drove for almost an hour before nearing our destination. Lightning Bolts shoved my head down toward my knees, preventing me from seeing any signs or structures. Maybe that meant they were going to let me live. I wouldn't be able to identify where I had been, but I would be alive.

Or he was just playing mind games.

It was hard to breathe bent in half like that, but I didn't complain. I closed my eyes and returned to my mantras and affirmations. I inhaled slowly and kept the panic at bay.

When we finally stopped, and I was allowed to sit up straight again, I hid how desperately I needed a full breath. I drew in a measured, deliberate amount of air and exhaled just the same. I wasn't going to let that bastard know how much he was hurting me.

I own my power, and no man can take it from me.

I was dragged out of the SUV like a sack of potatoes. I winced when my bare feet hit the gravel. I looked around the strange place they had brought me. It was some sort of industrial facility. From the harsh smell of chemicals, I deduced it was a production plant of some kind. That made me think we were still relatively close to Houston. North or south, I couldn't say, but close.

Lightning Bolts pushed me forward, and I managed not to stumble. He steered me with the handful of my hair he kept in his grip. My scalp had gone mostly numb from the tension. If I didn't end up with a bald spot, I would be shocked.

He shoved me toward a rusty metal building. The interior was damp, and there was so much noise I grimaced. Large machines clicked and hummed. The scent of exhaust filled the air. I didn't want to breathe too deeply. How much carbon monoxide was I inhaling? Too much, I figured, more than was safe.

He marched me across the building and through a set of double doors. He purposely banged my body into them, using my breasts and hip to force the heavy doors apart. I bit back another cry of pain.

Finally, he let go of my hair. He kicked my backside with his booted foot, and I tumbled forward onto the filthy concrete floor. I landed on my hands and knees, and my jaw rattled from the impact. I hurried to get back on my feet. Experience with Kiki had taught me that staying down was a sure way to end up with a broken rib or two.

"You stay in here until he comes." Lightning Bolts left me there in the dimly lit space.

He? Who the fuck is he?

Kiki.

It had to be him they were expecting. I was the prize he had been promised.

I looked around, trying to figure out if I could escape. There were windows up high, but I couldn't reach or fit through them. I tried the only door, shoving aside heavy plastic drums to get my fingers on the handle. It was locked from the outside, effectively trapping me in here.

This was some sort of rarely used maintenance storage room. I hurried to the shelves and started looking at the various bottles stored there. Solvents, detergents, and all manner of wickedly dangerous chemicals. If I wanted to make a bomb or mustard gas, I was in luck, but I didn't think that was really the safest option here.

What am I going to do?

I put my hand on the rickety metal shelf and lowered my forehead. The shelf wobbled, and I gripped it tighter to keep it from collapsing and spilling those chemicals. As I did, I felt a piece of the shelf come free. The jagged length of metal wasn't exactly the best weapon I could hope for, but it was something. The sharp end of it would make quick work of human skin.

I need a handle.

My gaze landed on a pile of dirty old rags. I grabbed two and wound them around the makeshift metal weapon. I gave the shaft of the piece a testing bend. It wasn't very strong, and I doubted it would get more than one or two good jabs before it snapped. The shorter length would still be useful for stabbing, but I needed something else.

The chemicals.

I knew enough about chemistry to decide which were the safest and which were much too dangerous to even consider. I picked out two bottles and stared at them. How would I use them? Take the lid off and throw it in my attacker's face? It would be difficult to control the liquid, and I would be at risk of getting splashed or inhaling the fumes.

Last resort, I decided. If it came to that, and there was no other way I could survive, I would use the chemicals.

I walked the perimeter of the room looking for more weapons. I found a broom handle that I stowed in a place I could reach easily. Before I hid it, I glanced at the double doors that were guarded by two of the men who had taken me from the cabin. They kept their backs to me, but I didn't want to risk them catching me squirreling away weapons.

There were a few more violent implements I scavenged—a length of pipe, a screwdriver, a hammer. I hid them around the room, making sure they weren't evident to anyone but me. The dim light in the smelly old room helped.

Tired and thirsty, I sat down against the wall and waited. For what, I didn't know. Pain, probably. Fear. Torment. Despite those troubling thoughts, the exhaustion of the last few days took hold, and I nodded off to sleep. For how long I couldn't be sure. A while, it seemed. Long enough that I felt a surge of energy when the sound of the doors being unlocked woke me.

I clambered to my feet and grimaced at the pain caused by the pressure of the dirty floor against my wounds. I nervously eyed the nearby pipe and the length of jagged metal I had hidden. Two steps to the right or five steps to the left. Whichever direction was safest, I could protect myself.

The doors lurched open, and the sound of shuffling feet filled the space. Like a paralysis demon from my nightmares, Kiki appeared in front of me. My gaze locked with his, the swirling pits of his demonic eyes boring right into my soul.

But as he shuffled into the room, the fear I had expected didn't come. He wasn't the big, mean monster I remembered. Gaunt, sallow, waxy—he looked like a Halloween prop.

"You really are sick," I said, remembering what Eric had told me about the prison moving Kiki to a hospital unit.

"And you got big as a whale," Kiki snarled meanly. "Look at you." He curled his lip. "You're fucking disgusting. I bet you can't even find your pussy underneath all those rolls of fat hanging off your stomach." He pointed a trembling finger in my direction. "This is exactly what I warned you would happen. I told you without me there to keep you in line you would turn lazy and fat."

"Are you done?" I asked, no longer moved by his cruel jabs. "Or do you want to keep throwing verbal stones this way?"

"Well, look at you," he mocked with a laugh. "Standing up to me finally. How much did that shiny new spine cost?"

"More than you can ever imagine." And I wasn't talking about money.

"I'll never forgive you for that." Kiki scowled menacingly. "You killed my baby."

"*You* killed *my* baby," I corrected. "You strangled me and beat me and then shot me through a fucking door."

Kiki rolled his eyes. "Always with your hysterics. None of that would have happened if you hadn't tested me! All I ever did was try to help you be a better woman, but you and that thick fucking head of yours were unteachable."

"What's it like living in this fantasy land you've built for yourself?" I waved my hand in his direction. "Do you actually believe the garbage you spew, or do you just keep repeating stupid shit because you don't have anything else worthwhile to say?"

"When you've spent almost a decade in solitary, locked away in a cell with only an hour of sunlight and fresh air a day, you can talk to me about building fantasies."

"You put yourself there. Not me."

"Loyalty, Nisha!" Kiki shouted, and I could see the spray of spittle from his lips. "You were my wife! You were supposed to be loyal to me!"

"You were my abuser! You were a murderer! You didn't just kill my baby. You killed those girls. You cut off their penises and testicles and kept them in a fucking box in a shed in the backyard! You are a monster!" I spread my hands in front of me. "And I don't owe you a fucking thing, least of all loyalty."

"I was helping them!" Kiki screamed at me. "I was giving them what they wanted! I took away the most disgusting parts of them and made them the perfect little girls they wanted to be!"

I reeled back in horror. In all the years since Kiki had committed his crimes, he had never once given his reason for them. He had never said a word except to deny he had been the killer. Now, hearing it from his own mouth, I wanted to puke.

"You're insane."

"Probably," he agreed and then took an aggressive step toward me.

"Don't you come near me!" I warned, pointing a finger at him. "I'm not the girl you used to beat on, Kiki. I'm a grown woman, and I know my power."

He laughed right in my face. The stink of his breath, of neglected teeth and rotting insides, nearly knocked me on my ass. I recoiled at the stench. "I mean it, Kiki!"

"I might look like I'm dying, and I probably am, but I can still beat the shit out of you." He took another step toward me and then another. "I'm going to teach you your final lesson tonight, Nisha."

A gunshot echoed in the building. Then another. And another. And even more.

Kiki turned his back and walked toward the door to see what was happening. I snatched my chance. I grabbed the metal pipe from the shelf where I had hidden it, strode toward him, and with every bit of strength I had, swung at his head as if I were Serena Williams.

He crumpled at the knees, and I took another swing, this time catching him on the side of the face. The reverberations of the impact jarred my elbow and wrist, and I was sure I had injured myself. I didn't care. I barely even felt the pain.

All those years of abuse. All those years of swallowing the pain and the torment. It all came bubbling to the surface like a geyser.

Kiki fell forward onto his hands and knees, and I switched arms, taking hold of the pipe in my left hand this time, and began to wail on his back. Rage and fury burned through me like wildfire. I wanted him to hurt. I wanted him to suffer.

"I hate you!" My primal scream echoed off the walls of the room. Outside, I was vaguely aware of gunshots. I didn't pay them any mind. My business was in here, now flat on his stomach, bleeding out on the concrete floor. "I hate you!"

Muscles burning, I screamed again and tossed aside the pipe. Kiki was still alive and managed to roll himself over onto his back. He looked up at me—and he laughed. He laughed like a lunatic and egged me on to kill him. "Do it, Nisha. Show me what you really are inside. Show me all the dirty, dark, ugliness that I left inside you."

If he thought that would discourage me, he was wrong. I turned to get the jagged length of metal with the makeshift rag handle. My breasts heaved as I tried to catch my breath. My head pounded, and my hands ached. My feet continued to leave bloody footprints on the floor.

I paid all of that no mind. I was focused solely on the task at hand.

But then I heard shuffling. I turned, and he staggered to his feet. He swayed and coughed up blood. The sight of him so obviously injured did nothing to me. I didn't feel empathy. I didn't feel sympathy. I felt nothing but a black hole of hatred.

"You don't deserve to die in prison with a needle in your arm." It was the one thing I had never been able to accept, even after his guilty verdict. It was too good an end, too gentle, too kind for a heinous serial killer like him. All the things he had done, all the pain he had caused, he needed to pay for those crimes in blood and suffering.

"You're probably right." Kiki rushed me, startling me with the burst of energy he managed to compel from his battered body. I was heavier, but he caught me off guard. I stumbled back into the shelf, slamming my back into the rough metal. I felt it slice my back open, and I cried out in pain.

"That's it, baby. You sing for me," Kiki urged, his disgusting breath choking the air right out of my lungs. His words took me back to the countless times he had abused me in our bedroom. He always called my screams and begging singing.

"She's going to sing for me later," he'd tell people when we were at parties. They would think it was something sweet like I was going to serenade him with a love song. That tickled him. He enjoyed it when others laughed or encouraged his abuse of me, ignorant of it as they were.

"No." I spit right in his face, and it felt good. He punched me right in the gut, burying his fist deep in my abdomen, and I gasped for breath. It was the kind of hit that would have dropped me, but he was weaker now. It hurt, and it set me back. But I didn't go down.

"I'm going to have to find another place to hit you, *gordita*." Kiki scowled at me. "Too much fat protecting all your soft, vulnerable spots."

"And not enough protecting yours, *flaco*." I slammed my knee right between his legs, cracking his dick and balls as hard as I could.

He fell forward into me, his face smashing into my neck. I knew it was coming before I felt it, but I couldn't move fast enough. He sank his brown and yellowed teeth into my neck, biting through my flesh like an animal.

I shrieked. The pain was so bad, and I felt him chewing at my skin, gnawing on me like a beast with a meaty bone.

I reached back, clawing at the shelf and trying to feel the jagged metal I had hidden there. Finally, I felt it. Gripping the metal in my hand, I drew it off the shelf and roughly shoved it into his side, jamming it through tissue and muscle and right into his belly.

His jaw sagged with the shock of it. His blood spilled over my hand, the hot liquid scalding my skin. Our eyes were locked, and I saw the flicker of fear in his.

He's afraid. He's afraid to die.

"Finish it, Nisha," Kiki urged. "Kill me, you fat bitch."

Grabbing the metal with both hands, I rammed it the rest of the way through his body. I tore through the viscera, gutting him and leaving him to die in agony.

Kiki staggered back on wobbly legs. His gaze never left my face. Blood and worse poured from his belly, soaking the front of his shirt and jeans and puddling on the floor. I stood there, completely oblivious to all that was happening around me. All I could see, all I could hear, was Kiki dying in front of me.

"You know," he said, voice raspy and weak. "I don't think I ever loved you at all."

"I know I didn't." I watched him fall to his knees and then slump forward onto the concrete. The metal sticking out of him scraped against the floor and held his body up at a strange angle. He jerked and twitched as his blood pumped from his veins and out of the wound. His eyes closed, and his breathing grew labored.

I didn't move. I stood perfectly still. I watched and waited for the end.

When the double doors burst open, I reluctantly tore my gaze away from Kiki. Ten stood in the doorway now, filling it with his broad shoulders. The panic in his eyes fled as soon as he saw me standing there, but then his expression turned to worry as he took in the blood soaking me from neck to toe.

Kiki's last breath drew our attention. He made a rattling noise that I would never forget—and expired.

Gone.

He's finally gone.

It was over.

He can never hurt me or anyone else ever again.

CHAPTER TWENTY-NINE

17 Weeks Later

"HEY! NO!" TEN rushed to intercept Lev before he could grab the chess pieces off Nikolai's board and stuff them in his mouth. The little boy squealed with delight as Ten swept him up off the ground. Wanting to hear that laughter a few seconds longer, he shifted Lev in his arms and flew him around the library like an airplane. "Flight E-LEV-EN coming in for a landing."

Vivian appeared in the doorway as he swooped Lev down and then right back up again. She smiled at their antics. "Oh, no! Did our landing gear fail to deploy?"

"No, but something else did." Ten made a face as he caught a whiff of something that was definitely no longer part of his job description. "Time to land at Terminal Mommy."

"Oh, lucky me." Vivian accepted her son with a grin and nuzzled his chubby face. "Stinky boy! Perfect time for a bath so you'll be nice and clean when Lana gets here to take over for the evening."

"She's good with him." Ten had been uncertain about letting Lana, the girl Kostya had found in a motel and who had worked part-time at Allure ever since, take on the position of nanny for Lev. Kostya and Holly vouched for her, as did Nisha who was glad that Lana was doing work more in line with her long-term career goals. The girl wanted to be a preschool teacher, and Lev was sure to train her right.

"She's wonderful with him." Vivian shot him a sad smile. "But you're irreplaceable."

"I don't know about that." He eyed Stas who hovered in the hallway. There had been some questions about who Nikolai would choose to take over now that Ten was leaving their employ. As far as Ten was concerned, Stas was the only choice. He had kindness to him when necessary, but he was no-nonsense when it came to following rules. He would keep Vivian out of trouble.

"Do you plan to be fashionably late tonight to your party?" Vivian asked as she carried Lev toward the grand staircase. "Or will you be annoyingly early as usual?"

"I'm coming from Nisha's place so we'll be fashionably late. She'll have to change her shoes at least four times before we make it out the door."

Vivian laughed and unlatched the baby gate at the bottom of the stairs. "Well, in that case, I will see you this evening, and I will not expect you through the doors of Samovar until fifteen after seven."

"Yes, ma'am."

She gave his arm a gentle pat before taking Lev upstairs to the nursery. When Stas didn't immediately follow, he growled, "Go. She'll need help keeping that feral child from running out the door."

"Right. Sorry." Stas hurried after Vivian, taking the steps two at a time to catch her. He struggled with the childproof gate at the top of the stairs but finally managed it.

Ten shook his head. Stas had a lot to learn if he wanted to be successful as Vivian and Lev's bodyguard.

"You're leaving?" Nikolai greeted when Ten stepped into the kitchen. The boss had brought in a basket of produce from his fall garden and was separating the vegetables into piles.

"Yes. It's time." In more ways than one.

"You're always welcome here in our home." Nikolai set aside two strangely shaped squash. "Just because you no longer work here doesn't mean you aren't family."

"Thank you. That means…." Ten cleared his suddenly tight throat. "That means a lot to me."

"You're practically Vivian's brother and Lev's uncle." Nikolai started piling produce into a smaller basket.

"Practically," he agreed.

Stepping aside and shifting his role in the Kalasnikov crime family felt natural now that his parole was officially completed, but it wasn't without some sadness. Even so, he was looking forward to taking over the trucking company for Alexei Sarnov. It was a piece of mafia business that straddled the line of legitimacy, but it meant he would be home every night, barring any emergencies. Being home every night meant he could finally ask Nisha to marry him.

"Did you get everything squared away with Zoya?"

Ten nodded at the mention of the jeweler's name. "It's at home in my safe."

Nikolai smiled. "She'll be a good wife to you."

"I hope I'm a good husband to her."

"You will be." Nikolai spoke as if there was no other option. Truthfully, there wasn't. If he fucked up, it wouldn't just be Nicky Jackson on his ass. It would be Holly and Savannah and Billie and everyone else at the salon. "Here. Take this home with you. We're drowning in acorn squash and beans. I let Lev help with the planting, and he went a little overboard with the seeds."

"He inherited his father's green thumb." Ten accepted the basket of vegetables. "Thank you."

"Better than other things he might have inherited from me," Nikolai reasoned. "We'll see you tonight?"

"Yes."

"I had the bar order in extra for your *retirement* party." Nikolai draped a dish towel over his shoulder. "I expect to see you dancing on a table before the night is over."

"Oh, Nisha will absolutely love that." Ten laughed at the image of Nisha pursing her lips and scowling up at him if he climbed up on their table.

"She'll get used to it." Nikolai clapped him on the shoulder. "Go on. Go before you get roped into chasing my wild son around the house again."

"He's upstairs having a bath."

"Ah, well, I suppose it's time for Stas to start the hard part of his on-the-job training."

Ten had a smile on his face as he left Nikolai and Vivian's grand manor for the last time as a bodyguard. He carefully placed the basket of produce on the passenger seat of Nisha's orange jeep. He had taken her vehicle for the day while his was in the shop having the tires replaced.

She had started leaving the salon early on Fridays for self-care. He wholeheartedly supported that decision and was glad to see her more relaxed and enjoying life. Now that he was looking forward to regular hours, they would have more time together.

No longer tied by the constraints of his parole, Ten could finally start working through the list he'd been keeping of places he wanted to travel and things he wanted to experience. Nisha had been going through the list with him, helping him prioritize each activity. She was most excited to take him to Disney World, a place she enjoyed escaping to once a year.

Only Vivian, Nikolai, and Zoya knew that he intended to propose there. He had already booked the resort and arranged everything with Vivian's help. Instead of flying out, he planned for them to drive and make that part of the trip as well, stopping at beach hotels along the way to enjoy some sun and sand.

I just hope she says yes.

He worried he might be rushing things. It was very quick. He had to admit that. Four months was nothing compared to some of the longer relationships other couples had before taking a step toward marriage.

But that wasn't their way. He and Nisha had done the will-we-won't-we dance for nearly two years before that first kiss. They had both spent a decade of their lives in prison, him in an actual honest-to-goodness cage and her in a mental prison of Kiki's making.

We're free now.

We did our time.

We get to live.

Kostya and Gabe had worked overtime to clean the scene of Nisha's rescue, making sure no one would know that they had been there. Nisha had been left to call 9-1-1 with a carefully crafted story that law enforcement accepted. They may not have believed it completely, but they accepted it.

He had been able to "prove" he had been in Houston while all of that went down with help from Kostya's spiders. Those women had terrifying skills, and he found himself questioning whether those conspiracy theorists who swore that the whole world was nothing more than a matrix might be right.

He had seen videos of himself in places where he had never been—a Walmart, a Dairy Queen, traffic cams, and a toll booth on the Beltway. It was fucking scary knowing that Fox could manipulate reality so cleanly that she could fool everyone.

But her skills had kept him from getting spanked for parole violations. They had allowed him to finish his program and earn his release. So, yes, if she ever came to him asking for a favor? He'd move heaven and earth to make it happen.

When he reached Nisha's house, he pulled into her garage and parked. As soon as he stepped inside the laundry-slash-mudroom, Wilford appeared, yowling and whining for a treat and pets. Ten bent down and gave the cat a scratch between his ears and a few strokes before leading Wilford into the kitchen. He took the lid off the treat jar, grabbed a handful, and placed them on the floor.

"Don't tell your mother I gave you all these extra treats." He eyed the cat with a warning look. "And don't come investigating any interesting sounds you're about to hear."

Wilford was more interested in his crunchy fish-flavored treats than what Ten had to say. Certain the beast would sneak into Nisha's bedroom to swipe at him, he made sure to shut the door firmly. The last thing he needed was another bite from those sharp teeth on his ankle while he was mid-thrust in Nisha.

"Nisha?" Ten made sure to be loud enough that she would hear him over the shower. "I'm home."

The bathroom door opened, and she stood there naked with one of those natural sponges she preferred in her hand. "I was just about to get in. You want to join me?"

"Like you have to ask." He already had his hand on his belt buckle, and he didn't miss the hungry way she stared at his hands. "How was your Pilates class?"

"Good." Her gaze lingered on his arms as he drew his shirt up and over his head, baring his chest for her.

"And Eric?" She had been planning to meet the detective for lunch.

"He's great," she said, tearing her gaze away from his body. "He looks so healthy and strong. He's been cleared, and he's back out on the streets doing what he loves most."

"Good. Houston needs him." Ten actually meant that. Decent cops like Eric were rare, and the city needed as man of them as they could get.

"Savannah comes back to the salon on Monday." Nisha's eyes brightened. "I'm so glad. We've missed her so much."

"I know you have." He sat on the bed and removed his boots and socks. When he stood again, he asked, "Did you and Tiara have a nice breakfast?"

"We did." She walked across the bedroom and placed her hands over his, drawing down his jeans and underwear. "I think she's finally starting to forgive herself. It's not as if she meant for it to go the way it did."

Stupid girl, he thought rudely. She had been fooled by Chad into feeding him information about Nisha. When she'd realized he wasn't the man he presented himself as, it was too late. She was embroiled in his scheme and couldn't get out.

"No," he agreed. "I suppose she didn't." He touched her hair. "Shower cap?"

She nodded. "In a minute."

He grinned and lowered his face to hers. Their kisses got better and better each time they practiced. She had learned to be bolder with him, to demand what she wanted and take what she needed. He was only too happy to give and give and give.

They eventually made their way into the shower, but there wasn't much cleaning happening at first. She was the perfect height for him, not too short, not too tall. He just had to bend her forward a little bit and her perfect pussy was right where he wanted it. Judging by the sounds she made as he fucked her, she was getting exactly what she wanted as well.

"Anton." Her fingers squelched against the wet tile. "Anton." She pressed back against him, meeting his thrusts with her powerful hips. "Baby, you're gonna make me come."

"I fucking better," he growled and then grabbed her breast. He squeezed her plump flesh, relishing her lush body and all its womanly softness. "Put your hand between your legs," he commanded. "Rub your clit. I want to feel you come on my cock. I want to feel you squeezing every last drop of cum out of me."

"Anton!" She followed his order, sliding her fingers down her belly and between her labia. She rubbed tight, fast circles, and he slowed his thrusting, holding back his own climax to make sure she had hers.

"When we get home tonight, I want you on my face." He lowered his head until his lips were near the shell of her ear. "I want to lick your cunt until your legs are shaking, and you've made a mess on my face."

"Anton," she whined, her pussy clenching.

"That's it, baby." He traced the outline of her ear before gently teething her lobe. "Then maybe if you beg for it nicely, I'll fuck a baby into you tonight."

"Anton!" She screamed as she orgasmed unexpectedly. "Anton!"

He pressed her against the wall, thrusting into her with short, deep strokes. His balls ached, and his toes curled against the tile. The water streaming down his back was an added layer of pleasure, and when he came, he wanted his filthy promise to come true. He wanted to make a baby with her, with the love of his life.

"Anton?" she asked a little while later as they dried off and exchanged silly smiles in the mirror.

"Yeah?" He rubbed his hair with the towel.

"Did you mean it?" She seemed suddenly shy.

"Mean what?" He wanted to hear her say it.

"That you want to have a baby with me."

"I meant it." He tossed his towel on the bathroom counter. "And not just one." He grasped her hips and drew her close. "As many as you want."

"Let's start with one," she suggested with a lopsided smile.

"Unless we get lucky like Bianca and Sergei."

Her eyes widened. "Twins?"

"Why not?"

"Slow down," she said with a laugh and patted his chest. "One is a perfect number."

"I suppose." He teased his mouth along hers. "I love you, Nisha Jackson."

"And I love you, Anton Vasiliev."

If you enjoyed Ten and Nisha's book, please consider leaving a review. I love hearing from readers!

Many of my books continue with FREE SHORT STORIES on my website.
www.roxieriverawriter.com/free-reads.html

Join my newsletter to receive notifications about new books, new free reads and upcoming events.
http://eepurl.com/sX-z1

Ten is part of my **Her Russian Protector** series that starts with the novella IVAN available here.
https://mybook.to/Y5do0r

Other books in my Houston underworld include COLLATERAL (Debt Collection, Book One) and In Kelly's Corner (The Fighting Connollys, Book One)

About Roxie

I am a New York Times and USA Today Bestselling author of steamy romances. I live in Texas on five acres with my paramedic husband, our special needs teen, a rambunctious preschooler, and a growing menagerie.

When I'm not writing or chasing after our kiddos, I dabble in flower farming with a special love for dahlias and lilies. I also enjoy firing up my sewing machines to make quilts and clothing. If I'm not in my studio/office or in the garden, you'll find me in line at Haunted Mansion at Magic Kingdom in Walt Disney World.

Find me online at www.roxierivera.com.
Facebook: WriterRoxieRivera
Instagram: RoxieWritesRomance
Newsletter: eepurl.com/sX-z1